The Legacy of
Hartlepool Hall

PAUL TORDAY

PHOENIX

A PHOENIX PAPERBACK

First published in Great Britain in 2012
by Weidenfeld & Nicolson
This paperback edition published in 2012
by Phoenix,
an imprint of Orion Books Ltd,
Orion House, 5 Upper St Martin's Lane,
London WC2H 9EA

An Hachette UK company

3 5 7 9 10 8 6 4

A CIP catalogue record for this book
is available from the British Library.

ISBN 978-0-7538-2883-0

Typeset by Input Data Services Ltd, Bridgwater, Somerset

Printed and bound in Great Britain
by Clays Ltd, St Ives plc

The Orion Publishing Group's policy is to use papers
that are natural, renewable and recyclable products and
made from wood grown in sustainable forests. The logging
and manufacturing processes are expected to conform to
the environmental regulations of the country of origin.

www.orionbooks.co.uk

The Legacy of
Hartlepool Hall

One

As a rule, Ed Hartlepool never opened letters unless they were invitations. These were opened and placed on the chimneypiece and marked with a tick or a cross to show whether he had found the time to answer them. Sometimes he even remembered to attend the wedding or drinks party he had been asked to: although for the last few years, living in the south of France as a non-dom, invitations had become scarce and his attendance scarcer.

Other post was usually left unopened. No member of his family had ever thought it worth their while to read correspondence from accountants, lawyers or bankers. Letters of this sort had been arriving at Villa Laurier with increasing frequency and remained in a pile on his desk. Every now and then he would open a few at random, glance at the first sentence, and then throw them away unread.

Ed never opened emails either – unless they were jokes. He used his computer to play on-line poker and couldn't see the point of it otherwise. His correspondents had long since learned it was hopeless trying to reach him in this way.

His father, Simon Aylmer Francis Simmonds, the fourth Marquess of Hartlepool, had died a few years ago. He had given Ed only two pieces of advice. The first was that if the opening sentence of a letter wasn't interesting, then the rest of it didn't deserve attention. The second recommendation was: '*A gentleman should only need to move his bowels once a day.*'

Ed began his day at half past nine with a cup of coffee and a couple of cigarettes on the terrace. As usual, at that time of the morning, he was clothed only in his dressing gown, preferring to swim before he began reading the English newspapers that his housekeeper would soon bring from the village.

Next it was time to obey his father's advice. He took his morning's post to the only room at Villa Laurier that in any way resembled home. When he had moved to France on his trustees' advice he had taken the house on a ten-year lease. Most of the furniture and decoration had been acceptable. However, Ed had not found French ideas on domestic sanitation to his taste and in this one room he had made changes. The best of English glazed ceramic sanitary ware had been imported and fitted; a lustrous mahogany loo seat and lid added. To complete the illusion, Ed had hung his old school and house photographs on the walls. He gazed at the sea of half-forgotten faces at this time every morning without thinking anything much about them. They were there merely as a silent audience while Ed performed his morning functions.

As he sat there, he opened the first letter. It was from Horace, the butler at Hartlepool Hall. Ed couldn't remember the last time he had received a letter from Horace and the shaky handwriting was at first unfamiliar to him. The letter began with the intriguing sentence:

'A Lady Alice Birtley has come to stay with us, and I do not recollect that your Lordship left any instructions in respect of her visit.'

Ed had never heard of Alice Birtley. He put the letter to

2

one side, promising himself he would read the rest of it later. He had certainly not invited a Lady Alice, or anyone else, to stay at Hartlepool Hall. The second letter was from his accountant in London and almost went straight into the waste-paper basket. But this time some instinct made him open it. The first sentence commanded his attention straight away; and the next, and the next.

The letter informed Ed that his five-year exile as a non-dom had come to an end. A settlement had been reached by the trustees of the Hartlepool Estate in the enormous and costly row with Her Majesty's Revenue and Customs that had arisen following the death of Ed's father. The figure that had been agreed was so large that Ed could not at first grasp it. It didn't seem as if the amount of money in the letter could have anything to do with him or his affairs. It was simply too large to understand.

Ed's father had followed a long family tradition of leaving his affairs in a dreadful tangle. The wealth of the Simmonds family had been colossal; it had survived generations of mismanagement. But somehow the taxman's demands had always been met or else avoided; to improve matters, Ed's father and his advisors had designed a series of trusts, in turn owned by overseas trusts in Guernsey, in turn owned by other trusts in Lichtenstein. As a result, the fourth Marquess had paid no inheritance tax on his own father's death; and little or no income tax during his lifetime. The arrangements that had been constructed to help him avoid all this tax were so complex it was probable that no single human being fully understood them.

When Ed's father died, Her Majesty's Revenue and Customs had taken Ed's trustees to court, and Ed had been advised to

3

move abroad. Now the matter had been settled and the bills were coming in.

Ed knew as soon as he read the opening sentence of the letter, that his life was about to change. Decisive action had to be taken. The responsibilities that had fallen to him on his father's death must now be taken up. His inheritance, the large Hartlepool estate and its enormous house, on the borders of Durham and Yorkshire, was finally his and his life of leisure was over. For five years he had done nothing; trod water, in a manner of speaking, whilst other people had written him letters either seeking instruction, or giving him information. He had almost never replied. How could he be expected to understand letters that began with sentences such as: 'You will recall the judgement in the case of Rex v. Chorley Settled Estates in 1934'?

Ed sighed as he thought of all the trouble that lay ahead of him, then went outside into the heat of a late spring morning in Provence.

The sun was climbing in the sky. Ed walked along the path to the swimming pool, which was about fifteen metres long and made of white marble, surrounded by an area of terracotta tiles. Sun loungers sat along its side, and there was a small pool-house at the far end. Here were lilos and beach balls and other objects that Ed never used. They were provided for the use of the villa's occasional tenants: sometimes Ed went back to England in the hottest part of the summer and let the villa to friends.

He wound back the pool cover, took off his dressing gown and flung it onto the nearest sun lounger. The blue water sparkled in the spring sun that had just cleared the tops of the surrounding trees. Dew glinted on the freshly mown grass. Ed picked up the skimmer and removed from the surface of the water a few dead leaves, a couple of drowned wasps and a large spider whose legs were still flailing. He emptied the contents of the net into a corner of the garden, then lowered himself slowly into the water.

At first the temperature seemed cold, but within moments, as he swam the first of twenty lengths, it was refreshing. The water felt like cream against his skin, and it lapped gently against the sides of the pool or gurgled in the overflow pipe. He made a turn, pushing underwater and changed from a medium-fast crawl to breaststroke. After a few more lengths he turned on his back and began a gentle backstroke, half closing his eyes to keep out the water, which was salty, like the sea. Now, as he lay on his back, the sun was a distant golden dot. The endless blue sky arched over him, warming his limbs. He turned again and swam with a steady breaststroke, smelling the fresh air of late spring, the scent of newly cut grass, the tang of salt.

Ed was at his happiest at this hour of the day when life was at its simplest. All he had to do was get from one end of the pool to the other, and count off the lengths as he did so. He swam with the grace and fluency you would expect from a man who had been swimming like this most spring and summer mornings for the last five years.

Fragments of thought went through his mind as he turned and swam and turned and swam.

'I shall miss all this ... there's nowhere to swim at Hartlepool Hall. The lake is full of blanket-weed and far too cold.'

Then another fragment, of a different kind.

'I wonder if the beech trees are in leaf yet at home?'

He felt as if he was no longer in a swimming pool, but being carried on some mysterious tide, sweeping him on to a

5

destination of which he remained, for the moment, ignorant.

He finished his swim and climbed out of the pool. The water continued lapping and gurgling after he got out, as if it were calling him back, in a watery language he could not fathom. Perhaps it was asking him to stay a while longer; but as he dried himself with his towel he knew that this morning's letter, unlike all the others, could not be ignored. He must return to England.

Ed spent a night in London on the way home. Then he took an early train from King's Cross and arrived at Hartlepool Hall in a taxi, around mid-morning.

Spring comes to the north of England later than it arrives in the south of France. But when it arrives, it comes in the blink of an eye. The young winter wheat had emerged in the fields; every tree in every wood seemed about to burst into leaf. The willows and the birch trees were already out; the horse chestnuts unfurling their waxy green spikes. The hawthorn was white in the hedgerows and wild cherry flowered everywhere in explosions of white and pink.

Approaching Hartlepool Hall from the station, the visitor travels at first through a region of flat water meadows. Slow streams wind their way listlessly towards a distant sea, leaving oxbows to the right and left of them. There are flat expanses of oilseed rape or wheat; or else grass fields trodden into mud by grazing lambs or pigs.

A few miles further on, the bones of the land begin to change. The contours begin to undulate gently, a foretaste of the dales further west where the land ramps up towards the crests of the Pennines. Woods and copses become more frequent, and the fields are smaller: green pastures bounded by dry stone walls instead of barbed wire fences. The villages

6

are no longer straggling rows of dull red brick buildings. Instead the houses are built from a grey limestone and clustered around a green, with a pub and a church. It is a landscape that has not changed as much over the last two centuries as other parts of Britain. Then the road turns a corner and there is the first glimpse, through the trees, of Hartlepool Hall. That is the view that takes the visitor by surprise: the unexpectedness of this palace in the middle of nowhere.

Ed's ancestor Henry Simmonds, a descendant of miners and forge masters from somewhere on the coast between Middlesbrough and Hartlepool, hired an architect and with him he visited various stately homes: Chatsworth, Castle Howard and Blenheim. In front of one of them − it is not recorded which − he is said to have given his instructions: 'Build me summat like that.'

The story is no doubt apocryphal, but even the Simmonds family enjoyed repeating it. In those days the family enjoyed immeasurable wealth, enriched by the expansion of the manufacturing industry caused by the Napoleonic Wars. They were hard men who worked with iron and steel. They knew the value of every penny they made, and when they loaned quite a large sum of money at the end of the Crimean War to an almost bankrupt Government, they made it plain that they expected a dukedom to go with the new house they were building.

The Secretary to the Treasury Bench, who was responsible for affairs of patronage, explained that a dukedom was not possible; the other dukes mightn't like it; but they could make Henry Simmonds a Marquess, if that would do?

After a bit of grumbling it was decided that it would have to do, and Henry Simmonds became the first Marquess of

Hartlepool just as the last sheet of lead was being laid on the roof of Hartlepool Hall.

The taxi drove through the lodge gates and then along the half a mile or so of drive that led to the house itself. Underneath avenues of wellingtonia and cedar, a mass of bluebells surged in drifts of a startling deep blue that seemed to shine with a light all their own in the gloom beneath the trees. The pale yellow of primroses showed here and there in small clusters.

Ed stepped out of the taxi and took a moment to look up at his family home. Indeed it *was* his home, and his alone. He had no close relations to share it with him: no sisters, no brothers, no wife or children. In front of him the cliff-like face of the building – a great façade of grey stone broken by countless windows – was graced with a central portico. Crowning the front of the house was a white marble dome that looked as if it might have been airlifted from Rome or Florence.

Behind the house was the ten-acre lake, where banks of rhododendrons were beginning to flower along the water's edge: luxuriant blooms of red and pink and cream whose reflections glanced upwards from the surface of the still water. Beyond the lake were the woods that encircled the house and its gardens and grounds, protecting them from curious eyes. This secret kingdom of limestone and glass, lead and marble, of lake and woodland, now basked in the hazy heat of a cloudless spring day.

Horace the butler was descending the steps while Ed paid off the driver. When he reached the taxi he said, 'Good morning, M'Lord.'

'How are you, Horace?' Without waiting for an answer, Ed bounded up to the front entrance. Horace struggled up the steps behind him with the luggage. Ed now stood in the great hall in the shaft of sunlight let in through the oculus, a circular window in the marble dome far above. The architect had borrowed this idea from the Pantheon in Rome, inspired by the family's treasured white marble statue of Romulus and Remus. This statue was now installed at one end of the hall and had originally been purchased by Percy, the father of Henry Simmonds, while on a grand tour in Italy during the first half of the nineteenth century.

It was good to be home.

'Get one of the gardeners to give you a hand taking those cases upstairs, Horace,' said Ed. Horace was wheezing as he set the suitcases down on the floor. Ed had forgotten how old Horace was. His pink, unlined cheeks belied his age: he must be eighty, Ed thought. He had served the Simmonds family since he was in his teens when his duties had consisted of polishing shoes in the boot room and taking the post down to the village. He had been his grandfather's, then his father's butler and personal manservant for at least fifty years and should have retired a decade ago. No one had remembered to tell him he could go, so he stayed on.

'Thank you, M'Lord,' said Horace. 'Will your Lordship be in the usual bedroom?'

'Yes,' said Ed.

'Lady Alice has asked me to say she would like to join you in the library just before luncheon. She has not yet risen. Lady Alice prefers to read the newspapers in bed. I am afraid it slipped my mind for a moment that your Lordship was coming home today, and I had the papers sent up to her. Shall I get someone to go to the village and buy some more?'

'Don't worry,' Ed replied. 'I read all the papers on the train. But who on earth is Lady Alice?'

'I wrote to your Lordship about the lady.'

'Of course you did,' said Ed. The experience of coming back to Hartlepool Hall and knowing that, for the first time in his life, it was his alone to enjoy, freed from the arthritic grip of his father, had driven all other thoughts from his head.

'She's still here, is she?'

'The lady has not yet said how long she intends to stay,' replied Horace.

'Has she not?' said Ed. 'We'll see about that.'

He left Horace standing in the hall and wandered about the ground floor of the house. Nothing had changed: the drawing room was covered in dust sheets, and the shutters were closed, but the dining room and the library had been made ready. The curtains and windows had been opened and there were fresh-cut spring flowers in a vase; a drinks tray had also been set out, so Horace mustn't really have forgotten about his arrival. The rest of the house was asleep: windows shuttered, curtains drawn to protect the paintings and the furniture from sunlight, dust everywhere, a sleepy quiet broken only by the echo of Ed's footsteps as he went from room to room.

He unlocked the glass door that led onto the terrace overlooking the lake and stepped outside. After the cool darkness of the house the sunlight made him narrow his eyes for a moment and warmed his face: he could have been in France still. He walked across the terrace to the stone balustrade. Below were more rhododendrons coming into flower and a yard or two beyond them was the shore of the lake. Startled by his arrival a mallard was paddling away, followed by six ducklings so small they could only have hatched in the last day or so. Clouds of midges and sedge darted above the water and swallows swooped amongst them, feeding on the new life.

For a long time Ed stood there gazing at the view, resting his elbows on the lichen-covered stone of the balustrade and drinking in the extraordinary beauty of the place – last glimpsed on a wet November night some months ago. This was his inheritance; this place was all his now, to do with as he liked. A sound behind him made him turn. It was Horace, standing at the window.

'Lady Alice is in the library, M'Lord.'

Edward followed Horace back into the house. His eyes had difficulty adjusting to the gloom after the brightness of the sunshine outside. He had not decided on the best approach to take with this interloper: cold irony, or outright abuse? In the centre of the room stood a tall woman, wearing a grey dress.

Edward blinked. He realised he was looking at a woman in her late sixties in whose features and figure a faded beauty could still be detected. Lady Alice Birtley was not much younger than his father would have been, had he still lived. She was not yet pulled earthwards by gravity. She held herself erect and she was slim: no, not slim, painfully thin. She had tight silver-grey curls about her head that must once have been blonde ringlets. She had great dark eyes: no, they were not dark, but a watery blue. They looked dark because the sockets were deep and shadowed. Her skin was so transparent that the bones of her face almost seemed to show. It must once have been a beautiful face to look at: even now, it was remarkable.

'Good morning,' she said as Ed entered the room. Her voice was clear, with the cut-glass accents of an earlier decade. She held out her hand and Ed took it in a brief grasp. Her skin felt like old paper.

'Good morning,' said Ed. 'I'm Ed Hartlepool.'

'I know who you are. I recognised you at once, even though we have never met before. You have your father's looks.'

'Have I indeed?' replied Ed.

'My name is Alice Birtley,' said the old lady. 'I don't suppose your father ever mentioned my name to you?'

'No. He didn't.'

He waited for some explanation but none came. Then Horace appeared beside them carrying a silver tray on which there were two glasses of champagne.

'Horace spoils me,' said Lady Alice. She raised her glass in Ed's direction. 'Happy days.'

Who was this person in Ed's house? Who was this woman, acting as if she had lived there all her life, drinking his best champagne?

Two

When Annabel Gazebee heard that Ed Hartlepool might be coming back to live at Hartlepool Hall she went and told her father. Although she was in her early thirties, she still lived at home looking after old Marcus Gazebee. Her mother had died long ago. It was Annabel's policy, learned from bitter experience, that it was best to tell her father everything, and as soon as she heard it. In such a case the worst that could happen was that he would accuse her of repeating idle gossip, or of wasting his time with trivia. But if she failed to tell him any item of news, however slight, the consequences could be unfortunate. He had been known to accuse her of leading a secret life; of plotting against him; of not paying him the respect that was due to him. She dreaded his tone when he reproached her. Either icy and withering, or querulous and complaining: both were equally hard to face.

On this occasion he was in one of his better moods. All he said, when Annabel told him the news, was: 'Well, I daresay he has only come back in order to sell up. That young man has no interest in anything at all. Except spending money, of course.'

'Poor Ed,' said Annabel. Colonel Gazebee laughed. Age had brought a shrill note to his voice and the sound was more like the cry of a seagull than anything human.

'He will be poor, very soon. And poorer still if that builder you're seeing gets his hands on the house. Simon Hartlepool must be spinning in his grave.'

The 'builder' was what Colonel Gazebee chose to call Geoff Tarset, the man whom Annabel had been going out with for three months. Men of any sort were scarce in her life these days, and the opportunities to meet them scarcer still. Geoff was one of the few – indeed the only one in recent times – to have survived the chilly sarcasm with which her father greeted most of her visitors. But Geoff had, unfortunately for Annabel, said in her father's hearing that he wouldn't mind making an offer for Hartlepool Hall if it ever came on the market. There were rumours all the time that such a thing might happen.

Annabel was pleased at first when she heard Ed might be coming home. A lifetime – five or six years – ago, the two of them had been close friends. She, and Ed, and Catherine Plender, Eck Chetwode-Talbot, Mike Fearnley, and four or five others had been in and out of each other's houses. They had been her 'set'. Annabel had thought in those days that this tight group of friends were the only people worth knowing. Their parties were the best parties. They went racing together, or shooting on Ed's family grouse moor. They sat in one another's dining rooms and drank and talked into the small hours. There had never been anything between Annabel and Ed although, when his girlfriend Catherine Plender married someone else and was then killed in a car crash, Ed was for a time so vulnerable and lost that Annabel thought she might have stepped into Catherine's shoes. But it didn't happen, and then Ed went abroad and they saw each other for only a few days a year on his rare visits home.

Now she awaited Ed's return with a curious mixture of

anticipation and embarrassment. The anticipation was in the thought that once Ed came back, everything would be as it once had been. Hartlepool Hall would be opened up and the parties would start again: dinner parties at the house; lunches in the family box at York Races. Ed had always paid for everything, or nearly everything, as he had inherited the careless generosity of his family. Mrs Donaldson, the cook-housekeeper at Hartlepool Hall, would serve up delicious feasts or provide picnic hampers full of absurd old-fashioned delicacies, to be washed down by the best wines from the cellars of Hartlepool Hall. The house would become the centre of the world once more: all cares and worries were left at its door, and inside was nothing but pleasure.

The embarrassment that Annabel felt was to do with Geoff Tarset. Her father had brought her up to believe that she should mix only with people who had what he called 'background'. Quite what he meant, Annabel was never sure. She had, in the past, brought home young men whose upbringing seemed impeccable, even when measured against her father's exacting standards. However, few of them returned after their first visit to Lambshiel House: the prize was never quite worth the grilling they received from the old colonel. The look of deep dissatisfaction that appeared on his face when, under cross-examination, they revealed the name of the school they had gone to or the regiment they had served in or the City bank they worked at, would have weakened the resolve of much tougher specimens. Annabel herself was not bad-looking but she was no beauty. She was a tall, thin girl with features that might have been handsome if they had been more animated. She had good dark brown hair that fell to her shoulders and large brown eyes. But this was never quite enough for the young men who came; and once they had visited the house it was obvious to them that, if there was money in the family, it was well hidden.

Then she met Geoff. It was in a hospitality tent sponsored by Malcolm Skinner's firm of land agents at the Great Yorkshire Show in Harrogate. Skinner & Partners were the agents for Hartlepool Hall. Annabel went because she received so few invitations to go anywhere that even the modest temptation of a free glass of sparkling wine and the chance to get away from home was enough to persuade her to make the sixty-mile round trip. Geoff was there because, as he told her, he was 'quite a big client of Malcolm's'.

Quite how or why he picked on Annabel to talk to she wasn't quite sure. She knew she would never have started the conversation. But Geoff cornered her and then made sure her glass was kept topped up, almost as if it were his party and not Malcolm Skinner's. There was something compelling about Geoff Tarset, even at that first meeting: his gaze had a hypnotic quality and he was a fluent talker, with an attractive lack of self-awareness. He seemed capable of doing or saying anything he wanted to. There was also an air of dangerous glamour about him: not just the evidence of wealth supplied by the Rolex Oyster he wore and the thick gold chain around his other wrist, but the impression he gave with his sharp blue eyes and very white teeth and the glimpse of his tanned and hairy chest where the top buttons were undone, that he was some kind of exotic animal who lived by different rules to those that governed Annabel's life.

He managed to get her phone number and she was not surprised when he rang a day later and asked her out to dinner. She hesitated only for a moment. She knew what her father would say if he ever met Geoff; she also knew that the boredom of sitting opposite her father in their austere drawing room night after night was beginning to drive her mad. Geoff took her out to dinner. It was a very good dinner, and she was collected from her house in a chauffeur-driven Rolls.

Indeed Geoff turned out to be good company. He made her laugh; he had a dry wit, and he was a good mimic. He told funny stories about himself, and he treated Annabel with something akin to deference. He was proud of the fact his parents had been poor.

'Where I was brought up,' he told her, 'the rich kids were the ones with bikes. The rest of us walked to school.' He liked to talk about the two-up, two-down terraced house he had been born in, because when he later showed her the large and modern single-storey dwelling he had designed and built for himself, the contrast was all the more marked. He explained that he had left school at sixteen and joined a firm of estate agents as a scout, and then as a negotiator. From there he had risen, as he told her in all modesty, to become 'one of the larger property developers in this part of the world'.

He didn't make the slightest attempt to kiss her, or even touch her hand on that first date. Annabel was sent home in Geoff's Rolls-Royce full, content and chaste. The next four or five dates followed a similar pattern: except that now he picked her up and drove her home himself in his other car – a red Ferrari. She knew with absolute certainty that sooner or later he was going to ask her to go to bed with him. The longer he didn't try to kiss or even touch her, the easier she felt it would be to say yes.

By this time Annabel had dropped out of the lives of the old Hartlepool Hall crowd. She didn't think their paths would cross often any more: one had died, one had gone to live abroad, one had married and pulled up the drawbridge, others had gone south to live in London. She needed someone in her life and it turned out to be Geoff. If she had not been so lonely, and so fed up with her father, she might not have chosen someone so different to her, whose friends were not her friends, whose way of life seemed so foreign to her. Geoff's friends were other property developers; or else professional footballers, bankers or lawyers. The people in his circle were noisy, confident, rich and sometimes predatory. But Geoff drew her into his world; and when he had drawn her in, he became her lover.

The initial thought that went through Annabel's mind when she lay in bed with him for the first time was: 'His back is even hairier than his chest.'

Then he began his love-making and she forgot all about the hirsute qualities of her new lover. In a while she even wished that he was rather less energetic. Afterwards, he went to the bar, located in the large living space next to his bedroom, and mixed them both a powerful cocktail. Annabel was dying for a cup of tea, but she accepted the drink with every appearance of surprise and gratitude.

'Get this down you, darling,' said Geoff. 'You need to keep your strength up if we're going to have a night of passion.'

He grinned and drank down half of his own. Annabel thought: 'Oh God, are we going to have to do this all over again?'

Not that it had been unpleasant: far from it. But it was all rather tiring. She was saved by Geoff's mobile phone. He began striding up and down the room, quite naked, the mobile clutched to his ear, saying things like: 'Try Clydesdale Bank – they might give us a better rate on the senior debt.'

It was not very romantic. After a few more minutes of this

Annabel started to dress, and when Geoff looked across at her and raised one eyebrow, still in the middle of a conversation, she said: 'I must go – Daddy will be wondering where I've got to.'

He didn't try to stop her.

All the same Annabel grew fond of Geoff. When he finally met her father, an occasion Annabel had been dreading and had put off for as long as possible, his robust indifference to her father's sarcasm impressed her. No other man she had brought home had dealt with the old man quite so efficiently. She really began to wonder whether Geoff mightn't, after all, be the knight who would rescue her from her imprisonment. He was an improbable knight, with his Ferrari and his Rolls-Royce, and his BlackBerry winking its red light at him, but he might just do the job.

'Why do you stick around if he treats you like that?' was Geoff's question after his first visit to Lambshiel House. He spoke out of curiosity. 'Why don't you tell him to stuff it?'

'I can't,' said Annabel. 'Someone has to look after him.'

'Put him in a care home.'

'I haven't got the money.'

'What about your old man? He must have something tucked away.'

So Annabel told him about The Inheritance. The inheritance was Marcus Gazebee's nest egg: a sum of money, which was at various times described by her father as either 'a very substantial sum which I have at my disposal thanks to my careful management' or else 'a derisory amount of money considering I have given half my life in Her Majesty's Service.' He never gave any further details. What was certain, whether her father's savings were large or small, was that they had not been frittered away by any extravagance on his part. Life at Lambshiel House was conducted with an impressive sense of frugality. The central heating system was never used, except in the depths of winter; nor was the house overflowing with milk or honey. At their infrequent lunch parties, wine glasses were not often brought out and never overfilled; the amount of food on offer to guests seemed to suggest that they must have eaten elsewhere first. The only luxury Colonel Gazebee allowed himself was his daily glass of port, of which a few dozen bottles remained in the otherwise almost empty cellar.

Annabel put up with all this because she felt she had no choice. One day her father would die and she would inherit whatever was left to inherit. She would sell the house and move somewhere smaller and warmer. Before Geoff came along, and while Ed was still in the south of France, she used to dream about her father dying, of some condition that was not too unpleasant, but quite conclusive. Then she would sell up and buy a little house somewhere in Provence herself. And then one day she would accidentally on purpose bump into Ed and he would say: 'What on earth are you doing here?' and she would say, 'I live here now,' and then ... and then ... and then what?

But now Geoff was in her life and asking her to come and live with him and already speculating, on her behalf, about how much Lambshiel House might fetch on the open market. Her father, however, still clung to life like a tough old root. The house was not for sale, the Inheritance was still salted away in whichever building society or bank her father had left it, and Annabel would not – could not – *dared* not leave him.

She also wasn't quite certain about Geoff.

*

When Ed decided to come back to Hartlepool Hall, news of his return travelled ahead of him. It was Geoff, of all people, who told Annabel about it, one evening when she was with him in his house.

'I hear your old mate Lord Hartlepool is coming back home.'

Annabel was sitting in Geoff's drawing room, trying not to be distracted by the football match on the enormous TV. She was embroidering a tapestry cushion with the words: 'You Don't Have To Be Mad To Live Here, But It Helps': a motto which had taken Geoff's fancy. She looked up in great surprise.

'No, really? Who told you that?'

As she spoke she found herself feeling upset that it was Geoff giving her the news, rather than the other way around.

'Malcolm Skinner.'

'What do you mean, coming back home? For a weekend, or longer?'

Geoff paused for a second, as if weighing up how much information he was prepared to part with.

'What I hear – and it's only a rumour – is that the Hartlepool Estate has gone bust. Lord Hartlepool is coming back to try to sort things out, but the word is he hasn't a hope. The banks are going to pull the plug on the whole thing.'

'No, really?' said Annabel again. 'How dreadful. Did Malcolm tell you that?'

She did not know Malcolm Skinner well, but she did not like him. She was quite prepared to believe he was treacherous. Geoff was very vague.

'It's just gossip. But I've heard the same story from people who are not often wrong. It's a big property, Hartlepool Hall. I wonder what will happen to it?'

'Ed would never sell up,' said Annabel decisively. 'It's been in his family far too long. In fact, they built it. He wouldn't dream of selling.'

'He might not,' said Geoff, 'but it's what his bankers are dreaming that matters. They're probably dreaming about getting their money out. Several million pounds of it, from what I hear.'

'Poor Ed,' said Annabel. She did not like the thought that Hartlepool Hall, once the centre of her existence and the scene of the happiest years of her life, might in any way be under threat. She did not like it either that she was hearing this news from Geoff. And because she did not like it, she chose not to believe it.

'I expect he'll find the money somewhere. The Simmondses have always been frightfully rich.'

'Maybe,' said Geoff. It was that evening, when he dropped her off at home, that she told her father the news.

Two days later Geoff rang her and told her that Ed was back.

'How do you know?' asked Annabel.

'Malcolm Skinner told me. He arrived this morning.'

'Has Malcolm seen him yet?'

'No. He's going to break the bad news to him this afternoon.'

'Oh, Geoff,' said Annabel, irritated by this, 'the Simmonds family has always had its ups and downs. They are far too rich to get into real trouble. I must ring Ed and see how he is.'

'That's why I was calling,' said Geoff. 'Do you think you could invite him to lunch?'

'You mean at Lambshiel House?' asked Annabel.

'Where else? And do you think you could manage to ask me at the same time?'

Annabel was surprised. 'I thought you hated coming here.'

'I'd go anywhere to be with you, darling,' said Geoff in his breeziest tone of voice.

'Do you mean it?' asked Annabel.

'I want to meet Ed Hartlepool. I want you to introduce me.'

'Why? I wouldn't have thought he was your type.'

Now Geoff sounded irritated.

'What do you mean, not my type? You mean I might not be his type?'

'Of course not, darling,' said Annabel. But that was just what she *had* meant. 'Why on earth do you want to meet him?'

'I want to meet him,' said Geoff solemnly, 'to discuss an idea that might be to our mutual advantage.'

Annabel thought it a rather vulgar remark, but she couldn't afford to say so, so she simply asked Geoff which date he had in mind.

'Any day next week,' he suggested. 'He'll need to catch up with events. I gather he never reads letters or, if he does, he never replies to them. Malcolm Skinner will have to tell him just how bad things are. Then he might be in the mood to talk to someone like me.'

Someone like Geoff: someone who did deals, someone who – Annabel had learned – bought and sold whole housing developments across the North East. Someone who made money, in amounts Annabel could not begin to imagine. She heard Geoff on the phone or listened to him at dinner with his friends. He talked about 'half a bar' when he meant five hundred thousand pounds; his projects cost millions to develop. In restaurants, bankers, lawyers and other rich men would cross the room to exchange a word with him, would acknowledge Annabel because she was with Geoff, and would then pat Geoff on the back, or squeeze his arm in one of those gestures with which alpha males acknowledge each other's rank and status.

What would Ed think of Geoff, wondered Annabel? Whatever it was, he would keep his thoughts to himself. Ed had always been a master of the cool, blank look that, without giving offence or being in the least ill-mannered, made others around him check that their ties were knotted or their trousers zipped. Ed never thought ill of other people; the trick was to get him to think of other people at all.

Annabel knew she would have to find a way of explaining the whole Geoff situation to Ed before he and Geoff met. Maybe she would have to go to Hartlepool Hall first, and tell Ed how her life was these days.

Three

The dining room was cold and the table, even with all the stretchers taken out, could easily have seated ten people. Horace had laid a place for Lady Alice and Ed at either end. They sat down, and Horace poured Lady Alice a glass of white wine from a bottle that had been kept on the sideboard. Ed drank water. Lunch was fresh asparagus dressed in vinaigrette, new potatoes, and a lamb cutlet. There was a moment's silence broken by the scrape of knife and fork, while Horace stood in one corner so as to be at hand if the salt needed passing or if more wine needed pouring.

Lady Alice took another sip from her glass and said, 'You must be wondering why I'm here?'

'Well, I am,' said Ed. 'Since you mention it.' He smiled then dabbed his chin with a napkin to remove some oil. 'I'm sure you have a reason.'

'The last time I saw your father was not long before he died. We had lunch together. We hadn't seen each other for years. It was not an easy occasion. But he told me then: when I am gone, if you are ever alone or in difficulties, think of Hartlepool Hall as your second home.' Lady Alice's own chin gleamed with oil from the asparagus but she seemed to be unaware of it. Ed dabbed his chin again, hoping she would take the hint. 'He used to say if ever I needed a bolt-hole,

I was to come here. This was long after your mother died, of course.'

Horace coughed in the corner of the room.

'But this is your first visit here, isn't it?' asked Ed. 'Why now?'

'Horace asked me if I had been here before,' replied Lady Alice, speaking as if Horace were in some other part of the house and not, at that moment, by her side, refilling her wine glass. 'And I haven't. But I came north once with a group of friends your father had invited to shoot grouse. We stayed at Blubberwick Lodge.'

'Is that where you met him?'

'No, we met at a party in London. It was in June 1963. A friend of mine, a doctor, introduced me to your father, who was one of his patients at the time.'

None of this made any sense to Ed. As Horace cleared away the plates he noticed that Lady Alice had left most of her food. She ate like a bird. Ed had devoured his modest portion in a few mouthfuls. Travel always made him hungry.

'Some fruit, M'Lord?' enquired Horace.

'Bring me an apple,' said Ed. To Lady Alice he said, 'Where was the party? Can you remember?'

'It was in a big house, an enormous place with its own swimming pool. Some of those delicious grapes I had last night, please, Horace.'

Ed found that, once again, curiosity got in the way of the things he wanted to say.

'You met my father at a party and he asked you to come and shoot grouse?'

'There were a lot of people at that party. I can't remember who they all were, but there were pop stars, some quite famous ones, and also people of your father's sort. A great deal of wine was drunk and everyone became rather merry, your father included. He asked various people to shoot with him while I was in the room and then saw me and said, "You must come too."'

There was a silence. Ed peeled his apple and ate it. Lady Alice cut two grapes from the bunch Horace placed in front of her with a pair of gilt grape scissors. She ate them and then pushed the rest away. Horace took the plates and disappeared.

'I still don't understand,' said Ed, 'why, after all this time, you should decide to come here now that my father is dead.'

'I came because I wanted to get away for a while.'

'But I can't imagine why you haven't been here before, if you knew him so well.'

'Well,' said Lady Alice, 'I couldn't really come here while your mother was alive, could I?'

'Why on earth not?'

'It wouldn't have been proper. I'm not even sure that it is proper now.'

'Why wouldn't it have been proper?' Ed felt he had been thrown off balance by Lady Alice, and he didn't like it. 'Why wouldn't it have been proper?' he repeated.

'Because at one time I was your father's mistress.'

Ed could feel his mouth open in surprise. He closed it again. That old woman in front of him had been his father's mistress? Not possible. But then came the thought that nothing was more probable. Lady Alice must have been very good-looking when she was young – of that there was no doubt. And his father's infidelities had been an open secret, even amongst the family. Ed managed to find his voice again.

'My father's mistress?'

Lady Alice smiled at him. Once again her ghostly beauty

reappeared for a moment, in the animation of her features and the sparkle of her eyes – produced either by the wine, or by the trace of a tear.

'Of course, I was his favourite,' she added. Horace had reappeared behind her. He coughed again. Ed wondered how much of this conversation he had heard; indeed how much was already known to him.

'I have put a tray with the coffee things on the table in the library,' he announced.

After lunch, Ed wanted to continue the conversation that had begun in the dining room, but Lady Alice announced that she would retire for an hour or two.

'I sleep so badly at nights,' she said. 'It is my age, nothing else. But I must have a rest in the afternoons.'

When she had gone Ed asked Horace: 'How long has this been going on?'

'Going on, M'Lord?'

'How long has this lady been staying here?'

'About two weeks, M'Lord. Will there be anything else your Lordship requires?'

Ed knew that Horace also liked an hour or two to himself in the afternoons, so he waved him away and sat down to think. The last thing that he needed in his life at the moment, when he absolutely must sort out his own affairs, was a complete stranger. She might be genuine, or she might not: but she had to go. He knew he must find the courage to tell her to leave. In fact, he would do so after tea. There must be somebody about who could drive her to Darlington Station. She could pack her bags and go.

The phone rang. As Horace was not there to pick it up, Ed answered it himself.

'Hello?'

'Edward?'

Ed recognised the voice even though he had not heard it for six months. It was Malcolm Skinner, the land agent for the Hartlepool Estate.

The agent for an estate such as Hartlepool Hall is a very important person. He collects the rents, and manages the properties and the farms and – when the owner is absent – takes all the decisions that are needed to keep the place ticking over. In some cases, and in the case of Malcolm Skinner, he also manages the estate bank accounts. Malcolm Skinner had been managing the finances of the Hartlepool Estate ever since Ed's father died, with only occasional interference from the trustees. The trustees themselves were quite elderly and not much inclined to take an interest except when they were asked to sign documents.

Ed's relationship with Malcolm was a distant one. Malcolm had been his father's right-hand man for many years. When old Lord Hartlepool died, Ed had been compelled to become a tax exile, what his accountant called a 'non-dom', within weeks of the funeral. His relationship with Malcolm had therefore been limited to occasional phone calls and one or two meetings face to face. He was well aware that Malcolm regarded him as hopeless and had long ago given up trying to get Ed to answer letters or emails. One of the things Ed had least looked forward to on his return was speaking to Malcolm. His feelings towards Malcolm were similar to those he had once had towards his tutors at school, when he had failed to hand in an essay or turn up to a lesson. Despite the fact that if anyone was Malcolm's main employer it was Ed, the sound of Malcolm's voice made him feel both nervous and guilty all at once.

'Good afternoon, Malcolm,' he said.

'I'd heard you were expected back today. I'm coming out from Darlington to have a look at one of your cottages that has a cracked gable end. Something might need doing about that. Then I was going to have a drive about the place in case I see anything else that needs attention. Care to join me? We could have a bit of a catch-up.'

'Well, I've a lot of paperwork to get through,' replied Ed. 'But yes, I could spare an hour.'

'Good,' said Malcolm. 'I'm calling you from my car. I'll be with you in about twenty minutes.'

Ed put down the phone and sighed. He neither liked nor disliked Malcolm Skinner, but he knew that he could not do without him. He was a tall, thin, saturnine man with intense brown eyes, who – like many of his kind – was respected by the good tenants and disliked by the bad ones. He was up at dawn and went to bed late. The Hartlepool Estate was not his only client, but it was his biggest.

So Malcolm would have to be faced, and when he arrived he would bring with him endless problems for Ed to deal with. But that was what Ed had signed up for, wasn't it? He had come back to England because he wanted to have something to do, and because if anyone was going to run Hartlepool Hall and the surrounding estate, it ought to be him. All the same he felt tired just thinking about it. And when he had dealt with Malcolm, and put the old lady on the train, there would be a mountain of letters waiting for him in the office: from the trustees, and the lawyers, and the accountants, all demanding his signature, his attention, and no doubt his money. A great deal of money.

Ed lit a cigarette, went to the window and looked out. While he and Lady Alice had been having lunch, the cloudless blue of the morning had given way to greyer, colder-looking skies. He finished the cigarette then went to find a tweed coat. Outside, he waited on the steps in front of the house. In a moment Malcolm's green Land Rover Defender appeared around a distant corner of the drive. After a short while it emerged beneath the trees and scrunched across the gravel to where Ed was waiting.

As Ed climbed into the vehicle, Malcolm leaned across and shook his hand. He had a strong grip.

'Good to have you back,' he said.

'Well, I'm glad to be back,' said Ed and found, to his surprise, that he meant it. They drove around the side of the house, through the stable yard, past the old bakery and the walled kitchen gardens, past the ice houses and an abandoned apiary, the old hives stacked along the back of a garden wall. Then they continued along a rutted track through the fields, past the home farm, through a dark fir wood and on to a small single-track road. Here Malcolm turned left, saying: 'We're going to see Billy Thompson's old cottage. Do you remember him?'

'I remember Charlie Thompson,' said Ed. He did too: an old grizzled bear of a man. He had been a tenant farmer on one of the hill farms. Ed's father had liked him. He used to come and help out on shoot days as a picker-up. Of course there had been a son, hadn't there? Ed had not known the son's name but he remembered him standing beside his father behind the line, helping with the dogs and wringing the necks of the pricked pheasants.

'Yes, well, Billy is Charlie's son.'

'I do remember him slightly,' said Ed. 'Is he still farming?'

'No, he isn't. There's a story to that,' replied Malcolm. They arrived at the cottage before Malcolm could say any more. Dogs started barking in a kennel somewhere, but there was no other sign of life.

'He must be out and about,' said Malcolm.

'What does Billy do now?'

'He traps moles and helps with the picking up in the shooting season. In the spring and summer he does fencing. He's probably out doing that at the moment. He works all hours, a real grafter. We give him work whenever we have something that suits.'

They walked around the side of the cottage. It was an old building, but someone had recently tidied it up. The small garden was already mown, although the grass had only started to grow in the last week or two. The door and the windowsills of the cottage had been freshly painted. A new kennel had been built beside the coal shed, and inside two large springer spaniels were jumping up and down. A smaller dog, a chocolate-coloured cocker spaniel, was wagging its tail and whining.

'That's his new bitch, Millie,' said Malcolm. 'Pretty little thing. I've put my name down for a pup if she has a litter.'

The two of them inspected the exterior wall. It was stained black by smoke from the flue and a pronounced crack ran across the whole of the gable end.

'We'll have to tie that together with metal bars,' said Malcolm.

The sound of a car could be heard approaching. Then another, much older Land Rover turned into the yard. A big man got out. He had a black beard, shaggy black hair streaked with grey, and bushy eyebrows. He was wearing an ex-army camouflage jacket and trousers stuffed into work boots.

'Afternoon, Billy,' said Malcolm. 'You remember Lord Hartlepool.'

'Aye,' said Billy. He did not offer to shake hands but stood silently in front of them, neither friendly nor unfriendly. Ed nodded to him.

'We were inspecting your gable end, Billy,' said Malcolm. 'We'll get on to a builder and have something done about that.'

'Aye,' said Billy again. 'Bloody thing'll fall down, otherwise.'

'How's the fencing going?'

'I'm on stock-proofing the new plantation up at Cold Crag.'

'Good,' said Malcolm. 'Glad to hear it. Let me know when that's finished. We might have another job for you.'

The two of them left Billy standing in the yard gazing at the cracked gable end. As they moved off, he walked away in the direction of the kennel.

'Bit of a gloomy character,' said Ed. He didn't expect deference – he understood that the feudal customs of rural England had mostly disappeared – but he did expect good manners from his own tenants. Malcolm pulled the Land Rover to the side of the road and switched off the engine. They were out of sight of the cottage now.

'I'll tell you a bit about Billy. You might as well know something about the people who live in your properties. When his father died Billy inherited the agricultural tenancy. I don't know how well you remember that farm: fell land, very wet even in a dry year. Difficult ground. Billy took over his father's beef suckler herd too. He was doing all right in farming terms, which means he was just about keeping his head above water. That was as good as it was going to get, taking on a place like that. Then he married a local girl: Kate Hamblett.'

'I remember her,' said Ed. 'She was rather good-looking. Used to turn up when the hunt met at Hartlepool Hall.'

'Absolutely. She was very pretty. Everyone was quite surprised when the two of them married. She adored hunting and wanted to keep horses. Well, Billy's income in a good year was ten thousand pounds. In a bad year it would be half that.'

'How on earth could he afford it?' asked Ed.

'He couldn't. He started to try different things. No doubt he thought he could improve his farm and get a quart out of a pint pot. He planted a few fields of barley. Two years in three it was no good: the land was just too wet. He went into sheep, then back into cattle, then back to sheep again. He lost money year after year. He fell behind on his rent. His lambing shed blew down in a winter storm. He couldn't afford to rebuild it and there was a problem with the insurers, so he lambed in the field after that and lost a fair few to the cold, the foxes and the crows.'

Ed said nothing. This was not a world of which he had direct experience.

'Anyway,' said Malcolm. 'The inevitable happened. When foot and mouth came in 2001, his farm was one of the infected ones. The men from DEFRA arrived and his flock was slaughtered. They piled the lot of them up on top of the fell and then brought in a big JCB, dug a trench, tipped the carcasses in and burned them. The smell was awful. The whole countryside was covered in the smoke that year.'

'I remember,' said Ed. 'If you went outside, you could see cinders floating past in the wind. I remember the smell too.'

'You don't forget things like that, do you? Anyway, Billy got his compensation claim in but as soon as he received the money the bank put the boot in. They called in his overdraft.

Billy had been running on empty for years, limping from one bad year to the next, and the bank had had enough. So they called in their loan and Billy had to sell up. There was an auction of his bits and pieces. It didn't fetch much, so he had to declare himself bankrupt. That meant we had to terminate his tenancy.'

Malcolm paused in his storytelling. Land agents, like most other professional people, couldn't afford to be sentimental. Indeed few of them were. But Billy's story was something that had stuck in his mind. Ed wondered whether he was being told for his own education, or whether Malcolm wanted to get it off his chest.

'Next thing his wife left him,' said Malcolm. 'She went off with a man who farms about ten miles from here. It's his own place, about five hundred acres of arable, and he could afford to keep Kate and keep her horses. There was a bit of feeling about that locally. Billy may not say much, but he's well liked. I remember being in the Simmonds Arms a few weeks after it happened. Kate and her new man came into the bar. I was there having a drink with someone who does a lot of thinning and clear-felling for us in the woods, trying to agree a price for a thousand tons of timber. Anyway Kate comes in with her new fellow, and there's a silence.'

Malcolm gave a grim laugh.

'Then somebody put "Stand By Your Man" on the juke box – you mightn't remember it: an old country and western number. Tammy Wynette sang it. Kate went bright red. She got the message. She and her new fellow left a minute or two later. They didn't even finish their drinks.'

Malcolm started the engine again.

'So what happened to Billy?' asked Ed.

'Oh, he went to New Zealand for a few years. Quite a lot

of men who lost their jobs did that. Scanning sheep, shearing, shepherding work: that sort of thing. Then he turned up here again this winter and put a deposit down to rent the cottage. And here he still is. I wish him luck.'

Something in Malcolm's voice made Ed feel that Billy was still finding it difficult to make ends meet.

'Most of our farming tenants struggle to pay the monthly rents. Billy isn't the only one,' said Malcolm. 'Quite a few of them are in arrears. You couldn't meet a more decent man than Billy Thompson. But one of these days we may have to chuck him out.'

'Why?' asked Ed in surprise.

'Because we may need to sell this cottage. We're struggling to pay the interest on our loans from the bank, let alone meet the repayment schedules.'

As he released the handbrake and steered the car back into the road, Malcolm said, 'Ed, the Hartlepool Estate is in bad shape. You need a day or two to get your bearings and catch up with some of the correspondence in your office. Then we will have to arrange a meeting with the bank.'

'Why?' asked Ed again.

'Because it's better to ask them for a meeting than for them to call us in.'

When Ed arrived back at the house he had a headache and was in a bad mood. Being reminded of all his responsibilities did that to him. He knew he ought not to react like that. He ought to be interested; he ought to be making notes and lists of things to be done; he ought to be ringing up Teddy. Teddy was the Earl of Shildon, and the senior trustee, indeed the only one who showed any interest in the affairs of the Hartlepool Estate. But Ed hadn't called anyone yet. He hadn't even been to say 'Hello' to his own housekeeper, Mrs Donaldson, even though she had been only a few yards away from him in the kitchen while he sat in the dining room at lunchtime. Just as that thought occurred to him he met her crossing the hall with a tray.

'Oh hello, Mrs Donaldson,' he said. 'How are you?'

'Good afternoon, M'Lord,' replied Mrs Donaldson. 'How nice to see you home again. I hope you will be with us for a while?'

'Yes, it's good to be back,' said Ed. 'Where are you taking those tea things?'

'To the library, M'Lord. Lady Alice likes a cup of china tea in the afternoons, and a cucumber sandwich. I've made enough for you, M'Lord, although I wasn't sure when you would be back.'

Lady Alice! Whose house was this? He followed Mrs Donaldson into the library.

Lady Alice was half sitting, half lying, on a sofa in front of the fire. There was a novel open on her lap and she was covered in a rug from the waist down. As Mrs Donaldson set the tea tray on a table beside her, she said, 'Ah, thank you, Moira. How kind you are. And you've cut the crusts off the sandwiches for me. Dear me! You remember all my little likes and dislikes. How thoughtful!'

'Shall I pour, Lady Alice?'

'No, I shall do it. And here's Edward! I'm sure you'd like a cup of tea too, wouldn't you, dear?'

Mrs Donaldson left the room. Ed sat down on the sofa opposite Lady Alice.

'I'd like a cup, please.'

'Now Moira told me you like the milk in first, is that right? Do stop me if I've got it wrong?'

Ed said nothing, so she poured the tea. What else had 'Moira' been cajoled into telling this stranger, Ed wondered? What colour boxer shorts he wore? The tea was poured. Ed stood up, collected his cup from the tray and stood with his back to the fire.

'It's a very refreshing drink, isn't it, dear?' said Lady Alice. 'My father used to call it a "grateful drink". You must need it. I hear you have been out and about with the agent. It's always a shock to the system when you come back from your holidays.'

'I haven't been away on holiday,' said Ed. 'I've been living in the south of France for the last five years.'

'Are you very fond of France?'

'Not especially. It's not a bad place to live, though. But I had no choice, as it happened.'

'Oh dear,' said Lady Alice. 'I'm sorry to hear that. Still, there's no place like home, is there, dear?'

Ed wished she would stop calling him 'dear'. He put his cup and saucer on a table.

'Lady Alice,' he asked, 'how long are you thinking of staying here?'

'As long as it takes. As long as I am not overstaying my welcome.'

Ed was mystified.

'As long as what takes?'

'As long as it takes for me to tell you a little about myself, and about your father, and how we met. I have a great deal to tell you, Edward. I know your father wanted me to do this.'

Ed was sure of no such thing. Suddenly he lost his temper.

'If you must use my first name, for Christ's sake call me Ed. No one calls me Edward.'

He was so embarrassed by his own behaviour that he had to leave the room. Behind him he heard Lady Alice say, in a tremulous voice, 'I'm so sorry if I've given offence.'

After that Ed didn't dare go back to the library, although it was a cold evening and the rest of the house felt like a giant icebox. Instead he went to the office in the wing overlooking the stable block. There was his father's huge desk, and opposite was a smaller table with a computer terminal that Mrs Budgen, the secretary, used on the two days a week she came in. Ed's post had been opened and piled up for him in a tray. He picked up the document on the top. It was a letter from the Estate's accountants and addressed to the trustees with a copy to Ed. The title was discouraging. It read: *Further tax implications arising on proposed asset sales to fund the provisional settlement with Her Majesty's Revenue and Customs.*

Ed scanned the first few lines. His stomach knotted in dismay. He put the letter back on top of the pile and left the rest unread.

He needed a distraction. He needed to see his own friends: not this unknown person who claimed to have slept with his father. On an impulse he picked up the phone and found that he could dial Annabel Gazebee's number from memory. When she answered he said: 'Annabel – it's me. Ed.'

Annabel Gazebee had been one of Ed's closest friends. In the last five years he had seen her from time to time on his visits home, but he felt that he had lost touch with her.

'Ed!' she said. 'I was going to ring you. How are you? When did you get back?'

'Just today. How did you know I was home?'

'Word gets around,' said Annabel in an arch tone of voice. 'There are no secrets for long in this part of the world.'

'You must come and have lunch.'

'That would be lovely. We can have a really good gossip. It's been ages.'

Annabel sounded as if she were sick with longing to see him again, but there had never been anything between them as far as Ed was concerned. She was not notably pretty compared with Catherine, his girlfriend back then, and she had rather a sharp manner.

'Are any of the others around?' asked Ed, meaning their circle of friends from five years ago.

'Well, Eck's around, but he's gone and wed his cousin, and there's a baby. I never see him nowadays. He's become very much the married man.'

Ed laughed.

'Oh well, it'll be just us,' he said.

'That will be so nice.'

She sounded delighted to hear from him and, at the same time, a little constrained. But when he asked her to lunch the day after tomorrow, she accepted straight away.

Four

Alice did not appear at dinner that night. When Ed enquired where she was, Horace, who was pouring him a glass of wine, answered: 'Lady Alice is indisposed, M'Lord. She asked me to say she was sorry not to be able to join you.'

His tone was funereal, as if announcing the death or grave illness of a member of the Royal Family.

'I'm sorry to hear that,' said Ed. He was sorry. He felt guilty. Poor woman: she was eccentric, even annoying, but he shouldn't have spoken to her so sharply. With his napkin he mopped up two or three drops of wine that Horace had spilled on the table. Then he applied himself to the roast pheasant on the plate in front of him.

He wanted to get Lady Alice out of the house as soon as he could, but there was no reason to be unkind to her. When he had finished eating he stood up, declining the Welsh rarebit that Mrs Donaldson had cooked as his savoury, or anything further to drink.

'Which bedroom did you say Lady Alice was in, Horace? I might just look in and see how she is.'

Horace's features lightened.

'She is in the Blue Bedroom, M'Lord.'

Hartlepool Hall consisted of two wings joined by a large central block. The family rooms were in the West Wing, overlooking the lake and the gardens. The East Wing was used for guests, when there were any, and overlooked the drive and the stable block. The Blue Bedroom was at one end of the guest wing, and was unique in that it was a corner room and had a view over the gardens as well. No doubt that was why Horace had chosen it. Lord Salisbury had once slept in it when he had visited the North East during the election campaign of 1885. Now it was an undistinguished room. If it had once been blue, it was no longer, but was painted in cream and dingy brown, although the name persisted.

Ed climbed the staircase and walked down the corridor which was lit by feeble flickering bulbs in wall sconces. On the walls hung the dimly lit portraits of the less important Simmonds' ancestors. This part of the house had not been redecorated or rewired since God knows when. When Ed came to the door he knocked gently.

'Come in,' he heard Lady Alice call.

He put his head around the door.

'I hope I'm not disturbing you?'

She was sitting upright in bed, pillows plumped behind her. On the bedspread in front of her was a tray with a boiled egg in an eggcup and a plate with half a slice of toast on it. The egg had been eaten, the toast only gnawed.

'You're not. I'm feeling so much better. I was beginning to long for some company. Do stay for a moment. Sit down over there where I can see you.'

She pointed to a small armchair facing the bed.

Ed sat down and said, 'I'm sorry – I spoke to you rather sharply this afternoon. I shouldn't have done so. My only excuse is that I've come home to rather a lot of problems

42

that I've been putting off and putting off. Now they must be dealt with.'

'Dear Ed, there's nothing to apologise for. It must have been very trying for you to come back and find a complete stranger living in your home.'

As she said this Lady Alice gave a surprisingly girlish laugh and for a moment she looked so young and lively that Ed could quite see why his father might have fallen for her ... if the story was true.

'I love boiled eggs,' she added. 'I never get them at home.'

'Do you cook for yourself?' asked Ed.

'I used to cook a bit. I don't any more.'

'You're one better than my mother, then,' Ed told her. 'She had a wonderful education, the best governesses, and she went to finishing schools in London *and* Paris. But she was never taught to cook: not even how to boil an egg. There was always someone else to do that sort of thing.'

Alice laughed again.

'Did you know my mother?' asked Ed.

'No,' Lady Alice replied. 'We never met before she became engaged to your father. After that, of course we couldn't meet. She would never have stood for it. It was no secret that I was your father's mistress before she became engaged to him. She would have known all about me. I hope I'm not upsetting you, telling you this?'

Ed shook his head. Revelations about his father were not something he relished hearing, but he couldn't help being interested. He had not known his father well. Simon Hartlepool had been nearly forty when Ed was born. By the time Ed had finished school his father was approaching sixty. They had met from time to time on the family grouse moor, otherwise the relationship had been a distant one: Ed spent

43

his time on racecourses, whilst his father adored cricket. The two of them had few interests in common and the age difference was significant. His father was often away. He had liked to spend time in London when he was still well enough to be allowed out on his own: he went to all the Test matches if he could and spent weeks staying with friends during the shooting season. Maude Hartlepool had rarely accompanied him on these visits, preferring to stay at Hartlepool Hall, which she ruled over like a despot.

Only when she died did Lord Hartlepool start to spend more time at home, shuffling about in an old cardigan in the daytime, or in a smoking jacket in the evening, his feet encased in slippers. That was how Ed remembered his father: as a rather doddery old man, old for his age, who watched cricket on Sky with a decanter of port at his elbow.

'No,' said Ed. 'It's not a huge surprise.' Then he blushed. 'I'm sorry,' he added. 'But you know what I mean.'

'Of course I do. I wasn't his only mistress. But I was the first, and that was what mattered.'

There was a silence. Ed was beginning to find the room a little airless.

'After your father there really couldn't be anyone else. Mr Robinson, God bless him, took me in, so to speak, but it was never a great romance.'

She turned away her face, and dabbed lightly at her cheek with the cuff of her nightgown.

'I won't disturb you any longer,' said Ed, standing up. 'Will I see you at breakfast?'

'I never eat breakfast,' said Lady Alice. 'I take a cup of tea in my room. We will meet at lunch, I hope.'

Ed said he hoped that they would.

'It was sweet of you to come upstairs.'

'Goodnight, Lady Alice.'

'You must call me Alice, from now on,' she told him.

The next morning, however, Horace brought him a note asking him to have lunch with the Earl of Shildon. Teddy Shildon was now eighty and older than his father would have been had he still been alive, yet he remained a person of great vigour and almost indecent youthfulness. He farmed a few miles further north, living in a large and very dirty farm-house – his wife had died a few years before, so there was no longer any domesticating influence in his life. He strode everywhere at a speed that most people found hard to keep up with. He was well over six foot and broad chested, with wiry ginger hair on each side of his head, joined by a few strands brushed carefully over the central dome. He had a beaky nose and bright blue eyes that many people found uncomfortable to gaze into. A request to go and have lunch with him could not be ignored, so Ed left a message for Alice saying he hoped to see her later in the day, and at twelve o'clock he left the house and drove to Shildon Mains, the farm where Teddy lived.

He arrived at the farm at the same time as Teddy, whose old Isuzu Trooper roared into the yard from the other side of the house, scattering hens and ducks in front of it. Teddy scrambled out of the car and roared: 'Welcome back, Ed!'

He took Ed by the hand in a crushing grip, then abruptly let go, spun around and marched into the house. Inside they entered a large kitchen with a wooden table, on which a hen stood pecking at some crumbs of toast Teddy had left behind at breakfast. On top of the Aga various wet items of clothing were drying out: an enormous pair of jeans, and a flat cap. Nothing had been cleared away. A pile of dirty dishes from the night before was stacked next to the sink and there was no sign of lunch. Teddy removed the hen and put it on the floor.

'Sorry about the mess,' he said. 'My cleaning lady doesn't come in today. But don't worry. I had her put up some lunch for us yesterday. I think it's in the dining room. Let's have a drink first.'

On the far side of the kitchen door, the house assumed a veneer of civilisation. The floor was of parquet that had once been polished but was now bleached and scuffed, with a few well-chewed rugs cast over it. They entered a scruffy room that was Teddy's snug. In it was a bookcase, overflowing with volumes on sporting and agricultural subjects; two large armchairs, quite devoid of any springs; and a television set. A small fire was burning in the grate. On the walls hung several ancient and rather fine oil paintings, darkened by age and wood-smoke. Ed had often been in this room when he had last lived at Hartlepool Hall. It was smaller, and a great deal dirtier, than he remembered.

'Glass of sherry?' said Teddy.

'Do you have anything soft?'

Ed didn't like drinking in the middle of the day but Teddy Shildon had no such inhibitions. He ignored Ed's request and poured two very large glasses of pale sherry from a decanter.

'Take it,' he told Ed. 'You'll need a drink.'

There was a silence as they both sipped their sherry. It was obvious Teddy was thinking about something that bothered him greatly.

'Just finishing the lambing,' he said suddenly. 'We've had more singles than I can ever remember. Only about half the ewes had twins. Rest were singles. I can't understand it.'

'I'm sorry to hear that,' said Ed.

46

'Sorry won't help my bank balance ... It's on the subject of bank balances I wanted to talk to you today, Ed. I know you hate talking business and so do I. Nothing I like less. That's what accountants and solicitors are for. But sometimes one has to get one's own hands dirty.'

To illustrate the point, Teddy opened out the hand that was not grasping the sherry glass. It was huge, reddened by weather and blackened by grime from whatever task he had been doing about the farm that morning.

'Yes ... sometimes we have to confront reality, Ed. Grim reality. Let's go and have some lunch. Want more sherry? There isn't any wine with lunch.'

Teddy's own glass was empty. He picked up the decanter and tipped in another inch or two then offered the sherry to Ed.

'I won't, thanks.'

They went through into the dining room. This was the cleanest room in the house, no doubt because it was not often used. A small and well-polished round table had been laid up for the two of them. On the sideboard were two plates of limp salad and some rather wet-looking slices of ham, sitting beneath cling film. Teddy stripped off the plastic and put the plates on the table.

'I hope this is enough for you,' he said. 'You young chaps have appetites like horses, I know. I don't eat much in the middle of the day. A good cooked breakfast to get me started; then a roast pheasant or a steak in the evenings. But not too much lunch. At my age that's the secret of keeping busy.'

He attacked his ham with vigour. Ed wondered when Teddy would tell him what was on his mind. It was alarming when he chattered on like this.

'You were saying you wanted to talk about the trust,

Teddy,' Ed said after a moment. Teddy put down his knife and fork.

'Yes. Well. I'm afraid it's not good news, Ed.'

Ed put down his knife and fork too.

'Your father and your grandfather lived well. They did themselves proud, and they were generous to their friends.'

The thought had never struck Ed before. His father and grandfather had lived in the manner that was expected of them. They owned a grouse moor. They caused thousands of pheasants to be reared each year in the woods around the house for the winter shooting. His grandfather had owned racehorses. His father had kept mistresses. The house had always been run – as it always had been run. There were fires burning in the library and the drawing room even when there was no one to sit beside them. Food was cooked to the highest standard and there were three courses at dinner every night even if nobody was hungry. The cellar was full of wine but Ed's father had only ever drunk whisky, champagne or port. He considered wine to be a woman's drink, or else something you should give as medicine to anaemic children. Ed drank wine, but in a frugal way. There were still three gardeners, a cleaning lady and a housekeeper, as well as a butler and a gamekeeper on the grouse moor and another on the low ground shoot. In Ed's grandfather's day there had been three housemaids, between-maids, a housekeeper and a cook; two butlers, footmen and hall-boys when they entertained, under-gardeners and under-keepers as well. His grandfather would have considered the present day establishment a very tight ship.

'And the house eats its head off,' Teddy continued. 'In the old days the farming paid for the house, with a bit left over. That isn't true any more. The cottages produce decent enough

48

rents, but they always seem to be falling down and needing money spent on them. People are so fussy, these days. They want double-glazing, and central heating, and en suite bathrooms. En suite bathrooms! Can you believe it? There's none of that sort of nonsense in this house.'

'Yes, I know Hartlepool Hall is an expensive place,' said Ed, 'but what can one do?'

'Well, that's exactly it,' said Teddy. 'That's just the question we need to talk about.' He wiped his mouth with his handkerchief and pushed his plate away. 'Would you like some cheese, Ed? There's a Stilton I had in for Christmas. It's a bit ripe, but I believe it's still edible.'

'No thanks,' said Ed. 'The salad was delicious.'

'Did you think so? I call it rabbit food, but I eat it because then I can tell my doctor I'm eating healthily. All rubbish, isn't it? Anyway the problem, you see, is that your father spent far more than his income from the Estate. And he never provided anything for tax. He believed that the income from the trust was exempt from UK tax. Turned out it wasn't, or at least now that your father is dead, there's no one left who can remember why he thought that it was. So we've had to reach a settlement with the Revenue. We've had to, Ed. The trustees are personally liable. I hadn't realised that when I signed up. Your father told me it would involve a jolly good lunch and a bottle of port once or twice a year, and that would be it. Far from it, dear boy, far from it.'

Teddy stopped speaking, waiting for Ed to say something.

'I haven't quite grasped how much tax we have to pay. I saw something in a letter, but it didn't make any sense to me.'

'Seven million pounds, Ed.'

There was a long silence.

When Ed could find his voice again he asked: 'But have we got seven million pounds we can spare?'

Teddy slapped his leg with one hand.

'Just what your father would have said! He never knew how much money he had. Never cared. The Simmonds always had tons of money and that was all there was to it. Not like my family, we never had a bean.'

Teddy was very proud of his family, who had a title a great deal older than that of the Simmonds, and had never been in what he called 'trade'.

'But have we?' asked Ed again.

'Of course not! The Estate already has a huge overdraft. You'll have to sell something. The trustees believe you'll have to sell the grouse moor.'

Ed looked at him in horror.

'Don't be silly,' he said. Then he corrected himself: 'I'm sorry, Teddy, but sell the grouse moor? You can't mean it?'

The Simmonds' family moor was called Blubberwick. It had been bought in the mid-nineteenth century. Twenty thousand acres of heather and bog, up in the Pennines, it was home to thousands of grouse, not to mention a good few foxes, peregrines, hen harriers and other assorted wild life. From that time to this the grouse season had become a central part of Simmonds family life: their raison d'être, some might say. In Ed's grandfather's day the shoot had been a very grand affair: royalty had even thought it worth travelling to this wild place on the Durham and Yorkshire borders, in order to enjoy the thrill of shooting the Blubberwick grouse. And there was no thrill like it, thought Ed, no sport to match it, and no place so wild and beautiful in which to spend one's days.

Blubberwick Moor was far from any dwellings. Apart from

a few remote inns and taverns, once the haunt of drovers and shepherds, there was nowhere else to stay. The second Marquess had therefore built a large shooting lodge at the turn of the last century, to put up the guns, and their wives. Every summer the entire Simmonds' entourage had moved to Blubberwick Lodge for the start of the season on the twelfth of August, and shot grouse every day through until the end of the month, when there were grouse to be shot. Some years, after wet and dreadful springs, the keepers would shake their heads and look solemn and then the incumbent Lord Hartlepool would know that there would be no shooting that year. The stock had to be preserved. Grouse are wild and cannot be bred in captivity like pheasants. They will not always multiply according to the wishes of the landowners on whose moors they live.

Selling Blubberwick was worse than selling the family silver: far, far worse. Ed shook his head. He felt as if he wanted to cry, but he did not allow this to show in his face.

'What a bore,' he said. 'Are you absolutely sure?'

'There isn't anything else to sell,' said Teddy, 'that produces so little income and would fetch that kind of money. We will have to sell Blubberwick Lodge with it. No one's going to buy a moor in such a remote place without knowing they've got somewhere comfortable to stay. We hope we will get offers: more than one, anyway. Good grouse moors are scarce.'

'But haven't we any pictures we could sell instead?'

'Your family never had much taste in art,' explained Teddy. 'No Titians or Turners or anything of that sort on the walls. The Simmonds have always liked portraits of their dogs or horses; or at a pinch, of their own ancestors. I know there are a few Italian pictures in the hall but they aren't very special. Painted for the carriage trade and bought as a job lot by Percy Simmonds early in the nineteenth century.'

There was another long silence.

'Pity, isn't it?' said Teddy. 'I've spent many happy days at Blubberwick.'

'So have I,' said Ed. 'And I was looking forward to many more.'

'We've instructed Cruickshank and Morse to put Blubberwick on the market. They're specialists in the sale of sporting estates. They will get the best price for it, if anyone can. I thought I should tell you before word gets out.'

'Thank you.'

'But that's not all,' said Teddy. 'There are bank loans to repay as well.'

For Ed, the final bit of news was the worst. As he drove back to Hartlepool Hall he wondered what the point of it all was? Who had built that enormous house, and why? What on earth was the logic of a family labouring for many generations to produce such wealth, and then to build a house that would consume everything? The last and bitterest pill was this: the estate, even after the tax had been paid, no longer washed its face. The house cost more to run than the surplus produced – in the years when there was a surplus – by the farms and cottages. The bank had told the trustees that something had to be done about it.

'But what?' Ed had asked when Teddy gave him this final piece of information.

'Well, that's for you to decide, of course,' said Teddy. 'Once we settle the tax bill with the Revenue, the trust will be wound up and the trustees will resign. I must say, it will be a relief to me. I'm far too old and set in my ways. If

52

Hartlepool Hall is to survive, it needs a young man's thinking. That's your job now, Ed.'

And why is it my job? Ed asked himself. Why should I be the unlucky one who has to foot the bill? His father had never had to do a day's work, and neither had his grandfather. Nor did any member of the family, as far back as anyone could remember. They always had the Simmonds' fortune behind them. Once that had been thought to be limitless. Now it turned out it wasn't. And it was Ed's problem. On top of that he had to return to Hartlepool Hall and have dinner with that old woman and pretend there was nothing the matter.

On the way home he pulled the car over to the side of the road. He got out and was sick. It was the first time in his life he had ever had to worry about money, and the experience was unsettling to both body and soul.

Five

Alice was drinking white wine and soda in the library when Ed came down to dinner.

'It's called a spritzer,' she told him. 'It's very refreshing. You should try it.'

Ed poured himself a whisky.

'I need something stronger.'

'You look pale.'

'I've had,' said Ed, 'the most unpleasant conversation I think I've ever had in my life.'

Alice looked concerned. She put down her drink and came and kissed him on the cheek. It was like having a moth settle on his skin: a faint, papery sensation. A scent of lavender enveloped him for a second.

'Horace told me you were having lunch with the Earl of Shildon. I thought he was an old family friend. Was he horrid to you?'

'Oh, Teddy was all right,' said Ed. 'It's no good shooting the messenger. It's just this place is about to go bust. We have tax bills to pay that you wouldn't believe – but I shouldn't be boring you with all this.'

Alice went and sat down again, but Ed was touched by the concern she had showed.

She said, 'Your father was a very generous man when

he was young. I suppose he never had to worry about money.'

Ed sipped his drink. At that moment, he was feeling a great deal of resentment about the fact that his father and grandfather had spent his inheritance; and more besides. Why should he have to draw the short straw?

'When I met your father in 1963,' said Alice from the sofa. 'I was twenty-one years old. At the shoot he invited me to, there was a party of about sixteen of us staying at the lodge. It was the first time I had been anywhere like that on my own.'

Ed poked the fire and put another log on it.

'The night before the shoot there was a dinner party. Everyone wore evening dress. On the day of the shoot we had a picnic on the moor – what was it called?'

'Blubberwick,' said Ed. He could not keep the bitterness from his voice, but Alice did not appear to notice.

'Yes, Blubberwick. We had a picnic there in the heather. Your father organised it. We had the butler – not Horace, another man – and the footmen from the hall to help carry the hampers and open the wine and spread the rugs so that we could sit on the ground. It was a wonderful, sunny day. I remember that was the first time I'd ever seen or heard a grouse.'

'It can be nice up there,' agreed Ed. He topped up his whisky and put a bit more water in this time.

'Your father came and sat next to me on the rug. There were other girls there, but he singled me out. I could tell he was interested in me. I thought he had been the first time we met, but I was with someone else that evening. He was so charming and friendly. We hadn't really spoken to each other before, except when I had been introduced. That day at

Blubberwick, he talked to me about cricket. Then, suddenly, he asked if he could come and see me in London. Nobody else heard him ask, he kept his voice low.'

'What did you say?' asked Ed.

'He looked at me very directly as he asked the question. It made my heart beat fast. I said yes.'

As Alice said this she sighed.

'I don't regret it. The time I spent with your father was the happiest of my life. I knew he had not the slightest intention of marrying me then or ever and that one day he would leave me for someone else. I knew it even before he touched my hand for the first time. I realised that every day we spent together had to be marked off the calendar and that one day there would be no more days left.'

Horace appeared in the doorway and announced dinner, then withdrew. The two of them rose to their feet.

'Why am I thinking of this?' asked Alice. 'You couldn't know, but I will tell you. It won't take a moment. The first time he came to see me in London was the following month. It was September and very hot. Everybody who had a place in the country had left Town. But I didn't have anywhere else to go. No one had invited me.'

Alice paused and put her hand lightly on Ed's arm, as if to emphasise her plight in having no invitations that September all those years ago.

'It was a blazing hot day. I had a room in a house in Bayswater – north of the Park, not very smart – and your father came and rang the bell. When I opened the door – we didn't have a maid – the sunshine was dazzling. But your father didn't seem to be affected by the heat. He stood there in the sunlight while I stood in the shade feeling cool and excited at the same time. I remember that moment as if it were yesterday. There was a dog barking in the basement flat. Your father took no notice: he only had eyes and ears for me. He said, "I've brought you a little present."'

Alice stopped again, as if re-enacting the moment in her memory. Her hand still rested on Ed's arm.

'What did he give you?' asked Ed, fascinated.

'It was a small thing, wrapped up in tissue paper. It was a little white porcelain shepherdess. I think it was Dresden. Your father said: "It was the prettiest thing in the shop. It reminded me so much of you."'

Ed could not imagine his father doing anything quite so romantic and yet at the same time Alice's words conjured a vivid picture of his father standing in the doorway of a dark little flat, a hot and dusty London street outside. At that age, ten years younger than Ed was now, he had been tall, fair-haired and handsome with a moustache the colour of ripe barley.

'Come over here,' said Alice, 'there's something I want to show you.'

The library had one long wall entirely covered in bookshelves. Opposite it was the fireplace and on either side of the fireplace were glass-fronted cabinets filled with knick-knacks: objects collected by different members of the family over the years and too valuable to throw away, though not in themselves deserving of any special place. Alice pointed at one of the cabinets.

'Look in there,' she told Ed.

Ed unlocked the cabinet door and saw what she was pointing to. It was the white porcelain figure of a shepherdess. He had never noticed it before. He reached inside and took it out. The figurine was jewel-like, its glaze still pristine, an exquisite miniature of a pastoral beauty: on her china head was a china bonnet, the detail so fine you could see the ribbons fastened under her chin. Her eyes stared innocently as if at an Arcadian landscape of green pastures and gambolling lambs. She was clad in a smock and carried a small basket in one hand.

'When – much later – your father told me he had become engaged to your mother, I gave him back all his presents, including this one. But this was the only one I ever missed. I had quite a shock when I happened to be looking at the cabinet this afternoon, and saw it there.'

'It is very pretty,' said Ed. He replaced the figurine in the cabinet with care.

'Let's go through,' said Alice. 'Moira will be upset if we let the food go cold.'

They sat in the dining room with the candles burning. In the dim light Alice appeared younger again, as if memories of that hot London street had in some way brought back her youth. As Ed looked at her he experienced a new feeling. His father had enjoyed the love of this once beautiful woman, and, he knew, several others. And he had found the time to marry Ed's mother – not a beauty, by any stretch of the imagination, but well off and respectable – and produce Ed.

For the first time in his life Ed was suddenly touched by the fear of growing old. He should have been married by now, with children of his own. To take his mind off the subject he asked Alice: 'How did you meet Mr Robinson?'

'I met Samuel in London. Where I worked.'

'Why did you decide to live with him?'

'I was tired of being on my own by then. I had never been well off and I wanted a well-off man to look after me.'

'Was Mr Robinson wealthy?' asked Ed, amused. He sipped

the last of his wine. Horace was standing in a dark corner of the room and, unusually for him, did not appear to have noticed that Ed's glass was empty. Ed tapped it lightly with his knife, making the crystal sing. Horace started, as if from a dream, and came forward slowly.

'No,' replied Alice. 'But he could afford to keep both of us and I realised that was as good as it was going to get. I was no longer young.'

'And what was it that brought you together— What on earth are you doing, Horace?'

Horace was standing behind Ed, holding a bottle of claret and pouring a steady stream of wine straight onto the table, missing the wine glass by about six inches. Horace's face bore an expression of devotion, as if emptying a bottle of wine onto a dining room table was an everyday occurrence. Yet, as far as Ed knew, Horace had never been drunk on duty, or neglected his tasks for one moment during all the years he had worked for the family. A quivering pool of dark liquid had formed on the polished surface and now a stream emerged from this lake, heading towards the table edge, where it trickled in a small waterfall into Ed's lap. Ed pushed his chair back from the table.

'I'm soaked, Horace,' he said angrily.

'Oh, M'Lord,' said Horace. He seemed to wake up, and was appalled by what he had done. Alice stood up and so did Ed, the latter shaking wine from his napkin and mopping his trousers with it. Alice came around the table and took the butler by the arm.

'Come with me, Horace,' she said. 'Let's go next door to the kitchen where you can sit down for a moment.' She took the empty wine bottle from his unresisting hand and led the old man out of the dining room.

Horace walked with his head bowed, muttering: 'So sorry; so sorry. It was the 1994. An underrated vintage, M'Lord.'

Ed shook his head. He tried to soak up the rest of the wine with his napkin, and then threw the sodden cloth onto the floor. He couldn't think what else to do. Then he remembered that salt was supposed to prevent wine stains. He found the silver salt cellar and up-ended it over the remains of the lake. A little mountain of white crystals turning pink now marked the spot of the accident.

He should have been the one who helped Horace out of the room. The old man had had either a stroke, or some sort of mental breakdown. But Alice, twice Ed's age, had reacted first. Now Ed would have to decide what to do about Horace. The simplest thing would be to get rid of him. He would speak to Malcolm about it in the morning. The old boy was well past retirement age and should have been pensioned off years ago. How did one go about these things? There was sure to be some law or other. He went upstairs and changed his trousers.

When Ed came back downstairs Alice was waiting for him in the library. A coffee tray sat on the table in front of her.

'I hope the coffee is drinkable,' she said, as Ed came into the room. 'I made it myself.'

'I'm sure it will be.'

'Were your trousers ruined?'

'I expect the stains will come out. It's not the end of the world. How is Horace?'

'Moira took him upstairs to his room. He's very shaken by what happened. He said that he has never done anything like that in his entire career. I think you should go and comfort him. He is very distressed.'

'I'll speak to him in the morning.'

'How long has he been at Hartlepool Hall?' asked Alice.

'Oh, Horace has been here for ever,' said Ed. As he sipped his coffee, he tried to remember when Horace had come into his life. The truth was that Horace had always been there. He had started work for the family at the age of fourteen, decades before Ed had even been born, polishing silver and cleaning shoes. He had risen to the position of butler in Ed's grandfather's day, in the late 1960s, and had held the position ever since. It was – perhaps – unreasonable to expect him to keep working to his eightieth birthday, but Horace had never complained or spoken about retirement, so it had been more convenient to allow him to get on with his job. Now Ed realised that something would have to be done. He wondered what butlers cost these days, and where one found them. It was bound to be a lot more than Horace was earning. That was something Malcolm would know about. Then a horrible thought struck Ed: maybe he couldn't afford a new butler. Maybe he would become the first member of the Simmonds family for nearly two hundred years who would have to open his own front door.

When she had finished her coffee, Alice rose to her feet. As she did so she picked up a large book, like a scrapbook or photograph album, which had been lying on the sofa beside her.

'I mustn't forget this,' she said to herself, rather than to Ed.

'What have you got there?' he asked.

'Oh, just a few scraps, newspaper clippings and photos I like to keep by me.'

'I'd love to have a look sometime,' said Ed.

'It would bore you, I'm sure,' said Alice. 'Goodnight, Ed.'

Annabel Gazebee came to lunch the following day. She was brisk and bright, pecking Ed on the cheek and then going into ecstasies about how well he looked.

'You're so brown,' she said. 'Don't you miss the sunshine?'

'Come and have a drink,' suggested Ed. 'I've had five years of sunshine, Annabel. I'm quite happy to put up with a few cloudy days.'

'Will you be staying in England then?' asked Annabel.

'I don't know what my plans are,' Ed replied. 'There's an awful lot to sort out here. What will you drink?'

'Oh, I shouldn't. But a glass of white wine would be very nice. After all, one doesn't meet such an old friend every day of the week.'

Ed poured them each a glass. At first, he couldn't think of anything to say to Annabel after all this time.

'I've got someone staying with me at the moment,' he remarked at last. 'Alice Birtley.'

'Should I know her?' asked Annabel. 'I don't recognise the name.'

'No, she's a good deal older than us,' Ed replied. He wondered why he had started this line of conversation. 'As a matter of fact she says she was my father's mistress.'

'No!' exclaimed Annabel. 'How wonderful! Will she be joining us for lunch?'

'I couldn't persuade her to. She's quite reclusive.'

'What a shame. Perhaps I will meet her some other time. How long will she be staying here?'

'I've no idea. She's good company,' explained Ed. He was surprised to hear himself say that, but realised it was true. 'I rather like having someone to talk to in the evenings.'

'I must ask my father about her,' said Annabel. 'He knew

all about your Pa. I don't think my own father was quite as well-behaved a young man as he should have been either. He would certainly have known whom your father was walking out with. He was your Pa's best man.'

'How is your father?' asked Ed as they went in to lunch. He had forgotten old Marcus Gazebee was still alive.

'Where's Horace?' asked Annabel, appearing not to have heard him. 'Isn't he still working for you?'

'He's not well,' explained Ed.

'Do give him my love. Dear old Horace. Now, Ed, do tell me: who is the girl in your life at the moment? Some gorgeous French lady?'

'There isn't anyone,' said Ed.

'Not like you to live like a monk.'

'I haven't always been monk-like,' replied Ed. 'But there's no one at the moment. What about you, Annabel?'

Annabel's sallow cheeks darkened for a second. She looked down at the lamb chop on her plate.

'There is somebody, actually ...'

'Would I know him?'

Annabel looked uncomfortable but she raised her gaze and faced Ed directly.

'No, you wouldn't,' she replied. 'He's called Geoff Tarset. He lives near Darlington.'

'Tell me about him.'

'He's very nice, and very kind,' replied Annabel. 'Very kind to me, at any rate. He's our age.'

'Then why haven't I met him before?'

'Ed, Geoff's a bit different to us. He was brought up on a council estate. That's why you've never met him. He's frightfully successful now, and very rich.' Annabel stopped, perhaps conscious she was explaining a bit more than was necessary.

'I'm terribly fond of him,' she added.

'I'm so glad,' said Ed. 'But why you should worry about where he was brought up is beyond me.'

'Oh, Ed. You know what people are like. Always asking which school you went to, or who your father was. I knew you'd understand.'

Annabel seemed unable to continue for a moment. Then she pulled herself together and said: 'Geoff wants to meet you.'

'Wants to meet *me*?' said Ed. 'Well, of course, I'd be delighted. Bring him here if you like. But why does he want to meet me?'

'I told him you were one of my oldest friends, just like my father was one of your father's oldest friends so of course he wants to although, to be honest, it wasn't just that.'

Ed had learned a few things as he had gone through life. He had avoided a university education, and he had not learned many skills that were remarkable in any way over the last thirty-five years. But what he *had* learned was to be on his guard when people used the phrase: 'To be honest'.

'Oh yes?'

'Geoff knows Malcolm Skinner,' she explained. 'Ed, would it be awful if I asked for another glass of wine?'

Ed sprang to his feet. 'Of course. I'm sorry; I've been neglecting you. I keep forgetting Horace isn't with us.'

He poured Annabel another glass of white wine. She sipped it for a moment until she felt sufficiently fortified to explain about Geoff.

Geoff Tarset and Malcolm Skinner had done a few deals together. Malcolm's firm specialised in property – land agency, estate agency, and consultancy – and Geoff was a big client. It appeared that somehow Geoff had learned from

Malcolm of the Hartlepool Estate's need for cash.

'I'm sure Malcolm wasn't being indiscreet,' Annabel told Ed. Although this was not what she really thought, she felt she had to stick up for Geoff and that meant sticking up for Malcolm as well.

'Just doing his job, I suppose.' Ed wondered how much Malcolm had been telling people about his private affairs.

'Anyway, Geoff wants to meet you. He says' – Annabel exhibited a faint blush again – 'that you might want to discuss with him "something to your mutual advantage".'

'What on earth does that mean?'

'Oh, don't be horrid, Ed,' said Annabel. 'You know perfectly well. Geoff is a property developer. You're a landowner. I suppose he wants to see if there are things you can do together that will help the estate to make a bit of money.'

'And help him do the same.'

'Of course. That's what he does.'

By the time Annabel left after lunch there was an understanding that the two of them would meet again soon, and that next time Geoff would be there.

'I really would like the two of you to meet,' she promised Ed. 'But if you decide you want to talk to him about business, I will creep away like a mouse so that you won't be overheard.'

When Annabel left Ed felt a sense of relief. He had thought it would be much more fun seeing her again than it had turned out to be.

Six

After lunch Ed went back to the estate office and sat at his desk. It was the last thing he wanted to do. Outside it was another sunny day, with clouds scudding across the sky in a southerly breeze. What he would have liked to do most of all was go for a walk in the gardens, or talk to the keeper about the shoot, or do almost anything except what he ought to do.

He couldn't face reading all the trust correspondence just yet, even though he knew how vital it was that he should make an effort. If ever there was a time to buckle down, put his nose to the grindstone, face up to reality – all those phrases he remembered from his school reports – it was now. Still he could not bring himself to do it and instead distracted himself by looking through the pile of unpaid bills in the in-tray. There was a handwritten invoice from Billy Thompson, for trapping moles. There was a bill from someone else for cutting up a tree that had crashed into the road during a winter storm. There was a bill for roofing repairs to one of the cottages. There was an enormous rates demand. There was a bill for the supply of cut flowers to the house for the period from January through to the end of March. It amounted to several thousand pounds. Ed picked up the phone and rang through to the kitchen. After a moment, Mrs Donaldson answered.

'Mrs Donaldson,' said Ed, 'why have we been buying cut flowers all winter?'

'Oh, Lord Hartlepool, we always do that. Your father liked the house to look as cheerful as possible, especially in the winter when there's nothing coming in from the greenhouses.'

'But my father's been dead for five years,' Ed pointed out, 'and I've been living in France.'

'Oh, well, M'Lord, we never knew whether you mightn't look in for a day or two. We wouldn't want you to come home to a nasty, cold, dreary house.'

Ed thanked her. It seemed pointless to be annoyed by it. Before he could hang up, she added, 'The doctor's visiting Horace this afternoon. Did you want to see him afterwards, M'Lord?'

'Not at the moment. I'll look in on Horace later.'

Ed hung up and turned back to the pile of bills. There was a repair bill for the under-gardener's car. There were vet's bills for the horses that no one ever rode. There was a thousand pounds to pay for replacing broken panes in one of the greenhouses. There was an enormous bill – Ed could not believe it was possible that anything smaller than a cruise ship could consume so much fuel – for heating oil. While he was reading these, Malcolm Skinner came into the office.

'I let myself in,' he explained. 'No one seemed to want to answer the door.'

'Horace is ill.'

'Nothing serious, I hope?'

'I don't know,' said Ed. 'Have a chair. Do you want coffee?'

'No thanks. You might need something stronger in a moment or two, though.'

'Why?'

Malcolm Skinner paused. Ed had seen the look on his face before. It was the same expression he'd seen on the doctor's face when he told Ed his father wasn't expected to live beyond a week.

'I had a phone call this afternoon from the bank. They want a meeting, and soon. They want to call in the overdraft and they want proposals from us as soon as possible to show how we can reduce our outstanding term loans.'

Ed felt depressed.

'I wish I'd never come back. You seem to have nothing to tell me about but problems.'

'Well, they have to be dealt with,' said Malcolm. 'It's no good us moaning about it. The fact is that the bank has got wind of the trustees' settlement with the taxman. They've heard about Blubberwick Moor being put up for sale and want to make sure the bank gets its cash out before everything is sold off or goes up in smoke.'

Ed put his head in his hands.

'No one ever told me things were this bad,' he said in an accusing tone.

'You've talked to Teddy Shildon, haven't you?' asked Malcolm. 'You've been sent copies of all the correspondence while you were in France. You know you could have picked up the phone at any time and talked to Teddy or me. I'm afraid we're beginning to run out of time. Something drastic will have to be done, and we'll have to do it soon. Otherwise, whether you like it or not, the bank may put the whole estate into administration.'

How could Ed explain that, in all the five years abroad, he had never read any of those letters all the way to the end? How could he explain that bitterness at his exile, and then idleness, had led to a state of mind where he very often didn't open the letters at all, preferring to put them in a pile that even now sat gathering dust at Villa Laurier.

'It's that bad?' he asked, after a long silence.

'When your father died there was an overdraft of – I forget what, but somewhere north of two million secured on the arable land and the residential properties. Then there were various term loans. Of course, what's happened in the last couple of years is that the value of security has gone down and the amount of the lending has gone up. Suddenly the bank's cover on its loans to the estate looks very thin, and the trustees' decision to sell off the grouse moor at Blubber-wick has undoubtedly rattled them. That was additional security they thought they could get their hands on if they needed to. Now it's gone.'

Ed realised that Malcolm was annoyed that the trustees had decided to use another firm to sell off the moor without consulting him.

'So what am I to do about it?'

'Well,' said Malcolm. 'We will have to submit a plan to the bank. Are you busy tomorrow?'

'No engagements so far,' said Ed.

'I will email you my own proposals, but the final decision must be yours, of course. Don't despair, Ed,' Malcolm said as he stood up to go, 'we'll work something out.'

But how could Ed avoid a feeling of despair? Nobody had any words of comfort for him; nobody was on his side. Only his conversations with Lady Alice afforded him any escape.

'I need cheering up,' Ed said to Alice that evening.

He explained a little of what had happened over the last twenty-four hours. Alice was a good listener.

'I'm sure you will sort everything out, my dear,' she said.

'The Simmonds have lived at Hartlepool Hall for a long time, and they will be here a long time yet.'

'Was my father very extravagant?'

'He was generous to me.'

They were sitting in the library as usual, and the door onto the terrace had been opened. It was a warm evening after a day of sunshine and showers and a sweet fresh smell wafted in from outside. Alice was wearing a black evening dress and a shawl. She dressed every night as if she were dining at the Ritz and Ed was rather impressed by her sense of style. Alice never just came into a room: she made an entrance. Despite her age, there was an air of faded glamour about her, a hint of dances and parties from long ago.

'I went for a walk around the gardens this afternoon after Malcolm left,' Ed told her. 'I found one of the gardeners mowing the grass tennis courts, and the other one was putting down fresh white lines on the court that had just been mown.'

'How very nice,' said Alice, 'that things are being kept up properly.'

'I haven't played tennis here for about seven years,' said Ed. 'My father never played. The courts were always kept in shape in the old days because we used to have house parties in the summer. But why are they still being cut?'

'What else could you do with them?' asked Alice.

'I don't know. But that's a day's work every week during the spring and summer for the last seven years, preparing tennis courts that no one ever uses.'

They went in to dinner.

'You were asking about your father being extravagant,' said Alice.

'Yes, I was wondering about that.'

'I don't know what you would call extravagance,' replied Alice.

Ed did not reply. He thought that filling an empty house week in and week out with cut flowers might be one definition; a two million pound overdraft might be another.

'But I do know that he was very generous to me. After his first visit to my flat in Bayswater he wrote to me and asked if he could call again. I wrote back and said that he could, if he liked. The next time he turned up at my flat he had a taxi waiting outside. He said, "I want to show you something. It's too far to walk." I didn't know what to say, so I locked the front door and then drove for a few minutes through Hyde Park and into Hyde Park Gate. We turned into a little mews and stopped outside one of the cottages. It must have been an old stable before it was converted. It was absolutely sweet, with wisteria growing up the walls. "What are we doing here?" I asked. Your father looked at me. He used to brush his moustache with his finger and smile when he was pleased about something. "I've taken this house," he said. "It's for you. I want you to come and live here."'

When Alice described his father in this way Ed knew she was talking about someone quite unknown to him: his father as a young man.

'He rented that little mews house near Hyde Park for me, and had it furnished and decorated just the way I wanted. He didn't ask for anything in return. I kept expecting him to, but he never did.'

'You mean he just gave you the house and left you there?' Alice laughed.

'No, he didn't just leave me there. He used to spend a lot of time in the family flat in Cadogan Gardens. I went there once or twice before he was married. I don't think he got on very well with your grandfather. He wasn't often at Hartlepool Hall or Blubberwick, except in the shooting season. No, he used to call for me in the morning and we'd go riding together in Rotten Row. There were livery stables at the end of the mews, you see. We had such fun, riding in the Park together.'

Alice paused to dab at her lips with a napkin.

'Often, in the afternoon, he'd come and have tea with me. It was like playing house as a little girl. We became such good friends. We talked and talked.'

'What did you talk about?' asked Ed. 'I never heard my father talk much about anything apart from cricket, or the uselessness of politicians in general or the House of Lords in particular.'

'We talked about all sorts of things. Your father told me he wanted to make something of himself in the world. "I've been born into a well-off family, Alice," he told me, "and I've been trained to do absolutely nothing. We made our money a long time ago through hard work, and none of us has worked for three generations. But I'm not going to waste my life like my father did."'

Ed was fascinated by this glimpse into his father's character.

'What did he want to do?'

'He thought he might become a publisher, or a journalist: something that allowed him to travel and meet different people, people outside his own class. He loved the music of the day; he enjoyed mixing with pop stars and going to clubs like the Marquee or Ronnie Scott's. He was young for his age in some ways. He didn't really have very clear ideas, only that he didn't want to live the life he saw being mapped out for him by his family.'

Mrs Donaldson came into the dining room and removed the plates.

'I've cooked some angels on horseback for you both,' she told them. 'Or there's floating islands with a raspberry *coulis* if you'd prefer something sweet.'

'Oh, I really couldn't,' said Alice apologetically. 'I have such a small appetite.'

Ed saw that he would have to eat something if he were not to cause offence, so he asked for the savoury to be brought in. When Mrs Donaldson had left the room he told Alice, 'I wish she wouldn't cook so much food. I can't cope.'

'Poor thing,' said Alice. 'She's had no one to cook for for five years. She's thrilled you are back here, eating her food. And she's such a good cook.'

'She's not bad,' agreed Ed.

'Do you think you might like to come outside for a moment?' said Ed, after dinner. 'It's such a beautiful night.'

'Just for a moment, then,' said Alice, wrapping her shawl around her.

They went out through the doors onto the terrace. Beyond the balustrade were the dim shapes of rhododendron bushes, and beyond that the lake. An owl was hooting in the woods. Then it stopped and everything was quiet. A delicious, indefinable, heavy scent came to them on the gentle breeze.

'This is a heavenly place,' sighed Alice. 'You must protect it and look after it.'

'Don't make me feel any worse than I do already.'

'I'm sorry, my dear,' she apologised. 'I shouldn't have said that. It's none of my business.'

Ed found his packet of cigarettes, took one out then offered one to Alice. She shook her head.

'So when did it happen?' he asked.

'When did what happen?'

'When did you and my father' – Ed groped for the right phrase, and couldn't find it – 'get together?'

'What an expression!' laughed Alice. It was almost a giggle. After a moment's silence, she began to speak again.

'We became lovers one afternoon when it was raining. Your father came for tea. He was very restless. He got up and walked around the tiny sitting room and then stood by the window. I can still remember the sound of the raindrops striking the glass, and your father shifting about on his feet. "I hate this weather," he said. "What can one do? It's too wet to go out."

'"We could play cards?" I said.

'"What games can you play with just two people?" he asked me.

'"We could play honeymoon bridge," I suggested. "You'd like that."

'"I'm bored with playing cards," he complained.

'I remember his exact words because some devil got into me then and I said: "We could play a new game."

'"What new game?" he asked, turning around.

'"Draw the curtains and I'll show you."

'"Why do I need to draw the curtains? We won't be able to see what we're doing." He still didn't understand but he drew the curtains anyway. Then I stood in front of him, unbuttoned my dress and slipped it off.

'"Can you see well enough to play this game?" I said. I was so naughty that afternoon. I don't know where it came from. That was how we became lovers.'

Ed turned away from Alice and drew on his cigarette. The image of a young girl slipping off her dress in a darkened

74

sitting room on a rainy afternoon was so clear it was as if he had once stood there, and not his father. The thought disturbed him.

Alice shivered. 'Let's go in. My blood is thinner than yours. I'm feeling cold.'

Alice went to bed soon after and Ed stayed downstairs, smoking a couple of cigarettes on the terrace and looking out into the darkness. Alice was right: he had just been given all this. He mustn't lose it, the instant it finally came into his possession. He remembered the feeling of apprehension in France the day before he returned home from his exile: the sense of an enormous weight settling on his shoulders. Now that feeling returned to him stronger than before. What could he alone do to correct generations of idleness, extravagance and folly? He, who for the first thirty-five years of his life had been brought up to believe that he too would live free from work: a life given over to spending money and the pleasure of entertaining one's friends? He didn't know if he was strong enough to do anything about it.

That night he dreamed about Alice. A spotlight was shining on her as she danced across a wooden stage by herself. Somewhere a waltz was being played. She had no partner, but she danced with the assurance of one who is held in the strong arms of another, now old, now young, dancing the night away to the sound of distant music.

Seven

The next morning Alice came downstairs in the middle of the morning, as usual – it already seemed as if she had always lived at Hartlepool Hall – and found Ed reading the newspapers.

'You won't save Hartlepool Hall sitting there reading,' she said. Ed looked up in surprise.

'No, I suppose I won't. The trouble is, I don't know where to start.'

'If your mind is idle, nothing will occur to it,' Alice told him. 'You need to *do* something. Go and talk to Horace: he's been asking to see you.'

Ed was suddenly reminded of his mother. She had used that exact tone of voice, to which there was no answer except obedience. He stood up, trying to pretend it was his own idea.

'I was just thinking about Horace.'

Ed left the room and went up the main staircase and along the Long Gallery until he came to the smaller, steeper flight of stairs that led to the servants' quarters on the second floor.

He knocked on Horace's door. He thought he heard a faint sound in answer so entered the room.

'How are you, Horace?' Ed asked in his most cheerful voice.

'Oh – ah – oh,' said Horace.

He was sitting up in bed, propped against a pillow someone had plumped up for him. A forgotten mug of tea sat on the bedside table. He was wearing a very ancient pair of flannel pyjamas, his hair was sticking up in tufts and he had not shaved for at least a couple of days. His cheeks were grizzled with white beard and his eyes seemed to have sunk deep into their sockets. Ed hardly recognised him. All his life, since he was a small boy, he had only ever seen Horace in a black coat and striped grey trousers: the traditional uniform of an English country house butler. Horace had always been scrupulously well turned out. His shirts were white as snow; his shoes the deepest black; his hair, even when it had begun to thin, combed across his head. Now, seeing this frail, dishevelled old man, Ed could not think what to say. After a moment's silence, he said: 'I hope you are feeling better?'

Horace looked at him with a wondering stare. His watery blue eyes seemed unfocused. He lifted his right hand towards his head and touched his uncombed hair. Then his hand wandered down onto his chest, feeling the flannel of his pyjama top. His mouth worked for a moment but no sound came out, although a thread of saliva worked its way down his chin. Ed looked on, appalled. He wished he were somewhere else. But then Horace spoke.

'I trust your Lordship finds everything to his satisfaction?'

It was as if he had gone back in time thirty or forty years, when butlers really did say things like that.

'Everything is fine, Horace,' Ed answered. 'Has the doctor been to see you?'

'The doctor?' Horace appeared to struggle with the question. Then it was as if he had suddenly woken up. His eyes focused and he spoke again, this time in a clearer voice. 'I am sorry that you find me like this, M'Lord. I will be up and about again in no time. I do regret the inconvenience my absence must be causing.'

'Don't worry,' Ed told him. 'We miss you, but we're managing. Take your time. Don't come down until you feel well. Has the doctor been to see you?'

'I'm afraid I'm not sure. He may have been.' Horace hesitated. 'There was some wine spilled. I remember that. I am so sorry. I fear some of the wine may have splashed itself onto you.'

'It was nothing.'

'My memory is not what it was,' said Horace. The ghost of a smile appeared on his face. 'I can remember quite well when your father was still alive and Mrs Horton was the cook, but more recent events are harder to recall.'

'I'm sure everything will be all right in a day or two.'

'Lady Alice has been very kind,' said Horace. 'She has sat and talked with me twice now. She has been a great comfort. I don't remember what we talked about. The old days, I expect.'

As Horace talked he became more and more alert: now he was sounding and speaking like his old self. He would want to go back to work soon and that would be good, thought Ed. But then it occurred to him that perhaps now was the moment to talk to Horace about retiring. The subject had to be discussed sometime, so why not the present?

'You know, Horace, there's no particular reason for you to come back to work at all. There's only me in the house. Lady Alice will be leaving soon, and I don't need much looking after. Why don't you take life a little easier now?'

'Oh no, I couldn't do that,' replied Horace. He sounded shocked by the suggestion. 'There is always so much to do.

You don't see it all, M'Lord. There's the silver to be cleaned. If I don't keep an eye on the daily cleaners the dusting doesn't get done properly and the furniture is never polished. There are all the clocks to wind up every week. Who will do that, if I'm not there to do it? They all have their special ways, those clocks. If I don't do it, you'll never know what time it is again. Oh no, I couldn't possibly just stop working, M'Lord. The house would go to rack and ruin.'

'Don't worry,' replied Ed, alarmed by the effect of his suggestion.

Horace was exhausted by his outburst. He lay back on his pillow and closed his eyes for a moment. Then he said, 'I'm sorry, M'Lord. But I do worry so.'

'I'll go now, Horace, I don't want to tire you out.'

'Thank you for coming, M'Lord.'

Ed stood up to go. As he passed the bed, Horace reached out and touched his arm.

'I had pneumonia once,' he told Ed. 'In 1963. I was very ill. I was in bed for six weeks. Your father never came to see me. It just wasn't done, in those days.'

Ed left the room, closing the door gently behind him.

Ed sat in the estate office for the rest of the morning. He knew he had to come up with a plan to keep the bank happy, and soon. He waited for the lightning bolt of inspiration to strike him. It did not. At lunchtime he had some sandwiches brought in to him and sent his apologies to Lady Alice for leaving her to lunch on her own. In some obscure way he felt he was punishing her for her accusation of idleness that morning. He ate his sandwiches and picked up documents and put them down again. What on earth was he going to do? He had absolutely no idea where to start.

The phone rang. It was Malcolm Skinner.

'I've spent most of the morning on the phone to the accountants and the bank,' he said. 'I'd better let you know where we've got to. Do you want me to come to Hartlepool Hall, or can we do this by phone first? Then I can come over tomorrow when you've had a chance to think things through.'

'Let's do it over the phone,' said Ed.

'Fine. I can email you everything in writing afterwards.'

Ed sat and listened to Malcolm. It was not pleasant. Horace had to go, of course, and Mrs Donaldson was to be replaced by a part-time cleaner. Ed would have to cook his own food. The gardeners would be made redundant and a contractor brought in once a fortnight to cut the grass. The keeper would be made redundant at the end of the following shooting season.

'We can't get rid of him now,' explained Malcolm, 'we've already let a dozen days' shooting and it would cost us more to stop than to go on.'

Then Malcolm read out a list of cottages that would have to be sold. Amongst them Ed recognised the name of Springwell Cottage, where Billy Thompson was the tenant.

'Those are the only properties we have that are on shorthold tenancies and aren't already mortgaged. We can turn them into cash and pay down some of our borrowing.'

Ed felt that if he looked at himself in a mirror at that moment he would see a man who was all grey: bloodless skin, grey hair, a man whose life was draining out of him.

'Do we really have to do all this?' he asked.

'This is just the short-term fix. The bigger problem – how to manage the running costs of Hartlepool Hall and the interest on the remaining loans – is unsolved. But we might win a month or two's breathing space. I'm sending you the email now.'

Ed didn't wait for the email. He didn't want to read it now or later. Instead he left the office and wandered into the main house and the Hall of Sculptures. This was an inner courtyard that long ago had been covered with a roof of glass and iron. The light shone down on the black and white marble floor on which stood, like giant chessmen, several white marble statues: muscular men and women on plinths, clutching torches, or swords and shields, or wrestling with serpents, or suckling babies, their blank marble eyes staring at nothing. An earlier Simmonds had brought the statues from a factory in Carrara in Italy. At the far end of the Hall was an enormous stuffed animal: a white bull with horns that would not have disgraced a buffalo. It was a throwback, with more aurochs in its DNA than anything else. It had been the monarch of a herd of white cattle; genetic freaks that had somehow reincarnated themselves after their ancestors had vanished during the last Ice Age. These creatures had once lived in the grounds of the now ruined Hartlepool Abbey a mile or two away and this magnificent bull had been among the last of its kind. It had been shot by King Edward VII on a visit to Hartlepool Hall, on a day when it was too foggy to shoot pheasants, and the King had grown bored.

Ed walked past the door that opened onto the den where his father had sat for years, watching cricket on television and sipping his port. He went up a staircase and returned to the Long Gallery.

The gallery was filled with armchairs, card tables and chaises longues as if at least fifty people were expected at any moment to drink tea or play bridge or wander about looking at the pictures. Tall windows illuminated the gallery, through which one could look out at the Hartlepool woods. Although it was a dull day, the sky filled with ominous grey clouds, there was enough light to distinguish the subjects of the portraits that hung on the opposite wall. Between each pair of portraits was a full-length mirror, creating a disturbing effect of vast interior spaces, reflections of the windows and the world beyond. Ed could not remember this room having ever been used. It was too full of dead people.

Each portrait depicted one of Ed's ancestors: Simmondses, and their wives and children. The faces at this end of the room were of the earlier members of the family: those who had struggled and worked their fingers to the bone hewing ore in the iron mines of the Cleveland Hills; those who had been mine foremen and the first members of their family ever to own their own houses; those who had been harsh overseers of enormous factories. Their faces were pale, their eyes dark with reproach, their clothes sombre and modest.

As Ed moved along the row the faces and dress of the subjects changed. Here was Joe Simmonds, a hard-faced man in a black coat, with a prosperous air. Ed knew that he had started life as a miner in the iron ore mines near Middlesbrough in the 1760s. Later he had become a mine foreman, and still later had secured mineral rights of his own. Next to his portrait was one of his sons, also called Joseph: he had become a mine owner and then a manufacturer, as the ore ran out. The Simmonds Railway Company had been established in order to provide the first steel rails for the new railway industry. At the time many thought that Joseph Simmonds had abandoned common sense, betting his fortune on this strange new technology. But as mile upon mile of track was laid down, the profits from Joseph's business grew. A network of railways began to criss-cross the country, factory sheds multiplied across the counties of North Yorkshire and Durham, the labourers who worked in the Simmonds' enterprises, who had once numbered dozens, could be measured in their hundreds.

Other ventures followed the railway business. The second Joseph Simmonds had been a considerable entrepreneur: he started the Simmonds Forge Company that supplied forgings for the armaments industry; the Simmonds Plate Company that supplied iron and steel plate for the even newer phenomenon of iron-clad ships. As the family grew in wealth and influence its aspirations increased likewise. Joseph's son, Percy, became a Member of Parliament. Never an assiduous attendant in parliament, he was nevertheless considered an important man and, after a few years as an MP, was also created a baronet. He was the last Simmonds to be directly involved in the family enterprises, which by then were too large to be managed by any one man. Managers were appointed to run these companies on behalf of the owners. Now, thousands worked in their factories, labouring for long hours in order to produce the dividends that the family required to maintain their new and expensive way of life.

When Henry Simmonds was created the first Marquess of Hartlepool, the College of Heralds was asked to make a coat of arms and a crest for the family. The crest showed a pick and a hammer crossed, a reference to the origins of the family wealth that disgusted some of their contemporaries. Henry Simmonds did not care: he had the title; he had the house and the acres; he had the money.

Ed stopped now in front of Henry's portrait. Here was a man who had learned how to enjoy life. His features were rosier than the pallid faces of his forebears. His eyes twinkled in his pink face. He wore a frock coat, underneath which peeped out a waistcoat embroidered with gold and blue thread. A cravat was knotted around his neck. The little finger of his left hand was turned so that the spectator could clearly see the massive gold signet ring, with the new Hartlepool crest engraved upon it. This was the man who had built Hartlepool Hall.

Next to his picture was the famous portrait of his son, another Percy, painted by John Singer Sargent at the turn of the last century. It was one of the few distinguished pictures in the house. The elegant clothes and languid air of this figure were worlds away from the earlier family portraits. This was a man of leisure: a man at his ease in society. It was Percy Hartlepool who sold the last of the Simmonds' businesses just after the Great War, severing the remaining links between the family and the worlds of industry and commerce. In his time and ever afterwards, no member of the family had been made to endure any form of employment. They devoted themselves to sport; to travel; to the pleasures of simply existing, in the company of like-minded men and women. In Percy's day, it had been unimaginable that the money would ever run out. Bankers toiled and stockbrokers worked late into the night so that the Simmonds' fortune would multiply. For generations after Percy, no Simmonds had opened a bank statement, or bored himself with conversations with his accountants or lawyers — at least until Ed's father's time. Now and then they had called for more funds to be made available; the funds always arrived.

There was a movement at the other end of the room. Ed was startled. For a moment he wondered if one of the portraits had come to life and had stepped out of its frame in order to reproach him. But it was only Alice. They met in the middle of the gallery.

'I thought you would be resting,' said Ed.

'I couldn't settle. I came here to walk about.'

That was what the room had been built for, so that ladies and gentlemen could stroll about without having to risk the inclemency of the weather.

As they passed along the row of portraits, Alice asked, 'Why are there so many mirrors?'

They stopped and stared at their reflections: a tall, grey-haired old lady who had once been beautiful; a fair-haired man going thin on top with a strained, pale face. Ed realised with a shock that his reflection looked nothing like his own image of himself.

'I was once told that it was so members of the family could stand in front of the mirror and compare their likeness with the portrait alongside it.'

'How quaint!' said Alice.

'My own theory is that we didn't have enough ancestors to fill the space.'

Alice laughed.

'We all have any amount of ancestors, my dear. You can't think your family simply sprang into existence three hundred years ago.'

They walked companionably to the end of the gallery and then turned around and walked slowly back. Alice took Ed's arm to steady herself.

'Do you mind if we sit down for a moment?'

'Not at all.'

Ed pulled out two armchairs that were set against the wall, so that they could sit facing each other.

'How are your plans coming along since I saw you this morning?' asked Alice.

'Badly,' said Ed. He was silent for a moment. 'It seems as

if I have a choice between making other people homeless or being made homeless myself.'

'Well,' said Alice, 'there is one thing that's even worse than being homeless.'

'What's that?'

'Having a home you don't want to go back to. Having a home that is more like a prison.'

Ed raised his eyebrows, inviting explanation, but Alice would not say any more. Instead she pulled herself to her feet. Suddenly she looked her age: frail and elderly.

'I think I will go to my room now for an hour or two.'

Ed offered to accompany her but she refused, walking away slowly. It was something about this room, thought Ed. It made people feel their own mortality. The rows of faces expressed exhaustion, avarice, disapproval, loneliness, pride – every human emotion except happiness.

The next morning Malcolm arrived just as Ed was finishing his second cup of coffee. Ed invited him to have a cup.

'I won't, thanks.' His words were polite but his manner was peremptory. Ed had noticed how Malcolm's attitude towards him had changed over the last few days. It was as if he was the master and Ed the employee. But there was nothing to be done about it – Malcolm understood what was going on and Ed needed his help.

They went through the copies of the redundancy letters first.

'We're obliged to write and say we're consulting with the employees we want to make redundant before we actually do so,' said Malcolm. 'It's best to speak to people before writing to them. Do you want me to do that? It's only a formality.'

'I'd better speak to Horace myself,' said Ed. 'I feel I ought to.'

'Very well. I'll speak to everyone else after we've finished here. The letters will be put in the post tonight. Now let's look at the properties.'

They went through a list of cottages. When they came to Springwell Cottage Ed said, 'That's Billy Thompson, isn't it?'

'The mole catcher, yes.'

'It's a bit hard on him, isn't it?'

Malcolm stared at Ed for a moment and then replied: 'It's a bit hard on all of them. All the cottages will have to be sold with vacant possession and all the tenants will get notices to quit. Andy Felling was a shepherd in your father's time. He'll have to leave Cold Fell Farm. Gilbert Elliott, who lives at Long Barns, was a tractor man for your father and your grandfather. They've nothing but a state pension and your father let them have the cottages at a peppercorn rent because in those days it was generally recognised that agricultural wages were very low. Now they're too old to find work.'

'What will happen to them?' asked Ed.

'Not our problem. We need to be robust about this. Cutting costs is the easy part. The hard part is: what do we do next? The estate and the house simply aren't solvent. So what do we do about it?'

As Malcolm said this Ed realised that what was happening to him meant more than a few days or weeks of discomfort. It was more than a bit of belt tightening: a few economies in the kitchen and in the gardens, or remembering to turn off the television at night and not to leave the lights on all the time. It was not just a question of buying grapes at Tesco's instead of having them brought in from the greenhouse. His way of life, the only life he had ever known, the only life the

87

last four or five generations of his family had ever known, was about to change: fundamentally, and for ever.

'What can I do?' he said, but he must have been speaking to himself because Malcolm didn't hear him.

'What?'

'What can I do?' repeated Ed in a clearer voice.

'That's for you to decide,' said Malcolm. 'Of course we can come up with ideas, but it will be a question of what you are prepared to put up with.'

'Could we open the house to visitors?'

'That's been tried, as you know. We're still trying to pay off the bill for the tearoom and gift shop your father built. It never made any money. That's why we closed it down last year. I wrote to you about it.'

'Oh yes,' said Ed, although he didn't remember. 'We could do weddings?'

'We do weddings, and private parties as well,' Malcolm told him. 'We must have done ten functions a year while you've been away. But it's only scratching the surface of the problem.'

There was a silence. Then Malcolm said, as if an idea had just occurred to him: 'Do you know someone called Geoff Tarset?'

'I know of him. He's a friend of Annabel Gazebee's, isn't he?'

'He's a very successful property developer. Very innovative.'

'Meaning what?' asked Ed.

'Meaning nothing. But I think you should meet him.'

It was clear that he was not going to say anything else about Geoff Tarset, but Ed couldn't miss the clang of a hint being dropped. Malcolm rose to go but then turned back again.

'One other thing.'

'Oh yes?'

For the first time Malcolm looked uncomfortable and didn't quite meet Ed's eye as he spoke.

'Our firm's account. It's normally paid in arrears and we deduct it from your client account. I'd like to suggest that we are paid in advance from now on. I hope that's acceptable.'

Ed said, 'I quite see.'

'I'm glad you understand. Things being what they are. I'm obliged to protect the firm's position.'

'I understand.'

'I'll see myself out,' said Malcolm.

After he had gone, Ed sat for a long time in the office. Rain began to patter against the windows but, apart from that faint sound, the house lay still and quiet under the grey skies of a wet May day.

Eight

As if by magic, Annabel Gazebee rang the next day and asked Ed to lunch.

'It will only be me,' she told Ed, 'and Geoff. I'm so looking forward to you meeting Geoff. I'm sure you'll like him *very* much,' although she did not sound in the least bit sure. Then she added, 'My father will probably be there too. He never tells me his plans. If I ask him, he'll say no, and if I don't ask him, he'll join us anyway.'

Annabel lived with her father in a grim, square, stone house a few miles north of Hartlepool Hall. Long ago her father had been a colonel in the army. Now aged seventy-four, he was a little older than Ed's father would have been. He had not served in the same regiment, but he had been one of his cronies, often to be found sitting with Ed's father in his den clutching a glass of port. Ed had never liked him. He was a tall, thin, overbearing man who seemed to sneer at everyone and everything. No doubt it was an unfortunate physical trait over which he had no control. Annabel had never quite found the courage, or the money, to leave home and live somewhere on her own. It was rumoured that her father was one reason why Annabel had never married; it was said that he gave every man Annabel brought home such a hard time that they never came back. Ed thought that Geoff

Tarset must be unusually resilient if he'd survived more than one visit to Lambshiel House.

He did not look forward to the idea of lunch with Annabel but he could not refuse. She knew quite well he had nothing else to do.

'Why don't you bring what's her name?' suggested Annabel. 'Alice?'

'Yes. Then she can chat to my father about old times. He's bound to remember her when he sees her again. They can keep each other busy, while we talk.'

Ed began to wonder if he could invent an excuse to cancel this engagement. Annabel, without trying hard, had managed to make it sound a most unappealing occasion. But there was no way out.

'I'll see you tomorrow,' he said.

'About one,' Annabel reminded him. 'And not smart.'

When Ed asked Alice if she would like to come, she declined.

'But you must have met Marcus Gazebee,' said Ed. 'He was one of my father's oldest friends.'

'Your father never introduced me to his friends,' said Alice. 'I was meant to be a secret. I'm sure they knew, but he never took me to any of the places where we might have met.'

'Why was that?'

'He was worried about scandal, I suppose. I was his mistress, and he knew one day he would have to marry someone else. The less said about me the better.'

Alice did not sound bitter as she said this.

'I won't come, if you don't mind,' she added. 'Going about tires me and I don't like meeting new people.'

'Well, you've met me,' said Ed. 'And Horace. Oh God, that reminds me.'

'But you've gone quite pale. What's the matter?'

'The post,' said Ed. 'What time does the post come?' He looked at his watch. 'He'll have read the letter by now. I was meant to speak to him first, break it to him gently. Oh God.'

He ran out of the room and hurried to the kitchen first, to ask Mrs Donaldson if the post had arrived. But when he got there Horace was sitting at the kitchen table, a mug of coffee in front of him. He was no longer in his dressing gown and pyjamas but had shaved and dressed. He was wearing his butler's uniform except that his black coat was hanging on the back of his chair. Ed noticed with a kind of strange detached interest that Horace wore garters on his shirtsleeves to ensure his shirt cuffs were always the right length. He was reading the letter from Malcolm Skinner. When he saw Ed come into the kitchen he got to his feet, put the letter down on the table, and struggled into his black coat.

'I'm sorry you find me like this, M'Lord,' he said. 'I was hoping to start work again today. I'm feeling a good deal better and I know there is a lot to do.'

Horace still did not seem well enough to go back to work. He looked as though a gentle breeze might blow him away.

'I wanted to explain about that letter,' Ed said. 'I'm so sorry you should have got it without any warning. I meant to speak to you yesterday.'

Horace looked blank.

'You've read it?' asked Ed.

'Mrs Donaldson and I were just talking, M'Lord. We didn't quite understand what it meant.'

He held out the letter to Ed, who took it and scanned it. It was written in the impenetrable language in which such letters are often couched. Yesterday Ed had hardly been able to look at it when Malcolm had showed him the draft, let alone offer a literary critique. Sentences caught his eye amongst the dense thickets of text:

We wish to discuss with you the issues that the Hartlepool Estate is currently facing

and

Economic considerations may mean that the estate has to reduce its headcount by way of redundancy

and

You are entitled to attend a meeting to discuss the situation and to bring a colleague with you (or other person certified under the Employment Relations Act 1999).

He looked up at Horace.

'You don't understand what this means?'

'No, M'Lord. I'm very sorry, but it is all a bit complicated. I'm not very familiar with this type of correspondence, M'Lord.'

'Sit down, Horace; you too, Mrs Donaldson. I need to tell you something.'

They both sat at the table, like small children about to be scolded. Ed tried to assemble his thoughts but then gave up. His words came out in a rush. The estate was very hard up. There had been a row with the taxman and Blubberwick had to be sold. Cottages would also have to be sold. They would have to save money wherever they could. The long and the short of it was that they couldn't afford to employ Horace or Mrs Donaldson any longer. He was very sorry to have to give them such bad news.

'I've a bit put by, M'Lord,' said Horace. 'Gentlemen have been very kind with their tips over the years, and I've never had anything to spend them on. You would be most welcome to use the money, if that would be of any help.'

'Horace, that is so kind of you. I am deeply grateful. But

I am afraid it wouldn't make any difference. Your offer is very generous. But in the scale of things it wouldn't help and, even if it did, the estate could never accept such a gift.'

Horace bowed his head. 'Does that mean I will no longer be in your service, M'Lord?'

'I'm very much afraid that's what it does mean.'

There was a long silence. Mrs Donaldson offered to put the kettle on but neither of the other two answered her. Then Horace gave a gentle smile.

'As your late father would have said, I've had a very good innings. I can't complain. I'm grateful to have been allowed to go on working so long. When would you like me to leave, M'Lord? I can be out by this afternoon, but tomorrow morning would be more convenient if that is agreeable to you.'

'There's no question of your leaving so soon, Horace,' said Ed. 'There's all sorts of things to be sorted out. There's the money owing to you, and I need to know you've got somewhere to go to when you leave here. Stay at least another week. Stay a month.'

'That is very kind, M'Lord,' said Horace. 'I shall await further instructions in the matter. Now, if there's nothing else at the moment, I had better be getting on with my duties.'

As Ed turned to leave he saw a row of cheeses had been laid out on the marble slab underneath wire mesh covers. There was a whole Brie; half a Stilton; and a profusion of other varieties.

'Who is all this cheese for?' asked Ed.

'Lady Alice likes a morsel of cheese after dinner, so I thought I had better get some in,' said Mrs Donaldson. Ed noticed that a brace of frozen pheasants and what looked like a brace of woodcock were thawing in an oven tray.

'Are we expecting anyone in tonight?'

'I always like to have enough,' she replied, 'just in case your Lordship decides to have guests.'

Ed had rarely been in the kitchen when he lived at Hartlepool Hall; this was his first visit in some years and the generosity of the arrangements astounded him. Looking about him more carefully he saw other delicacies: enormous bunches of green and purple grapes sitting in a bowl of pressed glass; a row of purple figs on a worktop; a pair of pineapples; a pair of fish fillets covered in flour; a glazed ham that had just come out of the oven.

'Who eats all this stuff?' he asked Mrs Donaldson in surprise.

'Lady Hartlepool always insisted that there should be a choice of things to eat,' she explained, 'and that's always been my rule in the kitchen.'

'Well, fine,' said Ed. He didn't feel like entering into a discussion on household economics. He left the room feeling wretched and went to the library, where he found Alice doing *The Times* crossword. He poured his heart out to her.

'But you are doing Horace a kindness,' she told him. 'If you hadn't made him redundant you would have had to ask him to retire. The job was killing him. Walking around this huge house each and every day, polishing silver, winding up clocks, fetching wine from the cellar and heaven knows what else. They are all jobs that should be done by a younger man. It had to happen, one way or another. Especially after his stroke.'

'Did Horace have a stroke?'

'I suppose it was something like that,' said Alice. 'Thank heavens, I have never had one, so I don't really know. But that's what it looked like to me.'

Alice picked up the telephone beside her, rang through to the kitchen and ordered them both some coffee. It arrived a few minutes later in a large silver pot, together with a plate of freshly cooked biscuits.

'Just a little something to help you get your strength back, M'Lord,' said Mrs Donaldson as she put the tray down. 'I know how difficult it must be for you at the moment.'

Ed thought that of all the economies that now stretched in front of him, like rows of freshly dug graves in which all of his life's pleasures would soon be buried, the loss of Mrs Donaldson's homemade almond biscuits would be one of the hardest to bear. But after he had drunk the coffee and eaten two of the biscuits he felt a great deal better.

At lunch he talked to Alice about all the schemes he had been turning over in his mind to save Hartlepool Hall. He would let out the house as a conference centre in the winter months and go and live cheaply at his villa in France. He would build a golf course in the park and turn a wing into a clubhouse. He would promote Hartlepool Hall to all the film location companies and pay for its upkeep in that way. He would turn over the garden to the growing of herbs and spices for the supermarket trade. He would turn over the farm to the production of Highland cattle, whose beef he had heard was exceptionally popular in Holland and Germany, and fetched twice the price of ordinary beef. With an unaccustomed glass of wine at lunch, Ed was in the best of spirits.

To all of this Alice agreed with a smile. She contributed nothing to Ed's flow of ideas, but a great deal to his confidence. Here at least was one person who believed in him.

'Something will turn up,' she said. 'If you look for a solution, you *may* find one in the end. The only certainty is that if you never look, then you will never find.'

'You are so wise, Alice,' said Ed.

The next morning was bright and sunny. At half past twelve Ed drove the few miles north to Lambshiel House, which was located on the edge of Shortmoor, a former pit village built on top of a cold and windy hill; a single street with a few pubs, fish and chip shops, a post office and a butcher's. The ancient Saxon church of St Winifred's stood at the far end of the village, on the highest and windiest spot of all. It had been there long before the village had been built and might well still be standing after the other houses had fallen down. Lambshiel House itself was a former farmhouse that had been enlarged and expanded into something its original builders had never intended. A dining room and a drawing room had been added to the lower storey and above were extra bedrooms and bathrooms, so that it was now quite a bit larger than when it was first built. Nothing about the exterior of the house suggested either comfort or convenience would be found inside.

The house was situated on a ridge. To the south were featureless brown moors that, in a few months, would turn purple as the heather came into bloom and then, as winter approached, would fade to a dark brown that was almost black. To the north of the house was a good view of a forest of giant wind turbines. These enigmatic structures would occasionally flicker into movement in the fiercest of gales, otherwise they stood motionless: a monument of some sort, but to what? The house itself was approached through two stone pillars along a short tarmac drive flanked by beds of roses planted in very straight lines. These testified to a desire for uniformity above all else. Every flower was the same shade of red, but in all other respects the plants suggested a complete indifference to gardening on the part of the owners. Close-cut lawns made up the rest of the garden. Another car was already parked in front of the house: a red open-topped sports car with white leather seats. Ed parked his father's old Peugeot next to this vehicle, which turned out to be a Ferrari. When Ed got out of his car he saw Annabel staring at him through the drawing room window. She had obviously been waiting. Then she vanished and appeared an instant later at the front door.

'Good afternoon,' said Annabel in a bright voice. 'Come on in, Ed, and meet everybody.'

In a lower tone she added: 'My father has decided to join us. He's being a bit tricky. Do be nice to him if you can.'

They went into the drawing room, a room that like the garden displayed the values of the owner of the house: orderliness before comfort. Two armchairs were arranged opposite each other, on either side of an empty fireplace, with a hard and uncomfortable-looking sofa facing it. Behind the sofa was a highly polished sofa table with nothing on it. There were no ornaments or books or magazines to hint at what might be the tastes of the inhabitants, no flowers or cushions to add colour to the bare whiteness of the room or to soften its rectangularity. A few prints of battle scenes hung on the walls. If Annabel was capable of decorating and furnishing a room, she had not been allowed to use her talents here. The furniture did not look new, but nor did it seem as if this room was often used. There was a sideboard along one wall on which a number of bottles and glasses sat upon a tray of silver plate. Next to this a short stocky man, in a blue, open-necked shirt and tight black jeans, was struggling with a corkscrew and a bottle of white wine. Annabel skirted around him and headed for the fireplace where a tall, thin old man with very long legs sat in one of the armchairs. He was dressed in an old tweed suit of great elegance, and wore a regimental tie with a tiepin, in marked contrast to the informal dress of the other man.

'Daddy, you remember Ed?'

'I'm not senile yet, Annabel. Of course I remember Ed, although it is a very long time since we met. Your father's funeral, I believe. I won't get up if you don't mind. How are you, my boy?'

He extended a thin, bony hand for Ed to shake.

'I'm very well,' said Ed. 'I hope you are the same?'

'I'm not getting any younger,' said Marcus Gazebee. 'Although I've lived a good few years longer than your father. He never looked after himself, of course. Never took any exercise or did a stroke of work. Not that you would expect a man in his position to do either. Annabel, go and give what's his name a hand – he seems to be taking an awfully long time with the drinks. You'll take a glass of wine, Ed?'

'His name is Geoff, Daddy, as you very well know,' said Annabel with sudden fury. She went over to help Geoff at the drinks tray.

'Annabel's new chap, you know,' said Marcus Gazebee in a tone that might have been meant to be confidential, but was certainly audible from the sideboard. 'Very strange sort of fellow. Reminds me of a corporal I used to know in my old regiment who came and worked as my groom for a few years. Of course that was a long time ago. I had to give up hunting twenty years back. Couldn't afford the keep.'

Annabel returned with Geoff. She handed a glass of wine to her father and one to Ed. Geoff was clutching a large glass of gin and tonic with a lot of ice in it. He was smiling broadly, showing very white teeth in a tanned face. He had bright blue eyes and tight curls of grey hair. His shirt was unbuttoned exposing the top of a hairy chest.

'Geoff, this is my old friend Ed Hartlepool,' said Annabel. 'Ed, this is Geoff Tarset.'

Geoff pumped his right hand.

'How are you doing, Ed?'

Ed murmured a reply and tried to recover his hand but Geoff gripped it for a moment or two longer, gazing at him with an intense blue stare as if he wished never to forget this moment. When he let go of Ed's hand, it felt rather crushed.

'Ed, Annabel has told me so much about you,' said Geoff. 'I'm sincerely delighted to meet you at last.'

Ed could not think how to answer this, so he smiled. Annabel said: 'I'm sure you two will have a great deal to talk about.'

'Are we in any danger of being served lunch today?' interrupted Marcus Gazebee from his armchair. 'I'm sure poor Ed must be starving after driving all that way.'

'Yes, of course, Daddy,' said Annabel. 'Everybody come through into the dining room in about five minutes?' She left the room in a hurry. Geoff beamed at Ed.

'Well, well,' he said. 'This is a pleasure, Ed. Annabel has told me so much about your lovely home at Hartlepool Hall.'

Marcus Gazebee interrupted him in a loud voice: 'I hear you're having to sell Blubberwick Moor. Hard times, eh?'

'I'm afraid that's true,' replied Ed.

'Of course your father was always reckless with money, quite reckless, like all the Simmondses. It doesn't matter how much you've got, you can always burn through it if you know how to spend it. Isn't that right, Mr Tarset?'

'I don't know, I'm sure, Colonel Gazebee,' said Geoff Tarset, still smiling broadly.

'No, you probably don't,' agreed Marcus Gazebee. 'But I expect you will find out one day. Of course you are what they used to call a self-made man. Not used to handling money and not used to hanging onto it. But the Simmonds family,' said the old man, contradicting what he had said a moment before, 'was old money. Well, not exactly old money, but still, they made their fortune a good two hundred years ago. They should have learned how to hang onto it by now, don't you think, Ed?'

Annabel came back into the room. 'Lunch is ready, if you would like to come through.'

The dining room was as austere as Ed remembered it. A small table of polished mahogany was laid for four with a jug of water placed at the centre. Ed noticed Geoff Tarset helping himself to a surreptitious refill of gin and tonic as he and Ed followed Marcus Gazebee out of the drawing room. Geoff must have known what to expect: there was no sign of any wine with lunch. In front of each of them a plate had been set on which was a slab of some kind of pâté, garnished with a limp lettuce leaf. A rack of toast was beside Annabel. She handed it round. For a couple of minutes there was no sound but the crunching of toast. Then Marcus Gazebee asked in his nasal voice: 'What's this meant to be?'

'It's pork pâté, Daddy,' said Annabel.

Ed turned to Geoff.

'I gather you're in the property business?'

'Spot on, Ed. I develop properties, for my sins. Houses, offices, whatever comes along.'

'He's a builder,' said Marcus Gazebee helpfully, from the head of the table.

'Oh, Daddy,' said Annabel. 'You know what Geoff does.'

'I'm sure I don't,' replied her father. 'Not my world.'

They finished the starter. Annabel cleared everything away and then brought in plates holding dry slices of roast chicken, and overcooked carrots and potatoes.

'Yes, if you've got a minute after lunch, I've an idea I wanted to mention to you,' said Geoff Tarset to Ed. Although he spoke out of the corner of his mouth Marcus Gazebee overheard him.

'Want to discuss a little business, do you, Mr Tarset? Can it wait until we've finished eating, do you think?'

'Oh, Daddy,' said Annabel. She stood up and left the room. Ed thought she was in tears.

Marcus Gazebee said, unperturbed by his daughter's departure, 'How's old Horace? Is he still going?'

'Yes, although he's getting on a bit.'

'Getting on? He can't be much older than me. Still, it'll be hard to replace him when he goes. You can't find the staff these days, my friends tell me. Not that we've had any staff here for a long time. Annabel has to do it all. Still, she has time on her hands. Do you have trouble finding staff, Mr Tarset?'

'Not especially,' said Geoff. 'But we pay top rates so that helps.'

Ed was impressed. Geoff Tarset seemed quite able to hold his own against Annabel's father and did not appear in the least bit intimidated by him. Ed, on the other hand, found Marcus Gazebee just as daunting as ever. Annabel came back into the room and sat down again.

'We were talking about domestic staff, my dear,' said her father. 'I said you and I managed perfectly well without them these days. Annabel enjoys cooking. You can tell that, can't you Edward? Where did you get this recipe for roast chicken, my dear? Quite delicious.'

'It's the same thing we have every week, Daddy,' replied Annabel.

'Is it really? It tastes quite different this week. Do you have a good cook at Hartlepool Hall, Edward? Is Mrs Horton still there? But she can't be. She must be dead by now.'

The conversation continued in a desultory way until Annabel cleared the plates. Marcus Gazebee did most of the talking and when he spoke, it was mostly to Ed. The dry chicken was followed by a slice of apple pie with lumpy custard and then Annabel offered to make coffee. Everybody declined. Marcus Gazebee stood up and produced a small decanter, half full of a brown liquid, from the sideboard behind him. He placed it on the table.

'Port,' he said. 'Needs drinking. It's going over. You'll both take a glass with me.'

It was not a question. Annabel stood up again with an attempt at a girlish smile.

'I'll leave you boys to it. Don't be too long.'

She left the room. The port circulated. Ed sipped his. It had once been a wonderful drink but now, like its owner, was in the later stages of its existence. What had once been a rich wine had decayed into a liquid the colour of watery gravy.

'Fonseca 1948,' said Marcus Gazebee. 'There's not much left of it now. Your father had a very good port cellar, Edward. What's happened to it all, I wonder?'

'He drank most of it before he died, I think the trustees sold what was left at auction.'

'Are you enjoying your port, Mr Tarset?' enquired Marcus Gazebee, 'or would you prefer a cocktail of some sort? A dry

Martini? I'm not sure what we've got in the house. You'll have to ask Annabel. She's the quartermaster here.'

'The port suits me just fine,' said Geoff Tarset. 'I like port. We drink a nice ruby port at the golf club I'm a shareholder in, near Stockton. This is similar, isn't it?'

Marcus Gazebee said nothing and Ed thought that for once Annabel's father was lost for words.

Geoff stood up, drained his glass and said, 'Well, with your permission, Colonel Gazebee, I'm going to go outside and smoke a cigar. I know you don't like the smell of it in the house. Ed, come and join me.'

'You'd better go, Edward,' said Marcus Gazebee. 'Don't mind me. He wants to talk *business*.'

The two of them left Annabel's father gazing at his half-finished glass of port, and went into the garden. Geoff produced a large cigar from a case containing two. He offered the other one to Ed, who declined it. Geoff bit the end off his cigar, then lit it. It was windy, but he managed to get the cigar going after a moment. They were standing next to the cars.

'Nice car,' said Ed, indicating the Ferrari.

'You like it? I'll take you for a spin in it some day. That's my fun car. I've got a Roller as well, but I just use that for business.'

Geoff dismissed the subject of cars with a wave of his hand, as if it was beneath both of them to talk about such commonplace things as Ferraris and Rolls-Royces.

'I didn't want to say too much in front of that old fox inside. He picks up on things and then tries to wind people up. I don't mind it. I've met a lot worse than him in my time. But he's a bit hard on poor old Annabel sometimes.'

Ed thought that this description of Annabel by her lover

did not inspire confidence in the relationship. He said nothing.

'I wanted to meet you to talk about an idea I've had for developing Hartlepool Hall. It could make a lot of money for both of us and it could solve some of the problems the estate has.'

'What problems were you thinking of?'

Ed did not at all like the idea that his financial position appeared to be common knowledge.

'Oh, I think we both know what those are. I should say that Malcolm Skinner, your agent, is also a consultant for Tarset Developments, which is the name of my company.' He held up his hand as if to forestall protests from Ed, but Ed was too surprised to say anything. 'Don't worry, Malcolm hasn't betrayed any secrets. He hasn't said anything he shouldn't have. But he thought it might be useful if we met. And the north-east of England is a small world. The bankers all talk to each other. The lawyers gossip. The accountants do, too. If someone's getting in too deep, everyone finds out sooner rather than later.'

'So what exactly did you want to discuss?' Ed asked.

He disliked Geoff Tarset's calm assumption that he knew everything about the Hartlepool Estate and its problems. Perhaps he did, but Ed wished he hadn't said so in quite such a blunt manner. At the same time there was a hard edge to Geoff Tarset that compelled respect. He looked like a man who got things done, and got them done in a way that suited him best.

'Not here,' said Geoff Tarset. 'We can't stay outside too long otherwise the old man will get even grumpier, and then he'll take it out on Annabel after we've gone. But I do want to come and see you with Malcolm. Will you hear what I have to say then?'

'When did you have in mind?'

'Tomorrow. No point in wasting time.'

Ed agreed. He didn't feel he had much choice. In any case, he was curious about what Geoff Tarset might have to say. Geoff threw the rest of his cigar into the colonel's roses, and the two men went back into the house.

They returned to the drawing room, where Marcus Gazebee was reading the newspaper. When they came back in, Annabel jumped to her feet and offered them coffee again.

'No thanks,' said Ed. 'I must be going. Thank you for a delicious lunch, Annabel. And you too, sir.'

'It's kind of you to say so, Edward,' said Marcus Gazebee. 'We don't aspire to *haute cuisine* here, do we, Annabel?'

Just before he left Ed remembered something. He turned back to Marcus Gazebee and asked, 'I've someone staying at Hartlepool Hall you might remember. Did you ever come across someone called Lady Alice Birtley? This would be in the nineteen sixties?'

'Don't recall the name,' said the old man.

'She was one of my father's old flames,' explained Ed.

Marcus Gazebee gave a harsh laugh.

'There were quite a few of those. We used to call them either B.M. or A.M.'

Ed said, 'I don't understand.'

'Before Maude, or After Maude. He had quite a few flings before he met your mother. Marriage never slowed him down much. Which one was she? Alice, did you say?'

'Yes.'

The old man shook his head.

'Don't remember that name. Unless she was one of Mrs Bright's girls. Was she?'

Ed had no idea what the old man was talking about. He

wished he had not brought the subject up. A few minutes later he took his leave. Annabel walked out of the drawing room with him into the hall where she murmured: 'So nice of you to come, Edward. I know Geoff was *thrilled* to have met you. Thank you for putting up with my father.'

'Not at all. He was fine.'

'Not if you have to live with it every day,' said Annabel with sudden bitterness.

Nine

The lunch party had been a trial to Annabel. Her father was at his worst, making snobbish remarks at Geoff's expense and oiling up to Ed because of his rank. But despite her father's behaviour, Geoff had got his way. He took Ed outside where they must have talked business because when they came back Geoff was all smiles. After Ed had gone Geoff and Annabel were alone for a moment in the passage outside the drawing room. He kissed her on the ear and patted her bottom.

'Well done, sweetheart. I'm going to see Ed tomorrow and tell him how we can rescue Hartlepool Hall.'

Before Annabel could ask Geoff what this meant her father called out angrily from next door.

'Is anyone going to get me a cup of tea? Do I have to ask every time? Annabel? Where are you?'

'See you, darling,' said Geoff. 'Don't let the old man grind you down.'

Then, whistling loudly because he knew it annoyed Colonel Gazebee, Geoff left the house, slamming the door behind him and scattering gravel onto the grass as his car sped down the drive.

Annabel made her father his cup of tea and brought it to him on a tray. He took the cup and saucer in his hand and stirred the hot liquid for a second with a teaspoon. Then he blew on the surface to cool it and took a sip. Annabel waited for him to say something that would release her from his presence. She wanted to have time to herself. Instead, he asked, 'Are you sleeping with that builder man?'

'Oh, Daddy,' said Annabel, shocked by the unexpectedness of the question as much as by the question itself. She felt herself turn crimson.

'Well, are you?'

She tried to keep some shred of dignity. 'What I do is my own business. You seem to forget I'm thirty-three years old, not sixteen.'

'I'm only too aware of your age, my dear. And I can see you don't want to answer my question. In any case, your face has done the talking for you.'

Annabel left the room. Her eyes were smarting as if she were about to cry; indeed one hot tear did run down her cheek, but she brushed it angrily away. She wasn't sure how much more of this she could take. She had looked after her father for fifteen years, since her mother died. She used to be able to picture her mother with absolute clarity but now the image in her mind resembled an old photograph that had been left lying around in the sun: it was bleached and faded. She could no longer hear her mother's voice in her head as she once did.

Her mother had died in a car accident, returning from Darlington, when her car had inexplicably crossed the central reservation on a stretch of dual carriageway and been hit by a lorry coming from the other direction. For fifteen years Annabel had been doing her mother's job.

But what could she do about it now? Her father sat upon her shoulders like the Old Man of the Sea; he clung there and could not be shaken off. Annabel had no income except the money he gave her. None of their relations offered to help: relations there were, but they had made it very clear they were not willing to share her burden.

She went upstairs to her room and sat on the bed. It was covered in a tartan bedspread her mother had given her years ago and at its foot was an enormous toy giraffe. A photograph frame, a telephone and a lamp occupied the bedside table. The frame held a picture of her mother standing beside her and steadying her as Annabel, aged six, sat astride her first, and last, pony.

The other furnishings in the room were an armchair, a wardrobe, a dressing table, a tallboy and a bookcase. The bookcase contained Annabel's little library of well-worn paperbacks. In the books Annabel read, charming and amusing-but-lonely girls fell for difficult but intriguing men, who often turned out to be surprisingly well-off. She used to sit here on the bed or on the little boudoir armchair, turning the pages of these novels, seeking clues to her future.

If she sat reading downstairs, her father would soon start to complain about some job around the house that needed doing, or demand she make him some tea.

Annabel was thinking about Geoff. It seemed to her that the relationship was about the best she could hope for. Their affair had only been going for a few months, but several things were already clear: Geoff had money; Geoff was considerate and so far had never shown the slightest sign of losing his temper with her. Annabel knew that sometimes she failed to get the point. She also knew she was inclined to say the wrong thing at the wrong moment, but if she had ever irritated Geoff, he had never shown it.

And then, Geoff was tough. He could cope with her father's

tantrums and sarcasm with an ease that astonished Annabel. He was completely impervious to her father's snide remarks about Geoff's origins, considered by Colonel Gazebee to be less than satisfactory, and his attempts to make Geoff conform with his own ideas of how a gentleman should dress, or behave, were simply ignored. Geoff was who Geoff was. He didn't give a damn about the old man's snobbery. In his world you were what you did; you were defined by your actions, and the consequences of those actions.

She knew she didn't love Geoff; that is to say, the emotions she felt towards him were not in the least bit similar to those described in the various books she read. The earth never moved; no fireworks went off inside her head when he kissed her; she had no photograph of him and if she had, she would never have spent hours gazing at it. She didn't need to: Geoff came to see her every other day. And she didn't believe Geoff loved her. He was affectionate, kind and generous but he could switch off and ignore her at a moment's notice, when his mobile phone rang – which it did often – or when he saw someone in a room he needed 'to network with'.

They had an adult relationship. Adult: free from illusions, free from the fog of youthful passions. Geoff could look after her and Geoff *would* look after her; sooner or later he would ask her to go and live with him and she could leave the dreadful old man downstairs to his fate.

Except she doubted she had the strength of will to do that.

If Annabel and Ed had become lovers she did not doubt her father would have been silent. No words of criticism would have passed his lips; no sarcastic remarks. She would have been with a man who even her father would have acknowledged was a gentleman, and the problem would have been solved. If Ed and Annabel were married – and there was no insurmountable objection to such an idea – then they could stick the old man in one of the attics on the top floor of Hartlepool Hall, somewhere so removed there would be little possibility of him disturbing them.

Only, Ed showed not the slightest interest in Annabel.

Before he had gone away he had always been spoken of in the same breath as Catherine Plender, at least until Catherine had gone off with a drunken software designer from Gateshead. Then for five years little had been seen or heard of Ed. On his rare visits home he had always been friendly to Annabel if they happened to meet, but had never by the smallest word or action suggested that he thought of her as anything other than an old friend. An old friend: like a favourite pair of slippers or an ancient pullover with holes at the elbows.

It was too late to think about Ed now. She had told him about Geoff; Ed had seen them together and appeared to accept the fact that they were a couple. Annabel had inherited enough of her father's military instinct to know that one strategic objective at a time was more achievable than two. Geoff was her destiny, not Ed.

It was only that these days Ed looked so vulnerable that when Annabel saw him, she wanted – she really wanted – to put her arms around him.

The meeting with Malcolm and Geoff took place at Hartlepool Hall the next morning. Before they arrived Ed went to the kitchen and told Mrs Donaldson that there would be two extra for lunch – he imagined they would chat through whatever Geoff's ideas were over a glass of wine and one of Mrs Donaldson's culinary creations. Then he went to his office and waited for the others to arrive.

If only there was someone he could trust. He wasn't sure whose side Malcolm was on and he knew Geoff would cut his throat – in a purely business sense – with a smile if he thought it necessary. He decided not to agree to anything before he had had a chance to talk it through with Alice. She would know what was best.

When they arrived Malcolm came in first. He seemed tired.

'Geoff's just behind me,' he said to Ed. 'Horace should be bringing him along in a minute.'

A moment later Horace appeared, announcing the presence of Mr Tarset. Geoff entered the room with the lithe step of a salsa dancer. He was wearing the same tight black jeans as the day before, but this time the shirt was striped blue and white, with massive gold cufflinks. He was carrying a huge roll of paper. There was a big oak table in the middle of the office that was used for meetings and as a general dumping ground. Malcolm cleared away unread letters and old newspapers and then Geoff unrolled his paper cylinder, weighing it down with books and paperweights. The document turned out to be an enormous floor plan of the house.

'What's all this?' Ed asked.

'I let Geoff have a copy of the plans when I heard what he had in mind. I thought it would save time.'

'Would anyone mind telling me what is going on?' Ed felt as if he was being given the smallest walk-on part in a drama in which he had expected to be the central figure.

'That's why we're here,' said Geoff. 'Right. Here we have Hartlepool Hall. Big house, yes?'

'Fifty something rooms,' agreed Malcolm. 'Not counting the outbuildings, stables and so on.'

'Right: a very big house, with a big front hall. I mean you could fit Darlington Town Hall into that.'

Ed said: 'I suppose it is quite large. One gets so used to it, though.'

'Full-time occupants, not counting staff?' asked Geoff.

'Just me, at present,' said Ed.

Geoff got out a magic marker, and then, consulting a smaller plan he took from his inside pocket, started drawing thick lines on the print on the table.

'You see, if we knocked down these walls here – and here – and used the space in the hall and in this gallery on the first floor ... and made a few other alterations here and here –' the marker pen stabbed at walls and staircases, halls and billiard rooms; it snaked over the dining room and the Hall of Sculptures and obliterated Ed's father's den '– then you get something that looks like this.' Geoff waved his hand triumphantly at the plan, which was now covered in enigmatic black scrawls.

'I'm afraid I don't see,' said Ed. 'What exactly are you getting at?'

'We turn an almost empty house that is costing you money, into flats that will earn you money.'

'Flats?' asked Ed in amazement.

'Yes, flats. Six of them, maybe eight if we get lucky with the planners. We might get a million and a half for each one, perhaps even two million. Depends on the spec. What do you think, Ed?'

'I don't know what to think,' said Ed. 'It's a bit of a shock.'

'Think about it. Hartlepool Hall is eating its head off. Something's got to be done. You could try and sell the whole place, of course. But where would you find buyers at the price you need? There might be a few Arabs or Russians out there with that kind of money, but the market for big country houses is crap at the moment. Of course, you could get lucky. But then you'd have to move.'

'I'd have to move anyway,' said Ed, 'if you're going to tear the house down and sell it off in bits.'

'Just listen to Geoff, Ed,' said Malcolm, a warning note in his voice. 'This is a scheme we can sell to the bank. Hear him out.'

Geoff glanced at Malcolm. His look made it clear he neither needed nor wanted help in explaining his ideas. Softening his expression with a smile, he turned back to Ed.

'It's perfect for you, Ed. What we do is this: I form a new company to develop Hartlepool Hall. I buy the property from you. Actually the cheque would go to the bank as they have first charge over the house and farmland. But here's the sweet part: the bank lends the money straight back to me, to help finance the development. That is the only way they can get their money back – if they fund this project. It's the best chance they've got. In fact, it's the *only* chance they've got. You too.'

Geoff sounded so sure of himself that Ed wondered if he hadn't talked to the bank already.

'Anyway, I take care of the bank; you get the Hartlepool Estate mortgages off your back. We start on Phase One. We convert the Hall into as many flats as we can. Our company rents one of them back to you so that you can go on living here. That's part of the deal. I need you as an anchor tenant to help me market the rest of the properties. The others are sold on fifty-year leases. Then we're up and running.'

Geoff paused as if he expected Ed and Malcolm to burst into applause. When neither of them reacted he continued.

'So, we move on to Phase Two: we build an eighteen-hole golf course with a clubhouse in the stable block.' Geoff's finger stabbed at the plan again. 'We'd put in a bar, a decent restaurant, and a spa facility for the wives. It would be perfect: Hartlepool Hall would become a top-of-the-range residential and leisure complex and you'd turn your liability into our asset. Your share of the deal would pay off the bank loans that you need to deal with, and you would be able to stay in your home, or at least part of it.'

Geoff smiled and looked at Ed, his hands resting on the plan. He was enough of a salesman to know when to start talking and when to stop.

'Of course an artist's impression might make it easier to visualise,' added Malcolm. 'Geoff's diagram is a little rough and ready.'

'Yeah, we can do the artist's impressions and glossy pictures for the marketing campaign,' said Geoff, 'when we get to that stage. We'll use a top architect. It will all be done properly. But, to be honest, Ed, I didn't want to shower you with a load of paperwork until I was sure you wanted to buy in to the concept. It would have been taking a liberty.'

Ed felt that quite a lot of liberties had already been taken, but he tried to remain calm.

'There's a lot to think about,' he said at last.

'Oh, sure,' said Geoff. 'You'll need all the facts and figures. And a written proposal. I have people back at the office who can churn out stuff like that. What's important is, does it make sense to *you*? I mean, it's still your house.'

'It's the bank's house at present,' said Malcolm.

Ed could think of a million objections to this plan. He had never heard of anything so awful in his life. That his beloved Hartlepool Hall – his home, his inheritance – should be torn up and converted into flats and a golf club and a beauty parlour: the idea filled him with horror. He forgot that he had mentioned such an idea to Alice only a day ago.

'But would the planners allow it?' he asked. 'It's a listed building.'

'Don't worry about them,' said Geoff, tapping the side of his nose with his forefinger. 'I've found us a tame expert. He's quite happy to tell the planners that the building is of no historical or architectural significance.'

Ed was struck dumb by this remark.

'So what do you think?' asked Geoff, staring at Ed with his bright blue eyes. Ed felt almost as if he were being hypnotised, willed into unconditional agreement.

'Let's talk about it over lunch?' he suggested finally. 'You'll both stay, of course?'

'Sorry, no time,' said Geoff, briskly. He rolled up his plan and put it under his arm. 'Places to go, deals to do. We need to talk again soon, Ed. If we're going to get this project up and running I shall want an answer from you in the next couple of days.'

'And so will the bank,' added Malcolm. 'We can't hold them off much longer. We need to show them that we have a plan.'

Geoff shook Ed firmly by the hand, said, 'Cheers, mate,' to Malcolm Skinner, then left the room before Ed could say anything further.

'You'll stay for some lunch, Malcolm, won't you?' asked Ed. His tone was almost pleading. Surely his own agent had time to sit and discuss the proposed dismemberment of the family home? But Malcolm shook his head.

'I'm sorry, Ed. You don't seem to realise the pressure we're under. I'm getting phone calls about this morning, noon and night. I've got to go to our accountants in Darlington now, to help with a cash flow forecast we have to email to the bank by five o'clock tonight. There's an axe hanging over our heads, Ed, and you don't even seem to have noticed.'

'I'm aware that we have some difficulties at present,' replied Ed.

'Difficulties? That's one way of putting it. You want to go for this deal of Geoff's, Ed. It might be the only way out. Of course you'll lose some of the house, but you'll still have somewhere to live, and you might get to keep some of the farmland.'

'But I don't even know what figure Geoff is talking about,' said Ed. 'How can I agree, or disagree, without having a bit more information?'

'All you need to know is this,' explained Malcolm. 'Geoff will give you a deal that will pay off the majority of the bank loans. He'll rent you a flat on a lifelong tenancy. You'll have the income from a farm and a few grazing rents. You'll be able to afford to live here. That's about as good as it gets, Ed. It's that simple.'

When Malcolm left, Ed felt as if he had just awoken from an unpleasant dream. He walked through the house to the kitchen. On the table were plates of cold lobster, and a fishplate with a whole poached salmon on it, covered in dill and thin slices of cucumber. In a saucepan a mound of freshly cooked new potatoes steamed, with parsley and mint sprinkled over them. In another pan white asparagus was gently simmering. Boats of hollandaise sauce, and mayonnaise completed the ensemble. Mrs Donaldson was garnishing the cold lobster with teaspoons of caviar.

'Mrs Donaldson,' said Ed. He stopped for a moment as he took in the scale of the feast, which might have fed a dozen people, not just the four it was intended for. 'I'm afraid those gentlemen won't be staying for lunch after all.'

Ten

After dinner Ed and Alice sat in the library and talked about Ed's day. Ed's appetite had vanished after his meeting with Malcolm Skinner and Geoff Tarset, so he and Alice had eaten the lobsters and poached salmon for dinner – that is to say, Ed had dined while Alice had picked at the food on her plate.

'I couldn't believe my ears,' complained Ed. 'There was this man Tarset, whom I only met for the first time yesterday, calmly proposing to tear my house down and turn it into flats. And I am to be allowed the pleasure of *renting* one myself. Paying *him* to live in my own home!'

Alice leaned forward and covered his hand with hers. Her skin felt cold.

'I know you are upset, dear. But at least you'd have a home. And, wonderful as this house is, isn't it a little quixotic to keep it going just for the benefit of one person?'

'I might get married. You never know.'

'I hope you do, my dear. But even then the problems of maintaining an enormous house would still be with you. You might not like the idea and I know it doesn't sound very nice, but if this is the only way to keep the estate from being taken over by the bank, or to prevent the house from falling down through lack of funds, then you really must think about it.'

They were silent. Then Alice asked, 'You're not angry with me for speaking my mind, my dear?'

'Never with you, Alice,' replied Ed. Suddenly he added, 'Would you live here for a while, Alice? I do like having you about. And it would make it all so much easier to bear.'

He realised as he spoke that he had never asked Alice about her own circumstances. Apart from the fact that she had once known his father, and had then lived with the late Samuel Robinson, he knew nothing about her: not where, or how, or with whom she lived.

'I would so love to stay here,' replied Alice. 'You don't know how much. And it is sweet of you to suggest it. But it is impossible. I will be missed. I should have returned home already.'

'Couldn't you stay for just a few more weeks?'

'I would be in your way. It will be a busy time for you.'

'Where *do* you live, Alice?'

She shook her head.

'I want to forget about all that for the moment. It's best you don't know. I came here on a selfish whim, my dear. I shouldn't have intruded on your life and I won't want you to think of me, or to try to get in touch with me, when I go back home.'

'But why?' asked Ed. 'I know I was a bit grumpy when I came back from France and found a stranger living in my home. But now I'm very glad you're here. And you mustn't go without leaving me your address. I couldn't bear to think I would never see you again.'

Alice sat quietly in her armchair. In the light from the table lamp Ed saw a large tear form at the corner of her eye then trickle down her face. No more followed. Alice opened her handbag, took out a small handkerchief and dabbed her cheek.

'I wish my father had married you,' said Ed with sudden ferocity. 'How different everything would have been!'

He remembered his own mother without affection. A strong-minded woman, she had ruled over Hartlepool Hall in an uncompromising manner. Her iron sense of propriety had been her most obvious characteristic, unrelieved by the slightest trace of humour. She made no allowances for other people's weaknesses or bad luck. She had died when Ed was in his teens.

'Your father would never have married me,' replied Alice. 'I've told you that. Besides, it is very wicked of you to forget everything your mother did for you.'

Ed wondered why that might be. From an early age his nurture had been subcontracted to a string of nannies. At the first opportunity, he had been sent to boarding school, aged seven and a half. In the holidays his parents were often away and, as he grew older, his main companions were private tutors paid to teach him all the things he had not managed to learn at school. There had never been any strong sense of family. He had no brothers, and his sister had died as a baby before he was born. No more children had arrived after Ed.

'I wish he had, all the same,' repeated Ed.

'I was quite penniless,' replied Alice. 'Everyone knew, even in those days, that your father had to marry someone with money.'

'Then he went and spent the stuff as if there was no tomorrow,' said Ed.

'He had to marry money,' said Alice, 'and it was a perfectly sensible way of looking at it back then. Maude Portalbert was the heiress to the Portalbert Toffee fortune.' She laughed.

'"Toffee for Toffs" was what it said on the tins.'

Ed remembered the toffee too. It clung to the roof of your mouth; it discovered cavities in your teeth you hadn't known were there; its sickly taste stayed with you a long time after the sweet itself had finally dissolved. When he was a small child, tins of this odious delicacy were often handed round at family parties and it was considered the height of disloyalty to refuse to take one. He was twelve years old when the supply of toffee finally ran out, after the Portalbert Toffee Works burned down; whether that was by accident, or helped along by some disgruntled toffee worker, Ed could not remember. The destruction of the factory caused few regrets except, perhaps, amongst the dental profession.

But forty years ago Portalbert Toffee had still been a prosperous business and Maude Portalbert had therefore been a catch, notwithstanding her lack of looks.

'Did you know my mother?' asked Ed. 'Did you know what she was like?'

'No, I never met her,' replied Alice. 'I only knew that your father loved me, and not her. I don't think your father was a very demonstrative man, Ed. You must remember what he was like. But what love there was in him, he kept for me.'

Ed recognised Alice's description of his father: he never remembered him showing much affection. But then he never remembered his mother showing him any affection at all.

Sometimes he had been aware of hesitant overtures made by his father. Once he had turned up at a school sports day – without Ed's mother – and stayed for at least twenty minutes. He wore an expression, common on parents' faces at such events, of not knowing in the least why he was there mixed with a reluctant and embarrassed pride. He had stayed to watch Ed come fourth in the hundred metres sprint. When

Ed had looked for him after the race, his father had already disappeared. Another boy told Ed he'd seen him heading for the car park.

Then there were the presents. Ed's father rarely remembered birthdays or Christmas: presents were somewhat irrelevant in a house so full of luxuries. Still, now and again he remembered that it was usual for parents to give their children such things. Sometimes these arrived out of the blue; there had, for example, been the gift of ten years' worth of bound volumes of *Wisden Cricketers' Almanack*. On his twenty-first birthday Ed had been presented with a matched pair of twelve-bore sidelock shotguns, engraved with the Hartlepool crest. Once – perhaps twice – there had also been a hesitant pat on the back when Ed, in some obscure way, had pleased his father. Ed knew his father had not been good at expressing himself, and this diffidence was compounded by a degree of self-centredness that made him a difficult man to warm to. But there had at least been some form of affection there.

'I knew about Maude Portalbert before your father told me,' continued Alice. 'One day I saw a picture of them together at Ascot in an illustrated magazine. There was a caption underneath. It was the usual gossip-column line, rumours of an engagement. When I read it I didn't know what to think. I hadn't seen your father for a week and I was alone in my cottage. That wasn't unusual. That was just how life was for us – at least for me – and I accepted it. I knew that one day I would see a similar picture, or be told a piece of gossip and I had taught myself to be ready for it. At least I thought I had ...'

'Poor Alice,' said Ed.

As she talked he imagined a young woman alone in a pretty sitting room, her head bowed over a magazine. He pictured her turning its pages idly, not really concentrating on what she was reading, then suddenly sitting up straighter in her chair, flicking back through the pages. Throwing the magazine onto the low table in front of her, her lips compressed so tightly that pale marks appeared around her mouth. In his mind she did not cry. But her face was empty, quite empty.

Alice spoke again and the images inside Ed's head disappeared, leaving only a sense of bleakness.

'It was what I had been expecting,' Alice said, 'but expecting bad news never prepares you for its arrival. Your father called on me the next evening. I was very glad to see him. I said nothing about the picture in the magazine until he had taken off his coat and I had made us both a cocktail – I think we were going to the theatre that night. When he had sipped a little from his glass I picked up the magazine.'

Ed saw that Alice's hands had tightened into fists. She was no longer looking at Ed, but past him, as if she too were picturing the scene.

'Oh, I was so casual about it! I showed him the photograph and the words beneath it and said in my brightest voice something about him being very naughty. I can't remember exactly what else I said. All I can remember is that I was determined not to be angry or demanding. I suppose I was hoping that it would all turn out to be quite innocent – that this Portalbert girl would be someone he had met by chance ...'

'Can you remember what he said?' Ed asked.

'All he said was: "Oh, Alice!"'

There was a silence.

'He just said: "Oh, Alice" – and I knew straight away that it was all over between us.'

She stood up.

'I must go to bed. These memories do tire me so.'

'Alice, are you all right? Shall I see you to your room?'

She turned and smiled.

'Don't worry about me, Ed. I shall be fine in the morning.'

Ed sat in the library alone. For a while he thought about the story that Alice had told him. He wondered if it was true, if that was really what had happened. It sounded like his father and he wondered if he would have behaved any better in similar circumstances. Then his thoughts turned to the deal that was being offered to him by Geoff Tarset.

Ed suddenly realised that he was terrified of his own future. He knew that his education and upbringing had given him a somewhat specialised range of skills. For example, he knew that when seated at the dining table you should keep your elbows pressed into your side, for the greater convenience of your neighbours, with your hands poised above your plate, knife and fork held like delicate surgical instruments.

His table manners were good. The desire to shovel peas onto the concave side of his fork was unknown to him: he knew that peas had to be pushed up the convex face, two or three at a time, and at this he excelled. He did not think that he was capable of understanding a set of accounts or of reading a balance sheet or of filling in a form to obtain a grant for the farm. He had never changed a light bulb or looked under the bonnet of his car. He only knew that that was where the engine must be, because one's suitcases went in at the other end. He knew that you can shoot grouse from the twelfth of August and that you must stop on the tenth of December; that if you catch a salmon before the fifteenth of June in England or Wales it must be returned alive to the river; that tenants pay rent on quarter days; that the port decanter goes to the left; that gamekeepers and masters of fox hounds will never see eye to eye, no matter what anyone says. He knew all these things but he hadn't the least idea of how his affairs had become such a dreadful, tangled, unsolvable mess.

Most families in similar circumstances to his own – large landowners or those lucky enough to have inherited great wealth – had for generations produced clever politicians or bankers; or else men and women concerned only with improving the lives of their fellow human beings; or else good stewards who really understood how to look after the woods and fields and farms and houses they owned, and the tenants who lived in them. The Simmonds family did not have a history of producing such accomplishments. A long time ago one or two of them had made a lot of money; since then there had been no conspicuous family talent apart from spending it.

Ed didn't believe anyone would ever want to employ him. He had no idea how to make his way in the world. He lived in one of the largest houses in his county – indeed one of the grandest houses in the north of England – yet he was very nearly destitute. If Geoff Tarset did not buy Hartlepool Hall, Ed was beginning to think he would end his days in some back street in Darlington, Hartlepool or Middlesbrough. He couldn't see any way out of his problems. He couldn't see any future at all.

As he liked to on these warm early-summer nights, he opened the door onto the terrace and stepped outside. A green dusk was fading into night; midges danced above the water and moths fluttered in and out of the light that streamed from the room behind him. An object on the ground caught his eye: it was a bird. It stood at the edge of the light, its yellow talons gripping the edge of a paving stone. Its speckled feathers and the black bar above its tail left him in no doubt as to what it was: a young sparrowhawk, not much more than a fledgling. It was the time of year when the young are ejected from the nest by their parents. It must have been pushed out, or fluttered to the ground, from somewhere high up on the side of the building. Now the bird looked at Ed and held its ground: its black eyes studied the monstrous biped in front of it more in incredulity than fear. From time to time it turned its head to see if its parents would come and rescue it. They did not. Bird and man stared at each other, until the young hawk fluttered off into the dark, in search of a new life.

Eleven

That same day Geoff had told Annabel he wanted her 'to host a dinner party'. Annabel was not keen to go out as her father seemed unwell. But when she asked him what was the matter, he was so irritable she decided to accept Geoff's invitation anyway. Geoff never asked her to cook. He preferred to employ caterers. He liked the idea of having someone work in his kitchen while another girl in a black skirt and white blouse, helped to serve the food and drinks. Perhaps, having sampled Annabel's cooking at home, Geoff was cautious about giving her any such responsibility. She knew she was not a very good cook. She just wasn't very interested in food. Annabel's role at Geoff's parties was simply to be gracious to Geoff's guests and to keep the conversation flowing.

There were three guests that night. One of them Annabel had met before: Eric McGee, Geoff's accountant and closest friend. Eric was a very large man. His bald head seemed to come straight out of his shoulders, as if someone had forgotten to give him a neck. He wore a loose fitting striped shirt outside his trousers to hide the rolls of fat that spilled over his waistband. He was Geoff's fixer; the man who helped him raise the money for his projects, the one who watched the pennies and paid the bills and made sure the profits kept rolling in. Annabel did not like him.

The second guest was someone Annabel had heard Geoff mention before but had not met until this evening. He was called Peregrine Smith, a young architect with a growing practice in Newcastle. He was thin and wiry, with a pale face and an intense expression as if he was just about to say something of great importance. He wore a white linen jacket and dark blue jeans. When he was introduced to Annabel he took her hand limply and then let go of it as if it displeased him in some way.

There was a third guest, a small, dark-skinned man with something of the Inca in his features. Geoff explained to Annabel that this was a new friend: a footballer who had recently been signed by Newcastle United. It appeared he had been known in his native Peru – where he was regarded as something of a legend – as 'El Condor', in reference to his swooping action in midfield. Apparently the Geordies greeted the arrival of his small figure on the pitch with chants of 'Haway, Biggsy'. The Geordies had given him a nickname because they couldn't pronounce his real name, which was a Quechuan word, the language once spoken by the Incas.

When Biggsy was introduced to Annabel he said: '*Encantado de conocerle, señora.*'

Afterwards he did not speak again and simply gazed around the room from time to time in confusion.

At first Annabel could not understand why Geoff had asked three such different people to dinner. Eric was a regular visitor to Geoff's bungalow, but usually his other guests were property developers, the men Geoff did deals with, or else the bankers who lent him the money. Tonight was different.

It was not an easy evening. Eric was more interested in eating than talking, and the little Peruvian seemed to be having language difficulties. Peregrine Smith looked as if he found the conversation insufficiently stimulating to encourage any effort on his part.

Then Geoff steered the conversation towards the subject of Hartlepool Hall, and everyone woke up. Even the Peruvian looked more alert, although it was impossible to say how much, if anything, he understood of what was being said. After a few minutes Annabel realised she was listening to a conversation that must have begun at some earlier meeting of these four men.

'Will we get consent to convert it, do you think?' asked Geoff.

'I know it's a listed building,' said Peregrine Smith, 'but English Heritage won't want another enormous house added to their at-risk register. We need to get consent from the County Council as well, and the Victorian Society will have to be consulted. But I'm pretty certain the application will go through at the next committee.'

'What a lot of fuss about an old house,' said Eric.

'Yes, Newcastle Central Station has more architectural merit,' commented Peregrine. 'I'm afraid the architect who designed Hartlepool Hall was a journeyman: no talent at all. Of course, it is quite a prominent building and has been open to the public, so we have to handle the application carefully. But these conversions are done all the time.'

'*I* think it's a lovely house,' said Annabel. She hated hearing them discuss Hartlepool Hall like this, as if it were a joint on the butcher's slab, waiting to be carved up. Peregrine Smith turned and looked at her as if he was amazed she possessed the power of speech.

'Do you really?' he asked. 'Well, it's a matter of individual taste, of course. Personally I think it is a hideous building. If it were allowed I would tear it down and start again.'

'We can claim back the VAT if we call it all repair work,' suggested Eric.

Geoff held up his hands. 'Wait on, Eric, man,' he said. 'We're getting ahead of ourselves. Annabel, sweetheart, would you get the girl to clear away some of these plates? I want to show you something.'

He left the room for a moment while Annabel and the waitress cleared a space on the dining table. He came back with a rolled-up drawing – an unmarked version of the plan he had shown Ed earlier that day. Geoff spread it out and held it in place using a couple of ashtrays. Then he produced a transparent overlay that showed the proposed alterations. For a while Geoff and Peregrine discussed whether more living space could be squeezed out of the available floor area.

'We'll have to divide up the hall and the Long Gallery,' said Peregrine, 'but we can keep the library. That would make a feature for one of the flats.'

'You'll do the artwork soon?' asked Geoff. 'I need some pretty pictures to show the investors and the bank.'

'Sure,' said Peregrine.

'And I want a sample specification for each flat. All the kit we'll put in: double ovens, top-of-the-range dishwashers, ice-making machines, climate-control units for wine storage. The punters love that sort of stuff.'

Annabel realised that the scheme was well advanced. Geoff must have been working on it for months, and yet he had never mentioned any of these details before.

'And media rooms,' suggested Eric. 'Sixty-five-inch 3D screens, all the gadgets.'

For a while they discussed the accessories that would be

so essential to the comfort of any future residents of Hartlepool Hall. Annabel could bear it no longer.

'But it all sounds so *horrible*,' she said. Everybody looked at her. Eric McGee, whose eyes were already nearly invisible in his pudgy face, screwed them up so that they almost disappeared. Peregrine stared at Annabel with an expression between contempt and disbelief.

'I know I'm old-fashioned,' she continued, 'but it's such a beautiful old house. Can't you leave it as it is? Or, at least, tidy it up a bit but keep the hall and the Long Gallery. And do leave the gardens, please. They're so lovely.'

Geoff came and stood behind her and placed his arm around her shoulders.

'Don't you worry, sweetheart; it will be tastefully done. It's just that we can't afford to waste too much space, otherwise the numbers won't work. Do you see? And don't worry about the gardens. We'll keep one or two of the trees and the water features when we start to build the golf course.'

'But Geoff,' pleaded Annabel. 'Who will want to live in these *vulgar* flats?'

Geoff took his arm from her shoulders and went around to where Biggsy was sitting and patted him on the back. Biggsy glanced up nervously at him.

'Here's our first buyer. His agent has agreed on his behalf to buy one of the flats off-plan. It's good for publicity. With Biggsy in one flat and Ed Hartlepool in another, people will be falling over themselves to buy the other apartments. Living in a stately home, with a football legend and a Marquess as next-door neighbours? We'll be sold out! We'll have the money we need before the building work's even started, let alone finished.'

He turned to Biggsy, pointed at the plan on the table and grinned.

'*Su casa!*' he said, laughing. Biggsy laughed too, although it wasn't clear that he understood what Geoff was talking about.

Annabel did not reply. She was remembering Hartlepool Hall as it had once been: Horace serving drinks on the terrace on sunny evenings whilst everyone chatted or gazed at the lake; the dances that old Lord and Lady Hartlepool used to give when she was in her teens. There had been so many people at such events that the orchestra and dance floor had been housed in one marquee, drinks served in another, and dinner in a third.

She pictured the house as it had been a few days earlier – a little forlorn in the way places become when they are unlived in for too long. Despite the presence of so many gardeners, the lawns and borders were less kempt than when Ed's parents had been alive; the terrace mossy and invaded here and there by weeds, the shrubs and bushes and plants in the borders crowding each other out. But it was still the most beautiful place she knew. It had been at the heart of her life as she grew up. But that was before the old Marquess died, Ed went abroad and everything had changed.

Peregrine was speaking, his thin features twisted as if he were sucking a lemon.

'Hartlepool Hall is no longer functional,' he explained. 'It was built for a way of life that has ceased to be relevant. That's the trouble with this country. Archaic planning laws make it far too difficult to get rid of our old building stock. Yes, I know we have to preserve some of the larger stately homes because of tourism. But so many of these houses have no real merit at all and should simply be pulled down.'

Annabel looked at him in horror. But Peregrine went on with the first sign of real animation he had shown all evening.

'If we lived in Scandinavia or Holland or any other enlightened society, we wouldn't go to all this effort to preserve an obsolete structure such as Hartlepool Hall. Where's the climate control? Where's the low-carbon technology? Worse than that, this house is a reminder of a feudal idiom that is very bad for this country's image. We need buildings that use modern materials: glass, steel, composites. We need buildings that are contemporary and relevant. Hartlepool Hall should be pulled down or blown up. It doesn't belong in a modern society. As it is, everything we are discussing here tonight is simply compromise.' Peregrine sighed. 'Planners are very hidebound people. We won't get permission to knock it down. But, as long as we keep the façade intact, I think we'll be allowed to do the rest of the work.'

Annabel rose to her feet and turned to Geoff.

'What a lovely evening,' she said. 'But I really must be going now.'

Geoff looked at her in surprise.

'You can't go,' he said. 'We haven't even had coffee yet. Stay and have a coffee. Or a glass of wine.' He leaned forward and whispered into her ear: 'I was hoping you'd stay the night, sweetheart.'

But Annabel was too upset. 'No. I have to go.' Her voice trembled and she thought she might be about to burst into tears.

'What's bothering you, sweetheart?'

'It's too horrible, hearing you talk about Hartlepool Hall like that.'

Suddenly Geoff's face changed.

'I'm trying to rescue the place, for fuck's sake. Your friend and his family have ruined themselves, and they'll ruin the house too. If I don't step in and save it, the bank will seize Hartlepool Hall. Then they'll do what banks do best: they will board up the windows, and padlock the gates. They will make a mess of trying to sell it and the whole place will start to fall down. Believe me, I've seen it happen.'

Annabel had never seen Geoff angry before and it frightened her a little.

'I'm sorry, Geoff. I know you mean well. It's the thought of the house being torn up and turned into flats – it's just so sad.'

'Well, darling,' said Geoff. 'We've all got to make a living somehow: that is, everyone except your friend Ed. This is how I make mine, so get used to the idea.'

He turned away from her.

'Thank you for dinner, Geoff,' said Annabel to his back.

'You're still going, then?'

'I think I ought to. Daddy hasn't been well.'

'*Daddy hasn't been well*,' said Geoff, mimicking her. 'Then you'd better run home to Daddy.'

As Annabel left she heard Geoff give a hard laugh, and she thought she heard him say – although afterwards she couldn't be sure – the words, 'Silly cow.'

She drove herself home through the dark lanes, telling herself that Geoff's words were not the language of love. And Geoff, she now realised, must already have had the plans for Hartlepool Hall in mind when they first met.

Twelve

Horace still had a couple of weeks to go before he left Hartlepool Hall. He had been fortunate: he had been offered temporary accommodation in a flat on the ground floor of a low-rise block on an estate in Darlington and was on the waiting list for sheltered housing. He had decided to continue performing his duties as a butler until the day he was due to leave, and nothing anyone could say would stop him. He appeared as Ed was helping himself from the sideboard to breakfast; there was a choice of kippers, scrambled eggs and sausages.

'Lady Alice is unwell, M'Lord,' he told Ed. 'I think we should call a doctor.'

Leaving his breakfast untouched, Ed hurried upstairs. Horace had not been exaggerating. When Ed knocked on the door of the Blue Bedroom there was no answer, so he went in. Alice was lying in bed, her hair plastered against her head and slick with sweat. Her eyes were glassy and her face flushed.

'Alice?' said Ed. 'How are you feeling?'

She did not answer so he put his hand on her forehead. It was hot and damp with perspiration. Ed went to the wash-basin, found a cloth and moistened it. He sat on the edge of the bed and wiped her face in an attempt to cool her down.

Then he heard a cough in the corridor and went outside. Horace was standing there.

'Mrs Donaldson has called the doctor,' he informed Ed.

'Quite right.'

'She will come and sit with Lady Alice until the doctor arrives.'

'Good idea. I will stay here until then.'

Horace went away and Ed sat in the armchair facing the bed. It was astonishing how important this stranger had become to him in the last few days. It would be dreadful if anything happened to her.

'Run down to the off-licence, Sammy, and get us two cans of Guinness,' said Lady Alice in a clear voice.

Ed looked up in surprise. Her eyes were closed. She must be dreaming. But dreaming of Guinness? There was a knock at the door and Mrs Donaldson came in.

'I'll look after her now, Lord Hartlepool,' she said. 'The doctor will be here in about an hour.'

Ed went downstairs and walked along to the estate office. It was Mrs Budgen's day to visit and catch up with the paperwork and filing. Mrs Budgen was a bright, efficient woman in her middle years who did part-time work for Ed and for a number of other local farms and estates. Ed couldn't bear to think that she might ask him about the state of affairs at Hartlepool Hall. After all, she read the correspondence in order either to file it, or to check which bills needed to be paid. She must know.

'Mr Skinner rang,' said Mrs Budgen as he greeted her. 'He said he'd look in this afternoon for a few minutes. Said he wanted a word with you.'

Ed managed not to groan. He left the office and went back to the dining room to collect the newspaper, then poured himself a cup of lukewarm coffee and went through to the library. As he sat down on the sofa he saw that Alice had left her scrapbook on the table next to where she often sat. She had never left it lying around before. She must have forgotten to take it upstairs with her.

Ed picked it up and opened it. For a moment he felt guilty, like a schoolboy peeking at his parents' private papers; then he became absorbed in what he saw.

It was an old photograph album. Into it, Alice had pasted newspaper cuttings, scraps of letters, photographs cut from magazines. It was a random collection. There were clippings from *Tatler*, *The Queen*, *The Bystander*, *Picture Post* and *The Illustrated London News*. There were also articles on fashion, and the latest domestic appliances: odd items that must have caught Alice's fancy. But most of the cuttings formed a kind of journal of the English upper classes in the 1960s. There were articles about the Royal Family, with pictures of the Queen surrounded by her family, or with her corgis. There were pictures of girls dressed in Norman Hartnell dresses. None of the girls in these pictures bore any resemblance to Alice. Some were individual portraits; others were posed in groups. Ed recognised the features of his own mother, stern even at the tender age of nineteen. There was a glamorous picture of Princess Margaret and, next to it, another of her husband-to-be, Anthony Armstrong-Jones. There were pictures taken at a dance given at Blenheim: Ed could make out the tall figure and fair hair of his father at the extreme right of one of the photographs. There were more pictures of his father: at Goodwood, at Ascot, in a shooting party at Bolton Abbey.

Other memorabilia was pasted into the leaves of the book. There were two entrance tickets to the Marquee Club in

Wardour Street. Top billing was given to the Rolling Stones. There was a programme from Ronnie Scott's jazz club in Soho featuring Sonny Rollins and Zoot Sims. These scraps recalled a rather different world to the others.

Ed turned the final pages. There were more pictures and cuttings. Some were of people he knew or had heard of from his parents' circle. But some of the newspaper cuttings suggested an altogether less respectable world: nightclubs haunted by stars now dead or forgotten; pictures of shops with names like *Granny Takes a Trip* or *I was Lord Kitchener's Valet* recalling the generation who had first discovered the joys of marijuana and flower power. Of the person who had collected these images and pasted them in the book, there was not a single trace.

Towards the end of the book was a newspaper cutting from *The Times* dated 1964. The headline ran: *Police Raid Closes Down Harley Street Sexual Health Clinic*. The story reported on the closure of Dr Stephenson's Clinic for the Propagation of Sexual Health. The police stated that complaints had been lodged against Dr Stephenson and, acting on information received, the premises had been closed under Section 33 of the Sexual Offences Act 1956.

There was a picture of his mother and father, his father wearing a tailcoat, his mother's face obscured by an enormous hat. Underneath were the words: *Toffee heiress sticks to her man*.

Ed put down the scrapbook and went to the bookshelves on the opposite side of the room. He pulled down a large red volume entitled *Burke's Peerage*, and flicked through its pages. There was no entry for Birtley. He put the book back in its place and pulled down several more reference books and directories. There was no Alice Birtley listed in any of them.

Thirteen

The morning after her trying evening with Geoff, Annabel was up early. As usual she made a cup of tea and took it to her father. He was sitting up in bed, propped against his pillow, listening to the *Today* programme. He seemed better than he had been the evening before, and in a good mood too because all he said when Annabel handed him his tea was: 'Bloody politicians. They're all the same.'

She went downstairs and as she came to the final step the doorbell rang. It was unusual for anyone to call on them at any time of day, let alone before eight, and it was far too early for the postman. When she opened the door, there was a man holding an enormous spray of flowers wrapped in cellophane.

'Flowers for Miss Gazebee,' said a voice from behind the vegetation. Annabel took the bunch and thanked him. She could hardly get the bouquet through the door. She went into the kitchen and started snipping stalks and arranging the flowers in two vases. There were white and yellow roses, just coming out; pink orchids; oriental lilies; purple asters; red and white carnations, and assorted grasses. A card was attached to the wrapping. She opened it and read:

Sorry about last night. Love and kisses. G

She threw the card away with the wrapping and carried

the vases through to the drawing room. An hour later her father came down to breakfast. When he had finished he went through to the drawing room with the newspaper.

A moment later she heard him sneeze, then shout: 'Get these blasted things out of here! They're giving me hay fever.'

Annabel took the two vases back to the kitchen and placed them on the table. She could look at them while she was doing the washing up.

The phone rang. Her father never answered it so she picked up and was not surprised to hear Geoff at the other end.

'Did you get the flowers?' he asked, without preamble.

'Yes. They're lovely. Thank you.'

'I'm sorry about last night.'

'There's nothing to be sorry for,' replied Annabel coldly.

'Oh yes, there is. I behaved like a complete bastard. There's no excuse for it. The fact is that life is a bit stressful at the moment. I need to get this Hartlepool Hall project going and I've a couple of other big deals going through. There are a lot of balls to keep in the air. But like I said, that doesn't excuse me being rude.'

Annabel did not reply at first. It occurred to her that this might be the moment to get rid of Geoff. She wasn't sure about him and she couldn't quite think how he had managed to worm his way so far into her life. She didn't like his friends. She suspected – she was almost certain after last night – that in part Geoff was using her to get to Ed. Maybe that was all there was to it. She didn't love Geoff. In fact, at present, she wasn't even sure she liked him.

'Are you still there?' asked Geoff, his voice uncertain.

'I'm still here.'

'Look, Annabel, I want to see you again. Soon. I want to

make it up to you. I'm an insensitive sod sometimes, I know, but that doesn't mean I don't care for you.'

'Do you care for me?' asked Annabel. She amazed herself by what she said next: 'Or is it just because I can introduce you to people like Ed Hartlepool?'

'Do I care for you? Of course I care for you. I want to look after you. I don't care who you know or don't know. I admit meeting Ed's been useful, but I could easily have persuaded Malcolm Skinner to introduce us if that's all I wanted.'

'I see,' said Annabel.

'You don't think very much of me, do you?' said Geoff. That uncertain note was still in his voice, and Annabel softened her tone.

'I *am* fond of you, Geoff. I was just a little upset last night, that's all.'

'You've every right to be,' said Geoff. 'Every right. When can I see you? What about tonight?'

'I'll have to cook Daddy his dinner first.'

'That's my girl.'

After that, Annabel went about her morning chores with more of a spring in her step. She had just finished making the beds when the phone rang again. Thinking it might be Geoff, she let it ring for a moment or two then picked up the receiver.

'Yes?'

'Annabel? It's Ed.'

It was just as well that Ed had announced himself. His voice sounded quite different from his usual detached drawl. He seemed tense and worried.

'Ed? You sound funny. Is everything all right?'

'No, it's not all right. Alice is ill.'

It took Annabel a moment to realise who Ed was talking about.

'What's the matter with her?'

'I don't know. The doctor's just been. She has a fever.'

'Is there anything I can do to help?'

'No . . . I don't know. A funny thing has happened, Annabel. I wanted to talk to you about it.'

Annabel felt a warm glow spreading from her toes to the base of her stomach. Who did Ed choose to turn to when he was troubled about something? He turned to her.

'Tell me about it,' she said.

'Have you the time?'

'Of course, Ed. As much time as you like.'

It was an odd story. The doctor had called and examined Alice. He had decided Alice was suffering from malnutrition and had then caught a virus.

'She eats like a bird,' said Ed. 'It's not as if there isn't enough food at home. You know what Mrs Donaldson's like.'

Alice's life was not in danger, but she needed looking after. Her malnutrition was not something recent. While the doctor was with her he had managed to obtain from her the name of her own GP. He had rung the man straight away.

'The thing is,' said Ed, 'Alice's doctor told us that Alice has run away from a care home. They've been going frantic looking for her. They've been searching high and low for weeks. The police and Social Services have been involved.'

'My goodness,' said Annabel. She was genuinely cheered up by all the drama.

'So now they will be coming here, I expect. They will want to take her away. What on earth am I to do?'

'Well, I expect it's for the best,' replied Annabel. But that wasn't what Ed wanted to hear.

'How can it be for the best?' he complained. 'Who will keep me company? I like having Alice around. She's been a great comfort to me and she doesn't like her care home, I know she doesn't. She didn't tell me what kind of place it was, but she told me she felt trapped living there.'

Annabel was nettled. How on earth had this old woman become so important to Ed, when he could have turned for comfort and companionship to Annabel, the person who had known him since he was a child?

'Well, if they come to take her back then I don't see how you can stop them,' she told Ed.

'Don't you? I could just tell them to bugger off, couldn't I?'

They talked for a few more moments. Ed did say one other thing that intrigued Annabel.

'I don't know who she really is, either.'

'I thought you told me she was called Lady Alice Birtley.'

'Annabel, I've looked her up in all the books: *Debrett's*, *Kelly's* and *Burke's*. There's no such person as Lady Alice Birtley. There never has been. So who is she?'

'Well, you'll have to ask her that yourself,' Annabel told him. They hung up.

Annabel felt that it had been an unsatisfactory conversation. It was never rewarding to hear how wonderful someone else was, when what you wanted to hear was how wonderful *you* were. Of course Annabel was much too grown up to think of Alice as a rival. In the first place, she was quite content with her life. She was going out with Geoff Tarset and one day soon they would be married. Or something. In the second place, Alice must be at least seventy, so even if Annabel *had* been in the least bit jealous – which of course she wasn't – how could she possibly feel threatened by someone twice her age? More than twice, thought Annabel, trying to do the sum in her head.

At lunch she asked her father again about Alice Birtley.

'I've told you before, I've never heard of anyone who goes by that name,' he said. 'There was a Caroline. Caroline Romford. A lot of us were rather keen on her but Ed's father was the lucky chap who went out with her, for almost a year, if I remember. Then there was some woman he had in London. But that was after Simon Hartlepool was married, and we never heard too much about that. Someone saw them in Wilton's together, chucking oysters down their throats.'

'When Ed asked if you knew who she was,' said Annabel, remembering something, 'you wondered whether she mightn't have been one of Mrs Bright's girls. Who was Mrs Bright?'

For the first time, her father looked uncomfortable. He coughed and said, 'Mrs Bright? Did I say something about Mrs Bright?'

'Yes, Daddy,' said Annabel.

'I don't remember too much about her.' Her father was not looking at her as he spoke, but gazed instead at a picture of the Duke of Wellington that hung on the dining room wall. 'Some of the chaps used to go there. She kept a house in Bayswater.'

'What sort of a house?'

'Oh ... ah ... you know what I mean, Annabel. The sort of house men go to when they want to be with a girl.'

'You mean a brothel?'

'Oh, I wouldn't go as far as to say that,' said her father. 'Some of the girls were really rather nice. Not exactly young ladies, but very pleasant, I'm told.'

Annabel could see that she ought not to press her father on this point. He was looking furtive and angry at the same time, so they talked of other things. But later, as Annabel did the washing up in the kitchen, the thought that occurred was: 'Alice is a retired old tart trying to sting Ed's family for money.'

That night, Annabel cooked dinner for her father then went out to spend the rest of the evening with Geoff. Her father made no objection; he seemed detached and forgetful.

This time there was no Eric, no footballers or architects or lawyers to contend with: Geoff was on his own and was easy and friendly in the way he had been when the two of them had first met. When Annabel arrived he poured her a glass of champagne from a bottle that was resting in a silver-plated ice bucket. So like Geoff, thought Annabel, to go to the bother of owning a silver ice bucket. They talked of this and that, and Geoff produced two plates of smoked salmon and poured more champagne.

Then he said: 'I want your help with Ed Hartlepool.'

Annabel was quite ready to be angry with him. This was exactly what she had accused Geoff of: using her to get to Ed. But the way he said it made her feel somehow important. Instead she asked: 'What exactly do you mean?'

'He needs to understand I'm not one of the bad guys. He needs to understand that what I'm offering him is a genuine deal, better than he would get from anyone else.'

'What *are* you offering him?' asked Annabel.

'I'm offering to take on all the debts of the Hartlepool Estate. And all I'm asking is that he transfers the house and grounds and some of the farmland into the ownership of one of my companies.'

Annabel didn't understand how this would work, or whether it was fair or unfair. It sounded as if Ed would lose almost everything; but then, perhaps he already had.

'So what do you think I can do to help?'

Geoff put his arm around her.

'I know what an influence you have on him, sweetheart. God knows, you're a tremendous influence in my life. You're just one of those people that others look up to. If you tell him what I'm offering makes sense, I'm sure he'll go for it.'

Annabel knew that Geoff was flattering her, but mightn't there be some truth in what he said? People had always valued her opinion. That was why she had once been invited to be secretary of the local Red Cross committee. That's why Ed had called to ask her advice about Alice.

'So what exactly do you want me to do?'

'Go and see him. Tell him to sign the contract – it will be in the post to him tomorrow. Tell him we're working against time. The banks are in a very nasty mood these days. It's my way or the highway, to be perfectly honest.'

Geoff expounded on this theme for a moment or two, then he changed the subject.

'You're looking very sexy tonight, sweetheart.'

Annabel was wearing an old cardigan and a sensible tweed skirt. She didn't exactly feel sexy.

'Am I?'

'Yes. You're making me very excited.'

'I mustn't be too late,' said Annabel. 'I need to make sure Daddy gets to bed. He's been a bit shaky lately.'

But she allowed Geoff to draw her to him.

Fourteen

Every Sunday Colonel Gazebee went to church, and Annabel went with him. They always sat in one of the front pews. The Gazebees had no special connection to this church: they did not have the presentation of the living, they owned no land nearby, they did not go to coffee mornings or lunch clubs or wine-and-nibbles evenings to raise funds to preserve its fabric. Yet in every respect Colonel Gazebee behaved as if he were the local squire taking his rightful place at the very front.

He sat in the foremost pew with Annabel and looked neither to one side nor to the other. Instead he fixed the vicar with a penetrating stare, which became more intense as the vicar started on his sermon. He had been known, if the sermon exceeded ten minutes in length, to make a great show of looking at his wristwatch in a way that made the vicar stumble over his words.

The vicar liked to range over the problems of the world during his sermons. To him a Sunday morning was wasted if one did not muse about – within the space of one long sentence – our troops in Afghanistan; the poor people in Darfur; the effects of global warming on the planet in general and the prospects for the harvest in particular. To review the world's problems should have been the work of at least thirty minutes, not ten: but ten minutes was all that was ever allowed him by Colonel Gazebee.

One Sunday the vicar had invited the colonel to read the lesson. He was under the illusion that if he acknowledged Colonel Gazebee's standing in the community in this way, the colonel would make allowances for his sermons. Such a ploy did not work, however. The colonel took his invitation to read as another right that he could choose to exercise every month or so and soon the vicar found himself powerless to stop Colonel Gazebee from reading the lesson whenever he felt it was his turn, and reading it in such a way that old men and women trembled, and children buried their heads in the laps of their parents.

On this particular Sunday Colonel Gazebee read one of his favourite passages. It was an edifying text from the Old Testament: Kings I, Chapter XXII:

So the king died and was brought to Samaria, and they buried the king in Samaria. And one washed the chariot in the pool of Samaria, and the dogs licked up his blood ...

When Colonel Gazebee came to the passage about the dogs licking Ahab's blood, he liked to place great emphasis on those words, then pause and stare around the church as if to suggest that the congregation should expect a similar fate unless it mended its ways. But this time he paused on the word 'dogs', faltered, and then stopped. For a moment he seemed disoriented, as if he had *thought* it was Sunday and he was in church, but now wondered if it might not be Wednesday and he was somewhere else. Then, without finishing the reading, he shut the Bible with a bang and walked back to his place with unsteady steps. There was a silence, while the vicar caught up with events and then smoothly moved to join the congregation in prayer.

Annabel leaned across to her father and murmured: 'Daddy, are you all right?'

He did not answer, so she repeated the question.

This time he heard and replied crossly: 'Of course I'm all right. Why do you keep asking me?'

But Annabel was left with the feeling that something had happened to her father while he stood at the lectern, a feeling that persisted when her father was silent during Sunday lunch, and quite failed to criticise her for leaving the shoulder of beef in a moment too long.

That afternoon he dozed, and made no objection in the evening when Annabel told him she was just going to visit Geoff for a couple of hours. His passivity on the subject surprised her. It was almost as if he had either forgotten, or else no longer cared, who Geoff was. She went out, feeling a little guilty that she had left her father on his own.

When she got back to Lambshiel House, there was a light on in the drawing room. Annabel opened the door and was surprised to see that her father was still up. On closer inspection she could not tell whether he was asleep or awake. He was still wearing the tweed suit he had worn to church, but his shirt collar was open at the neck and his tie was loosened. Also she noticed, with something like disgust, his flies were unbuttoned.

'Daddy, why are you still up?'

Colonel Gazebee did not answer. For a moment Annabel wondered if he might be dead. Then his mouth opened and shut, although no sound came out.

'What was that, Daddy?'

This time there was audible speech, but the words did not make much sense.

'Your mother was a poor, foolish, silly woman.'

'Poor Mummy,' said Annabel. 'Why don't you go upstairs and get ready for bed? I'll bring you some cocoa to help you sleep.'

'And you're another one. Silly and foolish.'

'I'm only trying to do my best,' said Annabel. She was beginning to feel like leaving her father to make his own arrangements for getting to bed. For a moment she felt overwhelmed by the cruelty of it all: what remained of her youth was ebbing away while she looked after this ungrateful old man who happened to be her father.

'We all try to do our best,' he said. 'We all try, but so often it isn't good enough. Look at me. Look at how I've ended my life: sitting in an armchair with only a foolish girl for company. No one wants to spend time with you, once you're old. Never get asked anywhere. Old army friends don't want to know. The neighbours aren't worth it anyway. Passed over; passed by on the other side. I don't want any cocoa.'

'Come on, Daddy,' said Annabel. She bent over him and tried to lift him to his feet. Eventually he managed to stand and then the two of them staggered up the stairs. Something had happened to her father in church that day, Annabel thought again, as she shut the door on him at last. Was the next stage of her life already upon her? The stage where she combined her present tasks as cook, housekeeper and general servant with the new duties of a hospital orderly and nurse?

The next morning, however, her father seemed to have recovered. He was marching about the house complaining that everything needed dusting, that the pictures were crooked, that the whole place wasn't being run properly. Annabel put up with this for a while and then rang Ed.

'I've got to get out,' she told him. 'My father is driving me mad. Can I come and have a cup of coffee with you?'

It was a twenty-mile round trip.

'Come and have lunch,' said Ed.

'You're not too busy?'

'I ought to be in the office but it's too depressing.'

Annabel put some lunch in the oven for her father and then went to tell him when to take it out. He was asleep in his armchair, so she wrote instructions in block capitals on a scrap of paper and left it on the table beside him. Then she tidied herself up, borrowed her father's car and drove to Hartlepool Hall. Ed met her at the door.

'No Horace?'

'He's in Middlesbrough, filling in forms to apply for his new flat. Mrs Donaldson drove him there. So it's just us for lunch. I've made some sandwiches. I hope you weren't expecting three courses.'

'Sandwiches would be lovely,' said Annabel. Then she remembered to ask: 'And how is Alice?'

'The fever's gone but she's still in bed. She's sleeping a lot, so I suppose that means she's getting better. But I'm worried, Annabel. Social Services keep ringing us, asking when they can come and collect her. They ring more frequently than the debt collectors do, and they're just as difficult to deal with.'

Annabel wondered when Ed had started to have contact with debt collectors. She decided it must be recently acquired knowledge. They went through to the dining room. Ed forgot to ask Annabel if she wanted a drink, but she didn't say anything. Poor Ed had quite enough on his mind.

In the dining room Ed triumphantly pulled the cling film from a plate of misshapen sandwiches.

'I went to the kitchen as soon as you rang,' he told Annabel, 'and I made them all by myself.'

'Cold chicken and mayonnaise!' said Annabel, with as much enthusiasm as she could manage. 'My favourite.'

'Oh my God,' said Ed after a moment. 'You must be dying of thirst. I forgot to ask.'

Annabel protested that he need not worry, but he disappeared from the room and came back with a bottle of wine. It was rather a grand-looking bottle of claret and was so cold it was impossible to say what it tasted of. Annabel wondered how on earth Ed would manage if he had to live on his own.

After a glass or two of wine, she found the courage to pass on Geoff's message. She ended by saying: 'Geoff thinks that there isn't much time. You need to sign the papers as soon as possible.'

'He hasn't even sent them to me yet,' protested Ed gently.

'But when he does.'

'Would it be all right if I read them first,' asked Ed, 'or should I just sign them anyway?'

'Oh, I didn't mean ...'

'I know Malcolm Skinner and Geoff Tarset are cooking up this deal between them,' said Ed with a touch of bitterness. 'But I didn't realise you were in on it as well.'

There was a silence. Annabel changed colour from white to red and then back to white again. Finally she said: 'Geoff says that selling Hartlepool Hall to him is your best chance. I'm only repeating what he told me to. You know I'm on your side.'

Ed said nothing, but just gazed at her with his cool stare.

'I'll always be on your side,' repeated Annabel.

'I know that,' said Ed in a gentler tone. 'It's just that everything seems to be happening so quickly. The bank, the tax people, Geoff Tarset – they're all after what remains of my inheritance. It takes a bit of getting used to. I expect when it's all gone I'll feel better for it.'

'Oh, Ed.'

He put the remains of his sandwich down and stood up. He walked around the table and kissed Annabel on the cheek. Instinctively she reached up her arms to embrace him, but he had already turned away.

'I know who my real friends are, Annabel, and you are definitely one of them.' He sat down again and looked at the half-eaten crusts on his plate.

'These sandwiches aren't much good, are they?'

'They're lovely.'

'Now I know you're not telling the truth.'

They both laughed; but it was not a joyous sound.

When Annabel returned home her father was in a furious mood.

'Lunch was burned to a crisp,' he told her.

'I left you a note telling you when to take it out,' she replied. 'Of course it will be burned if you leave it in there for three hours.'

'*Note!*' he screamed, so suddenly that Annabel almost jumped with shock. 'Note? I expect you to put my lunch on a plate for me at one o'clock every day without fail. I don't expect *notes*. I can't eat *notes*.'

'But Daddy . . .'

'If I didn't have to keep you, I'd be able to afford a proper housekeeper: one who could cook; one who didn't mope about the house all day.'

A vein was throbbing in her father's forehead. Annabel watched it with interest. It was like a separate living thing.

'Any other woman of your age would have got married by now. If you had had an ounce of initiative you'd have found a man. But you can't be bothered, can you?'

'That's so unfair,' Annabel said.

'And then you take up with that builder. You don't seriously think he's going to marry you? I don't know what his game is, but believe me, men who make money that fast lose it just as fast. When he does, he'll be off. Mark my words.'

Suddenly he sat back in his armchair, out of breath, and started to cough.

'Water,' he gasped. 'Bring me some water.'

'Get it yourself,' replied Annabel.

She went into the kitchen shaking with rage, tears running down her face. Then she went to the oven and took out the charred baking tray with the smoking remains of the quiche and threw the lot into the bin. She opened the window to let out the smoke then ran the cold tap and poured a glass of water. Wiping the tears from her face, she marched through to the drawing room and slammed the glass down on the table beside her father. He had stopped coughing. He wasn't moving, just breathing a little heavily with that glazed look on his face she had noticed once or twice.

'Your water,' said Annabel.

He didn't reply, or acknowledge her presence in any other way, so she went upstairs to her bedroom and sat on her bed. She picked up the book she had been reading but it provided no comfort. The story no longer held the power to transport her from the grim world she lived in. She sat there trying not to think about her life, and what the future might hold for her. Her father was as tough as oak, as hard as stone, and might live for another thirty years. She might die before he did.

She rang Geoff on his mobile and listened to a recording saying: 'Hi there! Geoff Tarset speaking. I can't come to the phone right now, but leave a message and I'll get back to you as soon as I can.'

'Geoff,' said Annabel. 'I'm at home. When can I see you? Give me a ring.'

She hung up. Then, curling up on the bedspread, she fell into a doze.

When she awoke, her thumb was wet and the nail ragged where she had chewed at it in her sleep. She was chilled to the bone. She walked about her bedroom for a minute or two, trying to get her circulation going. She checked her voicemail but Geoff hadn't returned her call. It was dusk outside and she realised she must have been asleep for hours. She went to the bathroom and splashed some water on her face, then she went downstairs.

Her father was still sitting in the gloom in exactly the same position as when she had left him earlier. The glass of water was untouched. His eyes were open and his breathing was slow and regular. He did not respond to Annabel's entrance in any way, not even turning his eyes to look at her. They still had that curious blank look as if whoever was inside his head had gone away for a while.

'Daddy, are you all right?'

No reply.

'Do you want any supper?'

No reply.

Annabel began to worry. Had her father had a stroke? She bent down and touched his arm. He farted, but did not speak.

'Come on,' she told the inert figure, 'we had better get you upstairs and into bed.'

She put her arm under his and tried to raise him to his feet. He was not as big a man as he had once been but he was still almost too much for her. She might never have lifted him on her own, but some instinct made him stagger from his chair. He mumbled something and then, in a kind of three-legged dance, they made their way to the drawing room door and very slowly, step by step, up the steep and narrow staircase. Halfway up Annabel had to stop to catch her breath, the sweat pouring down her face.

Her father said quite distinctly: 'I'm very tired, Molly. Very tired.'

Molly had been Annabel's mother's name.

On the last but one step her father suddenly teetered backwards and only by the greatest effort did Annabel stop them both from falling down the stairs. She thought that if they had, one or both of them might have broken their neck.

He might have broken *his* neck.

Her father might have fallen backwards and he might have broken his neck. She might have been free of him at last. She might have been free and she might have inherited his money and got rid of Geoff and made a life of her own.

On the last step she let go of him. He swayed unsteadily. She pushed him gently. It was only a little push: hardly a push at all, more like a pat of encouragement on his chest, just to say, 'There, there, well done, we're nearly there.' But it was enough to send her father tumbling. Annabel watched as he did a complete somersault on the way down. He landed on his head at the foot of the stairs, the rest of him following with a crash that seemed to shake the world.

Annabel sat on the top stair and looked down at him. He did not move. His body was at a funny angle and it looked as if he might have broken his neck and one of his legs at least. But you never knew. Annabel sat there chewing her fingernails while her father lay sprawled at the bottom of the staircase. After a long time she found she was able to speak.

'Daddy?' she said.

There was no answer from the figure at the bottom of the stairs.

'Are you all right?' asked Annabel.

Still no answer. Perhaps he was too angry to speak?

Perhaps he was too dead to speak?

She ought to tell someone. She ought to ring the police, or the doctor. If she rang the doctor he would ask questions. Colonel Gazebee had been quite well at the last check-up. What had happened? How did he fall? Was he upset about something? Is that what had made him lose his balance? Had there been an argument? The doctor would ring the police.

The police would ask questions.

Ever since she was a tiny girl, Annabel had managed to feel guilty about one thing or another. It was a weakness her father had done little to correct. At school, she would blush if someone asked her who had thrown the ball that broke the window, even though it had had nothing to do with her. When she went through customs she always blushed, as if she were smuggling something, even though she was never extravagant enough even to use up her tax free allowance, in the days when such a thing existed. The police would come and ask questions about how her father had ended up dead at the bottom of the stairs.

'Show me, Miss Gazebee,' they would ask. 'Show me where he was standing.'

So she would have to show them.

'And where were you standing, Miss Gazebee? You couldn't stop him falling? Did you let him fall?'

She would blush, and then there would be more questions. She did not know how it would turn out for her. She felt very cold, sitting in the dark at the top of the stairs.

The doorbell rang.

The doorbell rang, and it couldn't be the police, or the doctor because she hadn't told them yet. They couldn't possibly know about the accident. The accident was what she would call it, and an accident could happen to anybody. But now she would have to explain it all to whoever was at the door. They would insist that she called the police. The doorbell rang again, and she heard Geoff's voice shouting.

'Annabel? Are you there?'

He knew she was there because the car was outside and the drawing room lights were on. If she didn't answer the door it wouldn't be normal. He would wonder why she hadn't answered, when the lights were on and the car was parked outside. It was important that everything seemed normal.

'Coming!' she called as loudly as she could. She ran downstairs and with a sudden, furious burst of energy, picked up her father's legs by the ankles and dragged him the few yards to the dining room. She pulled her father inside and laid him on the floor beside the table. Then she mopped her brow, went out of the room, shut the door and leaned against it, breathing heavily.

'Annabel?' Geoff called again.

'Just a minute,' she replied. After a moment she felt able to go to the door and open it.

'What kept you?' asked Geoff cheerfully. 'Can I come in?'

Annabel gave a grimace like a smile and managed to say, 'Better not. Daddy's ... not very well. If you can wait two minutes I'll tidy up and come outside.'

'I was going to take you out to dinner, but if *Daddy's not well* ...' Geoff didn't finish the sentence, but raised his eyebrows in a sardonic manner.

'Oh, I couldn't eat anything, Geoff,' said Annabel. 'But a drink would be nice. I'd love a drink.'

'Are you all right?' asked Geoff curiously, looking at her hard. Annabel blushed.

'Of course I'm all right.' He had come a few steps into the hall, but she pushed him back out of the house. 'Go and wait in the car. I don't want to disturb Daddy. He's trying to sleep.'

'Well, I've had a lousy day,' said Geoff. 'And I could *murder* a drink. Don't be long.'

A few minutes later they were sitting in the car together, the house locked and the lights off.

Geoff started the Ferrari and as he did so he asked, 'How was your day?'

'Oh, just average,' answered Annabel.

Fifteen

Ed decided to sit with Alice in her bedroom most mornings until she felt a little better. She recovered from her illness – whatever it was – only slowly. At first they talked of light, unimportant things but as Alice became stronger Ed told her about his own worries. The contract for the sale of Hartlepool Hall and the discharge of the bank's mortgages and loans had arrived. Ed was spending hours with Malcolm and a lawyer, going through the documents. He talked to Alice about the shame he felt that he should be the last member of his family to live in the house as its owner.

'Don't think about it like that,' Alice told him. 'You didn't create the problem. You just have to do the best you can with what you've got.'

Somehow this comforted Ed, although he could not say why.

Only when Alice was sitting up in bed again, and eating proper food instead of the tepid broths that Mrs Donaldson had been reviving her with, did Ed return to the subject of Alice and his father.

'Before you fell ill you told me about my father taking my mother to Ascot. Do you mind me asking you about that? Was that the end between the two of you?'

'Not quite,' replied Alice. 'I admit, I was shattered for a

while. You can't imagine what my life was like before I met your father. It was so comfortable and pleasant, living in that little house near Hyde Park. The thought of giving it all up, and never seeing him again was heartbreaking. I didn't know what would become of me without your father.'

'Couldn't you have stayed in the cottage?'

'No. Your father was quite clear that we would have to stop seeing each other and he would have to give up the lease. He said that people would talk, that people had already talked. The wedding wasn't far off and Maude's father had taken him to one side and told him "to get his house in order". Those were the very words your father repeated to me and I never forgot them. They made me feel like a criminal.'

'If it had been me, I would have married you. How could he have left you for my mother?'

Alice frowned.

'You mustn't say that, Ed. Your father may have married Maude Portalbert for her money, but if it hadn't been her it would have been some other rich girl. He had no choice.'

Ed thought about his own hopes of marriage to Catherine Plender, the girl who had been killed in a car crash. The marriage had been planned between Ed's parents and the Plenders when both the children were still quite young. The Plenders had been very well off.

'Why couldn't my father have gone out and got a job, then married whoever he wanted?'

'He couldn't get a job any more easily than you can,' said Alice. 'He wasn't brought up to work.'

'How did it end? Did you ever see my father again?'

'No more questions,' Alice told him. 'You'll have me in tears thinking about it.'

'Please.'

Alice smiled at Ed. It was a sad smile of great sweetness.

'He just stopped seeing me,' she said. 'Your father wasn't a brave man. I knew he couldn't bear to tell me to go. A couple of weeks after I saw the photograph of him with Maude Portalbert in the magazine, I received a letter in the post. There was a cheque for five hundred pounds and a short note. It just said: "I'll always miss you." It wasn't signed. The next day I received a letter from the landlord saying that I had to be out by the end of the month.'

'Five hundred pounds!' cried Ed. 'Is that all?'

'It was a lot of money in those days,' said Alice. She stopped speaking for a moment; then said, 'Ed, I'm going to have to leave soon.'

Ed jumped to his feet.

'You can't,' he told her. 'You can't leave me. I need someone to talk to. I need you to be here, Alice. I don't want you to go.'

He stopped, realising that he sounded like a spoiled child. Alice seemed different: withdrawn.

'It's best for you if I go,' said Alice. 'I can't stay here for ever. Social Services will begin to think you've kidnapped me. I'm sure that they will be very cross with me for leaving without telling anyone.'

'Why is it their business what you do?' asked Ed. 'Where will they take you? I don't have your address, Alice. How will I get in touch with you? Will you come back?'

'I'm never coming back,' said Alice. 'I only came here because I promised your father.'

'What did you promise him? When was that?'

'I saw him again after he married. And I saw him just before he died.'

'So the last time you saw him was over ten years ago.'

'I suppose so. I don't know how he found me. He must have looked me up in the book. He wouldn't say. He wrote to me and then we met for lunch in a quiet little hotel in Knightsbridge.'

Alice's eyes were bright and shiny and she picked at the bedspread as she spoke.

'I told Samuel I was going shopping. I didn't know what might happen. I didn't really think your father would turn up.'

'So what did happen?'

'It was what didn't happen,' said Alice. 'Of course we were both getting on by then. Still, I wondered if he would have taken a room at the hotel, and if he would ask me to go upstairs with him. That was before I saw him. As soon as I came into the restaurant I could see your father was already an old man: tired and red-faced.'

Once again Ed had that strange feeling of seeing events through Alice's eyes. He remembered how his father had been in those last years before he died: infirm and forgetful, always complaining. He pictured his father sitting in the corner of a quiet restaurant, watching Alice enter the room. Had he too seen Alice not as she was, but as he remembered her? Had her upright posture and her firm features recalled the girl he had known over forty years before?

'Lunch was a failure,' said Alice. 'Agreeing to meet him again was a mistake. I had expected to find the same tall, good-looking man he had been, only grey-haired. But he hadn't aged well. It hurt me to see how old he looked; how forgetful he was; how sorry he felt for himself. It was an agony getting through the meal until it was time to say goodbye. But he said two things that I will never forget.'

She paused.

'The first was this. When I told him how sorry I had been to read of your mother's death, he replied: "You know, we still shared a bed. I don't know why. I heard her stop breathing in the middle of the night. She hadn't been well. I heard her stop breathing."

'"What did you do?" I asked him.

'"I turned over and went back to sleep," your father told me. Then he said: "You know, I never loved her, Alice. I never felt the slightest thing for her. The only person I ever loved was you."'

Outside a pigeon had started crooning to itself in the trees. It was so quiet when Alice stopped speaking, its calls filled the room.

'I asked him: "But you do love your son?" Your father shook his head. "I've tried to be a good father," he replied. "But I've brought Ed up so that he is incapable of doing anything except spend money. I've never known how to show him affection." Then your father started to cough, and he couldn't speak for a minute. Everyone was looking at us. I gave him a glass of water and waited until he stopped. Then he said: "Promise me one thing, Alice. Promise me you'll go and see Ed when I'm gone. I know you'll outlast me. Look at the difference between the two of us now. Go and see Ed and tell him about us, tell him that I know I wasn't much of a father to him."'

Ed bowed his head.

'That's why I came,' said Alice simply.

'But why now?' asked Ed. 'Why has it taken you so long?'

'I never saw your father again after that lunch. I didn't want to. It was too awful to see how he had changed. I only thought about coming here when I saw his obituary in the papers. Then Samuel fell ill. A few weeks ago I woke up and realised that if I didn't come and see you soon, I never would. I would be too old, or forget, or something else would happen. And getting away from the place I live now isn't easy.'

'I'm very glad that you did.'

Ed did not ask her the questions he really wanted to ask: why were there no pictures of her in the scrapbook? Who was she? Where had she come from? He would ask her these questions when she had fully recovered, he thought. For the moment he would have to wait.

Over the next few days, the calls and letters from Social Services increased in intensity. People were constantly ringing the house demanding an appointment. Ed read the letters out of fearfulness for Alice, but did not reply to them. He stopped answering the house phone; luckily, they did not have his office number.

The tone of the correspondence was varied. One letter referred to the Mental Capacity Act 2005 and suggested that Alice might lack the mental capacity to look after herself. It suggested that a court might take the view that Ed was holding her at Hartlepool Hall against her will. Another letter asked him to set out his qualifications as a carer. Yet another letter asked him whether he had applied for his carer's allowance.

Then the tone became more threatening. A letter arrived from the Director of Social Services saying that the case would be referred to the Mental Health Review Tribunal. The next letter referred to powers given to Social Services under the Mental Health Act 2007, and announced that the case file had been 'outsourced' to a private contractor, Humanitas PLC.

All this made Ed feel rather tense. Then, even more disturbingly, all the letters and phone calls ceased.

As if that was not enough to worry about, there were calls several times a day from Malcolm Skinner. Did Ed realise the bank had set a deadline for the repayment of its loans? Did Ed realise Geoff would walk away from the deal if Ed didn't 'come to the table' as Geoff had put it. Documents; phone calls; incomprehensible emails with attachments that Ed couldn't open; threats, blandishments, more threats.

Ed was not enjoying life.

Sixteen

When Annabel returned home from her drink with Geoff, she wouldn't let him get out of the car.

'I don't want to wake Daddy.'

'You should do something about that old man,' Geoff told her. 'He's ruining your life.'

Annabel gave him a little wave as she stood under the automatic light by the front door, and forced a smile. She felt the wind on her face. It was a breezy night. She fumbled for the front door key, and waved again as Geoff turned the car and drove away. She let herself into the silent house. She flicked on the lights in the hall and then, taking her courage in both hands, she walked towards the dining room door. It was still closed. Of course it was still closed. Who could have opened it? She switched on the lights in the stairwell and went upstairs, her eyes fixed on the wall, not looking at the top step where Daddy had – accidentally – fallen. She switched on the lights in her bedroom and in the bathroom. She went round the house and switched on all the lights she could find.

Then she went downstairs again.

It had to be done. She forced herself to open the dining room door. She forced herself to look inside. She didn't know what she was expecting: an empty room? The grinning figure of her father, his head lolling to one side as he walked towards her? But there was only an old, dead man lying on the floor beside the dining room table. He looked smaller dead than he had done alive.

She couldn't leave him like that. In all the books Annabel had read, you weren't supposed to touch dead bodies. You weren't supposed to move them, or interfere with the scene of the crime in any way. But this wasn't a crime scene, was it? It was an accident. It had been only a very little push. He would have fallen down the stairs anyway ... probably. It was too late to worry about all that. She'd already moved him in her panic when the doorbell had rung. She couldn't leave her own father lying dead on the floor of the dining room, no matter how badly he had behaved.

She knelt by his head and put her hands under his armpits. With a great effort she managed to lift him into a sitting position. Then, straining until she thought her back might snap, she dragged him and manoeuvred him until she had perched him on the edge of a chair. He started to slip, but she tugged and pushed and pulled until at last her father was propped up in his favourite chair at the head of the table.

'There, that's better,' said Annabel when she had recovered her breath. 'That doesn't look so bad, Daddy, does it? Better than lying on the floor. Now I won't have to hoover round you when I clean the room. And you look more comfortable.'

And he did look more comfortable, even if he also looked deader than ever. It was something about the angle of his head. But now one could imagine – just – that he had been sitting with his port and had drunk one glass too many and fallen asleep. Annabel didn't think she wanted to touch him ever again. His hands and his face felt so cold, not like human skin at all.

She went back upstairs and put herself to bed. Outside the

wind had got up. It howled around the house. Annabel tried to go to sleep but every time she closed her eyes an image came into her mind of Daddy falling on his head at the bottom of the stairs. She opened her eyes and stared into the darkness. There was a rattle and a thump from somewhere downstairs. It had happened before – the windows were old and they rattled on stormy nights when the wind came from the east. That was what she was listening to.

Rattle; thump.

Annabel switched on her bedside light and listened more carefully. Was that a creak on the lower stairs? But it was only the wind; what else could it be?

She lay awake, her heart beating too fast and her eyes wide open. Thoughts raced through her head but she could not get them to arrange themselves in a straight line. She had killed her father; no, she hadn't exactly killed him, but pushing him downstairs like that hadn't been a good idea. Or had it? She couldn't believe she had done that. She thought in time she would come to believe that she *hadn't* done that. It had been an accident; an accident. Was it wrong that she cared so little about her father's death? All Annabel felt inside was a deep coldness, an absence, not a presence, of any emotion that she could recognise.

She must have drifted off to sleep because when she awoke with a start, the bedside light was still on. The wind had dropped. There were no noises now: the house was quite still. In the silence Annabel thought once more about what had happened that afternoon. It had been wrong of her to move Daddy after his accident, but she could explain all that. She could say that she couldn't bear to see him lying there at the bottom of the stairs. She could say she had moved him to the dining room as a mark of respect.

But wouldn't it sound a little odd?

Maybe she wouldn't tell anyone for a while yet. After all, nobody would be that interested. Most of her father's friends either were dead or could no longer remember their own names, let alone his. There were few callers to the house. For the last two years, after one of her father's economy drives, Annabel had done all the cleaning. In fact she did all the cleaning, all the shopping, and all the cooking. A gardener called once a week but he knew enough about Colonel Gazebee's disposition to keep well out of the way. When the gardener came he just went straight to the shed, took out the lawnmower or the shears or whatever he needed, and got on with his job. He wasn't even offered a cup of tea; he brought his own in a thermos flask and drank it in the shed. Nobody came in the house these days except Geoff and she could deal with him.

And then, thought Annabel, turning over in bed, there was no longer any need for economy drives. She had control over her own life at last. She would go through Daddy's papers and see if she could find out about the 'Inheritance'. He had banged on about it for years but she had never discovered whether he had money in the bank, or in a building society account; or whether he owned property elsewhere. But wherever it was she would find it. Her father had never owned a computer; any records would be on paper, and they would be filed, and she would find them.

She yawned and stretched and looked at her watch: half past three. Too early to get up and make a cup of tea. Her thoughts ran on. There was the question of this house. It was not a nice house. It was a typical Northern double-fronted farmhouse that had been extended: two large front rooms that were quite well proportioned, while the rest of the house was a bit of a warren. Annabel thought that, given the choice, she wouldn't live here. What she wanted was a sweet little cottage somewhere, with roses around the door, and a small garden, and friendly neighbours so she wouldn't be too lonely.

She started to doze again, and halfway between waking and sleeping she found that the cottage had grown slightly, because it now accommodated Ed as well. For some reason Geoff wasn't in this dream. Annabel and Ed lived in a little cottage with roses around the door, a little cottage – but not too little – that Annabel had bought with the money from the sale of Lambshiel House.

Annabel sat up in bed, her dream slipping from her grasp like water flowing from a shattered glass. She couldn't sell the house because it belonged to her father. She couldn't inherit her father's money, wherever it was, because he wasn't dead. Until she told someone he was dead, he wasn't dead.

The old man was sitting downstairs, as if asleep over his non-existent glass of port, and no doubt he would be smiling. Annabel was sure of it. He would be smiling at this last cruel joke he had played on her. He had made her push him downstairs; he had made her feel guilty, so that she had panicked and moved the body. Now she didn't know what to do.

Annabel climbed out of bed and put on her dressing gown and went downstairs. The dining room door was still shut. She went into the kitchen and, as the sky turned golden in the east, she put the kettle on to boil.

What on earth was she going to do? She couldn't tell anybody about her father's death. She couldn't *not* tell anybody. It was a job to know what was best to do. Of course in the end she would have to ring the doctor, and the doctor would ring the police, but she couldn't face all that this morning.

'I'm in shock,' she said to herself out loud. That was it: she was in shock. She thought she might as well stay in shock for a day or two yet. Something would occur to her. It was just a question of time. She looked down at the kitchen counter and saw that she had made two mugs of tea: force of habit. She would get used to living without Daddy after a while.

The only problem was, Daddy was still in the house.

Seventeen

It was midsummer. The long June days had barely faded into dusk before the first light of dawn appeared in the eastern sky. The weather was dry and cloudless and the farmers were praying for rain. In the garden the rhododendrons were nearly over; in the fields the crops were starting to change colour. Swifts darted, shrieking, above the chimneys of Hartlepool Hall while swallows dived low over the lake. Ed had carried chairs and a table onto the terrace so that he and Alice could sit and look at the lake while they drank their coffee after lunch or their wine before dinner.

By now, Horace had gone. Ed knew he was leaving and had arranged for Mrs Donaldson to bake a cake. There had been plans, well advanced, for a leaving party with the remaining employees of Hartlepool Estate gathered in the kitchen. Ed was going to give a speech, and had started making notes: 'long and faithful service'; 'the Hall won't be the same place without him'; 'a friend as much as a servant' and so on. This speech was never given because one morning, while Ed was out and about with Malcolm, looking at a cottage that was about to be sold, Horace simply slipped away.

'He didn't want any fuss,' explained Mrs Donaldson when

Ed, taken aback, tried to find out what had happened. 'He ordered a taxi and went.'

'Did he leave an address?' asked Ed. 'I should have so liked to say goodbye to him.'

'Now I wrote it down somewhere,' said Mrs Donaldson, 'to give to the wages people in Mr Skinner's office.' She started rummaging around amongst the roast pheasants, hams and pâtés that covered the large kitchen table.

'When you find it, let me know,' said Ed. 'You're doing a lot of cooking, I see. Are we expecting someone?'

'No, M'Lord,' she replied. 'But Friday's my last day too, and I just wanted to make sure you had something to be going on with. The deep freeze is full, M'Lord, so you shouldn't have to worry about food for a bit.'

That was it. From the end of the week Ed would be on his own in the huge house: on his own, apart from Alice. He would have to prepare his own meals. He would have to do the washing up. He would have to open the front door if someone came to the house. Ed realised that his life was about to change for ever.

In the end Mrs Donaldson went without much more fuss than Horace. She wept a little and hugged Alice, did a half curtsey to Ed, then left in a taxi with all her belongings. She had already found a job in a gastro pub a few miles from Hartlepool Hall. Ed worried about what her ideas on cooking might do to the pub owner's budgets.

Despite his dislike of the office, Ed now found he had to spend more and more time in it. There was the sale of the grouse moor at Blubberwick, which was nearing completion: a Chinese mobile phone millionaire had bought it. Teddy Shildon rang Ed to tell him that once the cheque was banked and the money owing to the taxman paid, the trust would be wound up.

'We tried to get old Marcus Gazebee to sign the papers,' he told Ed, 'but he simply won't come to the phone. Annabel says he's feeling a bit antisocial at the moment. That's nothing new. But he is a trustee and he ought to be prepared to do his duty.'

'I'd forgotten he was a trustee,' replied Ed.

'Well, you could be forgiven for that. He rarely bothers to turn up to meetings,' said Teddy. 'Luckily the trust deed says that any two trustees can sign, so I've signed everything, and the lawyer from Newcastle has countersigned. Once the Chinese fellow's money is in the account, our job is done.'

'I don't know how to thank you, Teddy,' said Ed. 'You've done so much over the years.'

'Well, you can give me that day's shooting you promised me in December. You haven't sacked the keeper yet, I hope?'

'No, he's going in February,' said Ed. 'We'll try to make it a day to remember.'

Next Ed had to deal with the house in France he had been renting. This proved more complicated, but in the end he managed to wriggle out of the lease and made arrangements to have his belongings shipped back home.

'I'd like to have gone out there one last time,' Ed told Alice, 'but I daren't leave home at the moment.'

They were sitting outside on the terrace contemplating their plates on which sat two partridges, burned black in the oven.

'I'm sorry about those birds,' Ed told Alice. 'I thought you had to leave them in for an hour and a half, like a chicken.'

'I like them well done,' said Alice. 'I'm just not very hungry at the moment.'

'You never eat anything. It isn't my cooking, is it?'

'No,' said Alice. 'Your cooking is fine, Ed. You will learn. Isn't it beautiful out here tonight?'

The sun was sinking low in the sky. It was a warm evening and a light breeze ruffled the surface of the lake.

'We'd better enjoy it while we can. The builders will be here before long.'

'Is it all settled, then?'

'No, but there's a meeting soon when I'm meant to sign contracts with Geoff Tarset. And the bank will be there. I'm dreading it.'

There was a long silence.

'I ought to have done something before now,' said Ed suddenly. 'I should have taken more interest in what was going on. I don't know why I didn't. I used to explain it to myself by saying that since Catherine's death I had lost interest in everything, but that wasn't true – I never had much interest in the first place.'

As he spoke he wondered why he had never understood this before.

'You need to love something to be interested in it,' said Alice.

'But I do love Hartlepool Hall,' protested Ed. 'That's what makes it so awful. I shall be the last member of my family to live here after nearly two hundred years.'

But as he spoke Ed realised that what he was saying wasn't quite true. He loved the *idea* of Hartlepool Hall, but he had never truly involved himself in it; in its upkeep, and in the conservation of the fading and stained furniture and the oil paintings which grew browner and gloomier each year. He had never visited the farms; he had never cut down or planted a single tree. He had never expressed any opinion about the state of the woods with their windblows and overgrown timber; or the fences that sagged, allowing animals to stray through them; or the crumbling stone walls along the fields and around the park that were being pulled down by ivy or overturned by tree roots.

Alice rose and said she was going upstairs to bed. As she left she put her hand on Ed's cheek.

'Don't reproach yourself, Ed. There has been no love in this house for a long time. It's not just you.'

Ed took her hand for a moment. Then he said: 'I've been looking through your scrapbook. I'm sorry, I know I shouldn't have, but there it was on the sofa. There were no photographs of you.'

'No,' she replied in a low voice.

'Then I looked you up in all the books: *Debrett's*, *Kelly's*, *Burke's Peerage*. There's no Lady Alice Birtley in any of them.'

She gave him a quick sideways look.

'No, I don't suppose there is.'

'I want you to tell me who you really are, and why you came here. Not now, we're both tired. But tomorrow – will you tell me then?'

'Yes,' she said after a moment. 'Yes, of course I will.'

After Alice went upstairs, Ed sat and smoked for a while. There had never been much love at Hartlepool Hall. His father hadn't got on with his own father, Ed's grandfather, and had refused to live there until he died. Ed himself had not liked to be at home unless surrounded by friends. When his mother was alive his father had been conspicuous by his long absences, spent travelling abroad or in the flat in London. After his mother died Ed had begun to spend more time here, and his father had withdrawn from the world, settling back in his armchair for year after year of television. Ed had filled the house with his own set of friends. Chief among these had been Catherine; but the chilly emotional atmosphere of the place and Ed's chronic detachment had forced her away, and she had jumped into the arms of a completely unsuitable man before her tragic accident.

Ed put out his cigarette and went to bed.

The next morning, while Alice was still in bed, Ed went to Darlington. He knew he was running out of time; that Hartlepool Hall could not be saved; that Geoff Tarset and Malcolm Skinner must be allowed to take it all away from the family that had lived there so long in order to rescue it from the bank. But Ed did want to have one last shot at trying to save the place himself. He didn't know how one went about these things, which was why he'd driven to Darlington.

Once he was there he parked the car and went into the main branch of the Royal Welsh Bank, which was the principal competitor to the bank in which the Hartlepool Estate held its accounts. Ed had never been inside before; there had been no reason to do so. It was one of those modern banks that looked more like an open-plan office – he could see no counters with cashiers behind them. A smiling young girl in a blue jacket and trousers intercepted him.

'How may we help you, sir?'

'Could I see the manager?' asked Ed.

'Do you have an account with us, sir?'

'No, but I'm thinking of opening one.'

'Would it be for business?' asked the girl. 'Or personal?'

'A bit of both,' said Ed. 'I think I'd better talk to someone about a business account.'

'I'll take you to our Business Team Leader,' said the girl. 'I think he's free at the moment.'

They walked across the office, past various cubicles, to a corner where a young man sat motionless behind a clean desk. On the computer was a screen saver celebrating the local football club.

When Ed approached the man sprang to his feet and shook Ed by the hand.

'Hi! I'm Terry Martin.'

This information was unnecessary since the young man's name was printed on a badge pinned to the lapel of his suit jacket.

'My name is Ed Hartlepool.'

'Hi, Mr Hartlepool. How may I help you?'

Ed wasn't quite sure where to begin. He thought he had better explain himself a little.

'I live at Hartlepool Hall,' he began.

The young man was busy opening up a program on his computer so that he could enter Ed's information. He paused and said, 'I'm sorry. I thought you said your *name* was Hartlepool. You must have meant your *address* is Hartlepool Hall. What is the post code?'

'Well, my name is Hartlepool too,' explained Ed.

'Wow. That's weird, isn't it?' The young man entered the information on the screen, then asked: 'And do you bank with us?'

Ed told him the name of the family's bank.

'And your name is Hartlepool and you live at Hartlepool Hall?'

'Yes,' said Ed again.

'I've been there,' said Terry Martin. 'The bank had a function there two years ago. You mean you *own* that place? I thought it belonged to the National Trust?'

'Well, it belongs to a *family* trust,' replied Ed. He did his best to explain the estate's financial problems. As he spoke Terry Martin became more and more excited.

'And you want to bank with us? I'm sure we'd be delighted to have you as a customer.'

'Yes, I was thinking about moving the account.'

'Were you thinking of making an initial deposit to open the account?'

Ed hesitated. This was not really what he had in mind.

'As a matter of fact I was wondering about a bank loan,' he explained.

'Did you have a particular sum in mind, Mr Hartlepool?'

Ed reached inside his jacket and pulled out his diary. He had written some numbers on the flyleaf.

'About six million pounds.'

Later, as Ed drove back to Hartlepool Hall, he admitted that he could have handled the interview better. He should have written beforehand; he should have taken his accountant with him, or at least somebody who was more fluent with numbers than he was. Terry Martin had been very apologetic, as well as rather flustered by the request for such an enormous sum of money. He explained that he had no authority above ten thousand pounds; there was the question of security; perhaps a meeting with his regional director in due course would produce an answer.

But there was no time left. With cruel insight Ed realised that there might have been a chance to rescue Hartlepool Hall if, at some point during the last five years, he had bothered to read his correspondence. If he had, just once, picked up the phone to Malcolm or his accountant; if he had tried to cut expenditure sooner; if he had found another, more tolerant bank than the one that was now on the point of declaring him insolvent, might he then have succeeded in changing the course of events?

Ed would never know.

When he arrived back at Hartlepool Hall there was a large people carrier parked on the gravel. As Ed got out of his car he could see a name on its side in black letters: *Humanitas PLC*. Underneath in flowing script was the motto: *Caring for the Elderly*. As Ed went in through the front door, he was surprised to be met by someone who was standing just inside the hallway.

'Mr Hartlepool?' The man was dressed in a tightly fitting dark suit with the jacket buttoned up, an open-necked white shirt, and white trainers on his feet. His head was almost completely shaven and he wore rimless steel glasses. To Ed's eyes there was something sinister about his appearance. He was carrying a clipboard.

'Yes,' replied Ed. 'I'm Ed Hartlepool. Who are you?'

'My name is Sam,' said the stranger. 'I'm from Humanitas PLC. I am here on behalf of the Department of Health and Social Services. I have an authority under Schedule 2, Paragraph 8 of the Mental Health Act 2007 to enter these premises and remove Alice Birtley to a place where she can be given proper care and medical attention.'

For a moment Ed was too surprised to speak. The stranger thrust the clipboard forward so that Ed could read the documents on it.

'What do you mean, remove Alice?'

'My medical operatives are checking the premises. We

believe Miss Birtley to be staying here. Questions will have to be asked as to whether she has been staying here of her own free will or not. Right now, our job is to return her to the care of the people who are legally responsible for her.'

'But she's perfectly all right,' said Ed, his voice sounding loud in his own ears. He realised he must have shouted, because Sam from Humanitas took a step back.

'I must warn you not to approach any closer,' said Sam. 'Unless you keep your distance I may find it necessary to call a police officer and have you charged with assault.'

The situation was not improved by the arrival of Alice at the other end of the hall. She was being half-dragged, half-carried down the staircase by two men in green medical scrubs. Her head sagged slightly.

'Alice!' cried Ed, starting towards her. He felt Sam grab his arm but shook him off.

'There you are, petal,' said one of the orderlies to Alice. 'We're nearly at the front door now, and when we get to the bottom of the steps there's a nice wheelchair for you.'

Alice lifted her head and gazed blankly at Ed for a moment. Her pupils were dark, and saliva ran down her chin.

'What's wrong with her?' said Ed, turning fiercely towards Sam.

'Now then, I won't warn you again,' replied Sam, producing a mobile phone and flipping it open. 'Any more trouble from you and I'm calling the police.'

'We had to give her a shot,' explained one of the orderlies. 'She was a bit agitated. Slows down the heart rate. Stops them worrying too much.'

Ed might have flown at the orderlies then, and tried to release Alice, but he was saved from creating mayhem by Alice who managed to say a few words.

'It's all right, Ed. Let them take me away. It had to happen. I will be better off back in my home. I'm only going to be a trouble to you here.'

Her words were slurred but their meaning was clear. Ed turned to Sam and demanded: 'Where you are taking her?'

'You're not a relation, are you? I'm afraid that is privileged information.'

Ed was paralysed by indecision. If he tried to stop them, it would be one man against three. He might have been able to deal with Sam, but the orderlies were burly, solid men. Anyway, it would only distress Alice. She might even be hurt. And then that idiot with the clipboard would call the police. By now, the orderlies were gently helping Alice down the steps, and Sam had skipped in front of them to the people carrier, from which he produced a folding wheelchair.

Alice was lowered into this and then taken to the back of the van and wheeled onto an hydraulic ramp. As she was raised from the ground she turned to face Ed once more. He could see tears running down her cheeks.

'Darling, I'm so sorry to leave you.'

'Alice – where are they taking you?'

But the sedative was working now. Her head slumped forward.

One of the orderlies said: 'There, flower. You have a lovely sleep now while we drive you back home.'

'Where are you taking her?' repeated Ed. 'I only want to come and visit her.'

He approached Sam, who backed away, holding the clipboard in front of him defensively.

'Now then, Mr Hartlepool . . .'

The orderlies had settled Alice in the back of the van and shut the doors. One remained with her while the other came around the side and said, 'Oh relax, Sam. He won't hurt you.'

'Can't you tell me?' Ed asked the orderly. 'I'd just like to know where you're taking her.'

'Not allowed to, mate,' said the man, amiably enough.

The two of them then climbed into the front of the van and soon it was disappearing down the tree-lined drive.

Eighteen

The vicar came to call on Colonel Gazebee.

'We haven't seen your father in church for a while,' he said to Annabel as she opened the front door. He smiled and made a sinuous movement as if he hoped to slide past her and into the house. Annabel stood in his way.

'He hasn't been himself,' she explained.

'We wondered,' replied the vicar. 'May I come in for a moment?'

Annabel smiled back at him but did not move. She was thinking hard. If she didn't let the vicar in, he might start asking questions around the parish. Who else had seen Colonel Gazebee recently? When had they last seen him? Annabel's father did not go out much, but apart from church he occasionally managed expeditions to the village shop and post office. She decided she had better invite the vicar in.

'What was I thinking?' she said. 'Do come in and have a cup of coffee.'

She let the vicar sidle past her into the hall and showed him into the drawing room. Then she went and put the kettle on. The smell that had invaded the house in the last few days was very noticeable. Annabel had not been into the dining room for several days. She had not studied the chemistry of putrefaction while at school, but she could picture only too clearly what might be going on behind the closed door. Sometimes she imagined that she could hear flies buzzing in the dining room; there were an awful lot about this summer. From time to time a childhood rhyme sounded in her head with a metronomic beat:

> *The worms go in*
> *and the worms come out;*
> *they go in thin*
> *and they come out stout.*

When the kettle had boiled, Annabel made coffee for herself and the vicar. The kitchen, like much of the house, smelled at one level of air freshener. Annabel had been to the local Co-Op and bought a selection: air fresheners that recalled the sea breezes of the Pacific Ocean; others that wafted the fragrances of Japanese tatami grass or the pine forests of Norway. None of these was quite able to dispel the underlying odour.

When she returned to the drawing room the vicar was wrinkling his nose, but was too polite to say anything.

'I'm so sorry about the smell,' Annabel said. 'We put some rat poison out and I'm afraid there's something dead beneath the floorboards.'

'Oh dear,' said the vicar. 'Still, better that you know it's dead. I have a particular dislike of rats. We were troubled with them in the vicarage garden last year, around the compost heap. But do tell me: how is your dear father?'

Annabel smiled. 'Daddy's taking things easy at the moment. It's nothing serious.'

'We thought he looked unwell in church last time he came,' said the vicar. 'Has the doctor been?'

'We haven't bothered Dr Mitchell,' said Annabel. She knew

it was probable the vicar had already asked the doctor, who was a regular member of his congregation. 'It didn't seem to be anything he could help with.'

'What didn't seem to be anything he could help with, my dear?'

'Whatever's wrong with Daddy,' replied Annabel. She felt she had tripped herself up. 'Not that there's anything wrong, of course. He's just very tired and doesn't want to see anyone.'

The vicar frowned for a moment. 'Perhaps I should sit and pray with him for a while?'

'I don't think so.'

'Many of my parishioners have said how much comfort it has given them when I pray with them,' persisted the vicar. 'Is he in his bedroom?'

'Daddy particularly asked not to be disturbed today,' Annabel said firmly. 'I really can't go against his wishes. He wouldn't be pleased, Vicar.'

The vicar knew Colonel Gazebee did not like to have his instructions on any subject ignored. He hesitated, then said: 'Perhaps another time. You will tell him I called and was asking after him?'

'Of course,' said Annabel. She stood up, so the vicar stood up too. He wrinkled his nose again as he caught a whiff of whatever was going on in the dining room.

'I do hope your rats don't return,' he said.

'I think the problem has been dealt with. So good of you to call, Vicar.'

'If there's anything you need ...'

'I'm fine,' said Annabel, ushering him to the front door.

She watched the vicar until he had got in his car and driven out of sight, then she went back to the drawing room and collapsed in a chair. When she felt calm again, she reviewed the whole conversation in her head. Did the vicar suspect that anything was wrong? She hoped not; but one could never be sure.

There had been too many such difficulties in the last few weeks. Considering what a reclusive existence her father had led in recent years it was surprising how many people had wanted to talk to him. The surgery had rung up asking why Colonel Gazebee hadn't been in to collect his prescription. Annabel had forgotten about her father's pills for a mild complaint, and had gone to pick them up. Then the woman at the post office asked why her father hadn't been in to draw his state pension, so she'd had to deal with that. Teddy Shildon had rung and had been most insistent that Annabel should call her father to the phone about some documents that needed signing. That had been tricky, and Teddy had asked a lot of awkward questions.

The fact was that sooner or later Annabel was going to have to tell people that her father had died. She was going to have to tell them about the accident and explain why she hadn't called a doctor, or the police, on the evening it happened. Worst of all, she was going to have to explain why she had dragged him into the dining room and seated him at the head of the table. She wasn't even sure she could explain that to herself.

Later that day Annabel went out shopping. There were still a few shops left in the village. The petrol station and one of the pubs had closed, but a small general store still offered a selection of dry groceries, bread, frozen food and the daily papers. Opposite it was a butcher's shop that had so far survived the competition from various superstores a few miles away. Annabel went in and ordered a lamb chop.

'That won't go far between the two of you,' said the butcher, wrapping it up for her. Annabel realised her mistake and quickly added a couple of slices of lamb's liver to her order. She would have to freeze that. She paid in cash. She was already running low: her allowance was handed to her by her father at the beginning of each month in twenty-pound notes, and she wasn't sure how she was going to manage when this instalment ran out.

When she returned home she decided the time had come to do some investigation into her father's finances. It seemed indelicate, somehow, to rummage through Daddy's papers when the poor old man was still in the dining room, but various questions had begun to occur to her that she ought to have thought of before. For example, how was the electricity bill paid, or the council tax? Was it by direct debit, or did her father write a cheque? She had never bothered herself with that side of domestic business. She had had enough to do, keeping the house up to her father's very high standards, and washing and ironing his clothes, without having to worry about all the paperwork as well.

But the paperwork might be important. What would she do if the lights went out, or the telephone was cut off, or if final demands started arriving for this or that unpaid bill? Was she meant to forge Daddy's signature on a cheque? She didn't think she could do that; besides, it would be breaking the law.

Apart from that, there was the question of her inheritance. She had always understood from her father that when he died, there was – somewhere – some sort of nest egg. Her father had often mentioned his own cleverness in putting some money away, but Annabel didn't believe that he could have saved much. He had retired from the army in his forties, and he hadn't done a great deal since then, apart from sit in his armchair, read the newspapers and complain.

There was one way to find out. Annabel knew that he kept his private papers locked up in a roll-top desk in the drawing room. He kept the key ... he kept the key ... where had she last seen it? Oh, on his watch chain. The key to the roll-top desk was on Daddy's watch chain, and that was in the dining room attached to him. Annabel found a screwdriver in the garden shed.

When she had opened the desk, without doing too much damage apart from splintering some wood, she started to sort through the papers. First of all she went through his bank statements. These were confusing. It seemed as if his council tax and phone bill and electricity were all paid by direct debit, so that was good. Coming in the other way was his Army pension, which, even given the frugal way of life at Lambshiel House, didn't seem like much. There was, however, a transfer from another account that occurred every month that more or less meant he broke even.

A little more investigation revealed the secret she was after, the money that her father had always hinted she would inherit one day. It was an investment portfolio worth about three hundred thousand pounds' that produced the additional income that helped to balance the books. There were also several hundred pounds' worth of Premium Bond certificates. Annabel went to the drinks tray and poured herself a stiff gin and tonic. She stood to inherit the house, which must be worth something, and an investment portfolio that, if carefully managed, might produce just enough income for her to live off. She was financially independent. She could sell the house and live somewhere smaller – the cottage with roses around the door – and manage rather well.

She sipped her drink and thought through the implications of all this. If she was financially independent, she didn't need Geoff. There was no particular reason to stop seeing Geoff. She quite liked him, although she did not warm to some of his awful friends. But she admitted to herself that she had allowed Geoff into her life because he represented the possibility of escape from Lambshiel House and the tyranny of her father. He offered, if not love, then the possibility of comfortable accommodation, good food, good clothes and two or three holidays a year. He might even buy her a decent car, if she asked him to. She had always liked the idea of a small BMW.

She topped up her drink with some more gin and thought about the new world that was opening up before her. She could stay with Geoff, and go and live with him once Lambshiel House was sold, and life would be ... acceptable. Or she could choose not to stay with Geoff. She could live on her own, in the cottage. She could live on her own and be independent and perhaps see a little more of Ed. Ed had his own troubles, of course. But one day he would sort them out and be in a better mood than he had been in since he returned from France.

The gin and tonic produced a kind of pleasant torpor in Annabel. She might easily have nodded off except that the phone rang. It was Geoff, asking her to have dinner with him that evening in a nearby Indian restaurant. Annabel said she'd love to.

'Sure Daddy won't mind?' asked Geoff. Annabel said she was sure. 'The only thing is, I'm tied up in meetings with the bank until quite late. Could you borrow your father's car and drive yourself over at about seven thirty?'

Annabel agreed, but as she put the phone down she

remembered that the car was very low on petrol. She looked in her purse to see how much cash she had left and saw that it was only forty pounds.

Forty pounds! Half a tank of petrol would cost at least that. That left nothing to live off. She had no idea where the money would come from when she had spent what was in her purse. Her own bank account had no money in it; the monthly handouts had been her father's way of keeping her dependent on him. Now she realised with awful clarity just how dependent she was.

Daddy wasn't going to give her any more cash. There was a small fortune tied up in the house and in his investment portfolio that Annabel would inherit when her father died. But her father couldn't die because he was already dead. Annabel couldn't inherit until she told someone about it.

And then there would be questions.

'Where were you standing when he fell, Miss Gazebee?'

'Why did you not inform the doctor or the police, Miss Gazebee?'

'Why did you move the body, Miss Gazebee? You must have known that a doctor should see him first? Why is your father sitting at the dining room table?'

She didn't want to have to answer questions at the moment. She might manage it later, perhaps, when she felt a little stronger. Pushing your father down the stairs took it out of you to a surprising extent.

She looked at her watch. It was two in the afternoon – enough time to drive into Darlington, or Richmond. She knew of a couple of antique shops in each town. With a sigh, but wearing a determined expression, she took the clock from the drawing room mantelpiece. It was a Georgian carriage clock. That ought to be worth something.

*

That evening Annabel met Geoff at the little Indian restaurant not far from his house. This was not his usual style. Geoff liked expensive restaurants where the plates were strange shapes, and the olive oil came from a single grower in Tuscany, and the wine lists were long and fabulously priced.

'I didn't see the Ferrari in the car park,' remarked Annabel as she sat down. 'I wasn't sure you'd be here yet.'

'Got rid of it,' replied Geoff. 'I've got a Freelander now. Much more practical.'

'Oh, that's a pity.'

'I was bored with it,' said Geoff, dismissing the subject. 'Let's have some poppadums. I'm starving.'

As the meal progressed Annabel noticed that Geoff was talking less than usual. He seemed morose.

'Is everything all right?' asked Annabel.

'What do you mean? Of course everything's all right.'

'I just thought you seemed a little down.'

For a split second Geoff appeared to be on the point of saying something unkind. Then his face softened.

'Even I have my bad days.'

'I'm sorry.'

'Money's tight, that's the problem. The banks aren't lending any more. I've got three developments lined up where I've bought the land but I can't even put a spade in the ground because I can't get project financing.'

'But you've got Hartlepool Hall.'

'Yes, thank God – as long as we can keep Ed sweet. He's not showing any signs of being difficult, I hope.'

'I never see him,' replied Annabel. 'I never hear from him, not since that day I went over and had lunch. That was weeks ago.'

Geoff frowned.

'The sooner we get those documents signed the better. I'm hoping we can get it done this week. Once that's up and running I'll get an injection of money into the business and things will look different.'

He seemed to cheer up. 'I'm going to have another Cobra,' he said. 'Fancy another glass of wine?'

When the evening was over, Annabel waited for Geoff to ask her to go back to his bungalow. She quite hoped he would. There would be the sex, of course. But once they'd done that, she could snuggle down beside him in the enormous king-sized bed. She wouldn't lie awake feeling lonely, and haunted. For once she would have a good night's sleep. She could make up some story about her father not needing her to come home that night. Geoff wouldn't pay any attention.

But he surprised her by saying, as they walked out of the restaurant, 'Do you mind if we call it a night?'

'What?'

'I'm knackered. I've got a lot on my mind and I've meetings from breakfast onwards tomorrow. Things to sort out; a bit of juggling required. Nothing I haven't done before. But I think I need an early night.'

'Oh, of course,' replied Annabel, trying not to sound hurt. 'I quite understand.'

Geoff kissed her lightly on the cheek.

'Love you, babe.'

'Thank you so much for dinner, Geoff.'

He was already walking away towards his car, not even bothering to wait until she had got into hers. Well, that was Geoff for you, thought Annabel. Old-fashioned manners didn't mean very much to him.

As she started the engine she wondered what was troubling

him. Was he growing tired of her? She thumped the steering wheel gently with her fist. How dare he grow tired of her! Geoff's car sped past and she heard him toot goodbye on the horn. As she watched his brake lights disappear down the road she decided he was just having an off day. Everyone was entitled to one of those now and then. Tomorrow he would call her, and everything would be back to normal.

Back to normal. She drove home to Lambshiel House and Daddy.

Nineteen

The meeting with the bank and Ed took a long time to arrange. The regional director of the bank was called Chris Higgins. He was, apparently, an old friend of Geoff's and was crucial to the proposed transaction. Without his support and participation it might never happen, so everyone's diaries revolved around his. But he was away on holiday. By the time he had been able to find a gap for this meeting, it was already August and the British summer, true to type, had brought dour skies and intermittent drizzle that swept across the valley in grey sheets. Geoff took Annabel with him to the meeting.

'Ed will be more comfortable if you're there,' Geoff told her the evening before. He had continued to be distracted by his business affairs for several weeks, and Annabel had seen less of him than she would have liked. It was not that she felt any great passion for Geoff. But these days she found that she craved company – the company of the living – and needed to get out of the house more often than before.

They had been out to dinner and now they were in bed together for the first time for several weeks, so that was good. But since they had undressed, Geoff had spent most of the time on his mobile phone talking to Eric about arrangements. That was less good.

'But none of it's any of my business,' protested Annabel, when he asked her to come along.

'Ed needs someone there who he thinks is on his side.'

This was probably true. Annabel had spoken to Ed on the phone several times in the last few weeks. He had sounded frantic at first, when Social Services had taken away Alice. Then he had disappeared from Hartlepool Hall for days at a time, and Annabel understood from the little he told her that he had been touring old people's homes across the North East in an effort to find her. Annabel couldn't understand why he would want to do that: it must have been a depressing experience and, so far, had proved unsuccessful. What was worse, in Annabel's opinion, was that Ed had devoted so much of his time to this pointless effort. He seemed to attach less importance to the break-up of his family home and estate, than he did to finding Alice. It was as if he simply didn't care about Hartlepool Hall any more.

The next day Geoff and Annabel drove past fields of damp wheat and splashy meadows where sheep huddled against stone walls for shelter. The rain was not heavy, but gentle and persistent. Geoff parked the car as close to the front entrance of Hartlepool Hall as he could but there were already a number of other vehicles there. Annabel recognised Malcolm Skinner's old Land Rover Defender; there were also two smart black Range Rovers and a black Mercedes 600 parked close to the steps.

'I see the bankers have taken the best parking places,' muttered Geoff.

They got out and hurried through the drizzle, up the steps and into the hall. Ed was waiting for them. Annabel noticed how thin he looked, and how pale. When he came back from

France he had been so brown it was impossible to imagine him otherwise; but the summer rain, or else the worry, had driven the colour from him.

'We're in the dining room,' said Ed. 'It's the only place where I can seat this many people. There seem to be an awful lot of them. The bankers have brought a team of lawyers. Malcolm Skinner has brought some lawyer from Middlesbrough to advise us, but he doesn't seem to know the time of day. Your man Eric's already here, Geoff.'

'Good to see you, Ed,' said Geoff, grasping his hand firmly. 'I know this is tough for you, but believe me, you're doing the right thing.'

'That's what everyone keeps telling me. It's rather worrying.'

Then Ed noticed Annabel.

'Hello. Are you on Geoff's team as well?'

'No, I'm on your team,' said Annabel firmly. She kissed Ed on the cheek and he returned it in a distracted manner.

'Well, that's good to know. You'd both better come through. Do you want coffee or tea? I've made a flask of Nescafé.'

'Oh, I can help with that,' said Annabel, wanting to appear useful.

They went into the dining room. A crowd of people were milling about as if at a drinks party. With the arrival of Ed and Geoff these loose arrangements resolved themselves into a more formal set piece. An array of dark-suited men sat along one side of the table. Opposite them was Malcolm, in his land agent's tweed coat and corduroy trousers; Ed, wearing a cream shirt, a blue pullover and jeans; a small man in a light grey suit and brown shoes, who was the lawyer from Middlesbrough; and Annabel, who went and sat beside Ed.

Geoff drew up the chair at the head of the table and sat down. Beside him was Eric. They muttered conspiratorially for a moment and then Geoff spoke.

'If we can all go round the table and say who we are, that will save a lot of time.'

The lawyers and bankers introduced themselves by turn. Chris Higgins made a little speech on behalf of the bank.

'I've already said "Good morning" to Lord Hartlepool today. I just want to use this opportunity to say how sad I am that our long relationship with the Simmonds family may be about to come to an end. But I am also pleased that the deal I hope we will complete today marks the opening of a new chapter for Hartlepool Hall.'

Piles of documents in spiral-bound folders sat on the sideboard ready for signature. One of the lawyers passed round sheets of paper on which there was an agenda of the outstanding points that needed to be agreed before the documents could be signed.

'Nothing of significance,' said the lawyer. 'Mostly just tidying up.'

These words announced the start of close combat between the parties. There was a perceptible heightening of tension around the table. Battle was about to be joined when Annabel said in a bright voice: 'Shall I be mother?'

Geoff and Eric both gave her irritated looks, but by that time Annabel was already handing round mugs of lukewarm Nescafé and tea from the flasks Ed had provided.

As the discussion got under way again Annabel studied the faces around the table. The lawyer from Middlesbrough, who was supposed to be advising Ed, looked like a frightened rabbit. Malcolm Skinner's sharp features resembled those of a fox. He followed the discussion with close concentration, every now and then stabbing the document in front of him with his forefinger. Chris Higgins's rosy cheeks and pursed lips betrayed no hint of emotion. He seemed content to let his attack dogs do all the work while he sat back in his chair and surveyed the proceedings. The three lawyers and the junior banker were all thin, intense-looking individuals. They did most of the talking on one side, while Malcolm spoke for the estate, with only occasional and apologetic interventions from his lawyer.

By now Ed looked pale to the point of illness, and seemed so detached that he might not have been in the room. He hardly spoke at all. Once he scribbled a note on a scrap of paper and passed it to Malcolm, who looked at it, then nodded.

Annabel had never attended anything like this, and she was quite certain she never wanted to spend a couple of hours like this ever again. It was all very boring. But then, every so often, Annabel thought she could detect a glance, a gleam in the eye, that went from Malcolm to Geoff to Chris Higgins, and then back again. At first she couldn't decide what this meant. It was like a secret code, a language of signs, of raised eyebrows and faint inclinations of the head, or a twitching of the muscles around the mouths of the three men.

'They're in it together,' she finally thought to herself. 'They've cooked this scheme up between them to get rid of Ed and pass the property into Geoff's hands.'

The meeting warmed up. Now even the Middlesbrough rabbit joined in. Noon came; and then one o'clock; but no sandwiches or canapés were brought in for the lawyers and bankers because Ed had forgotten to make any arrangements for food. He had not attended meetings of this sort before: he did not know the importance the legal, banking and accounting professions attached to the prompt arrival of sandwiches and fresh coffee or tea to keep their blood sugar levels up. The men around the table looked at their watches and glanced at the door, as if by magic caterers would arrive. The occasional rumble of an empty stomach could be heard. Perhaps a sense of privation sharpened everyone's mind, for soon after one o'clock the arguments came to an end, the outstanding points were agreed and minuted and then the signing began.

Documents were passed around the table, first to Ed, then to Malcolm, then to Geoff and then to the chief banker. By these means all the acres that had belonged to the Simmonds family for most of the last two hundred years were conveyed away from Ed. Every ancient stand of oak or beech; every dark plantation of pine and spruce; nearly every field of wheat or barley; every acre of green pasture or rushy fell – all these now were gone. The dozens of cottages and steadings; the home farm, the stables, the old bakery and the brewhouse; the walled gardens and the hothouses; the parkland and the broad lake and the streams that fed it – these too were gone from Ed. Last of all the house itself was conveyed, together with most of its furniture, statues, pictures and carpets. Only Springwell Cottage and a couple of hundred acres of farmland remained in Ed's ownership. So did a few items that had never been within the Hartlepool Estate: some furniture; the contents of his bedroom. The rest left the ownership of his family for ever.

Once all the documents had been signed they were put in a stack at one end of the table. Then the lawyers from both sides began phoning their banks. Millions of pounds were transferred electronically on their instruction from Geoff's account to the accounts of the Hartlepool Estate and the trusts. For a nanosecond Ed was rich once again, if homeless; and then the same amounts were transferred from the Hartlepool accounts to the bank, and Ed was no longer rich, just homeless. More phoning and then the final transaction took place when almost all of the money completed its circular journey, leaving the bank's account and reappearing as new loans in the accounts of GT Hartlepool Developments Ltd, a company set up by Geoff. It was all a little confusing, but everyone except Ed seemed content by the end of these processes.

When this was over the assembly marched out of the dining room into the hall. One of the lawyers went out to the cars and returned with some huge cool boxes. In these was champagne. Annabel found some glasses. There was a popping of corks, and the champagne that was not spilled on the marble floors was poured out and handed round. Chris the banker gave a toast; Geoff responded. The formalities over, everyone stood around chatting.

Annabel overheard Chris say to Geoff: 'I'd be quite interested in obtaining the sporting rights here. They say the pheasant shoot is very good, although I was never asked in old Lord Hartlepool's day. Can you imagine that? They used the bank's money for probably fifty years, and in all that time neither I nor any of my predecessors was considered fit to wipe our feet on the doormat here.'

'I dare say something could be arranged for a modest consideration,' replied Geoff. Annabel saw him wink at Chris.

'A very modest consideration, I hope, Geoff, since you are doing all this with our money.'

Ed stood apart. Malcolm went over to him.

'Well, Ed, I'm sorry our long association with your family

has come to an end. It's very sad to see everything go, but times have changed.'

'Thank you, Malcolm,' said Ed, turning away.

'I must get everyone out of here,' he said to Annabel. 'This is driving me mad. Can you stay for lunch?'

'I'll ask Geoff,' she replied. But at that moment Geoff came over holding a flute of champagne.

'Ed, I'm taking Annabel out for a celebration lunch. I'd like you to come. I know you mightn't feel like celebrating much yourself, but this is a fresh start for all of us.'

'I don't think I'll join you, thanks all the same,' replied Ed. Geoff took the rebuff well. He smiled and grasped Ed's arm.

'I understand. I'd probably feel the same way. Listen, Ed, I want you to go on thinking of this as your home, at least for the next few weeks. The builders will arrive in mid-September and then we may have to turn the water and electricity off while they knock things about a bit. When they come I expect you'll find it more convenient to live somewhere else for a while. Is there anywhere you can stay?'

'Springwell Cottage is vacant now that Billy Thompson's moved out,' replied Ed. 'I'll live there for a while.'

'But Ed, I'm counting on you to come back here into one of the new flats when they're finished. As you know, you're contracted to rent one of them as part of the deal, for the first five years.'

'Yes,' said Ed, without making it clear whether he had noticed that part of the agreement or not. Eric joined the conversation. In honour of the occasion he was wearing a suit, but his white shirt was not tucked in and could be seen poking out from the bottom of his suit jacket.

'Canny place you had here,' he said to Ed. 'But it's a bit

big for a lad on his own. We should get six or seven apartments fitted into this space.'

'Oh yes?' replied Ed. He did not sound the least bit interested.

'Aye, you'll be better off in one of those than in this big old place. We'll put broadband and a media room and a Jacuzzi in every flat. I wouldn't mind buying one meself.'

The party broke up. The bankers and the lawyers departed, and then Malcolm Skinner and his lawyer left too. At last only Geoff and Annabel remained. Ed came down the steps with them as they walked to Geoff's new Freelander.

'Look, the sun has come out,' said Annabel, as cheerfully as she could. She thought Ed looked ghastly and if she had been a bit braver she would have told Geoff to go and have lunch on his own. If ever anyone looked as if they needed looking after it was Ed at the moment. But she wasn't brave enough, so all she said was: 'Will you be all right?'

'So good of you to come, Annabel,' replied Ed, as if she had just dropped in for tea. It was not an answer. To Geoff he said: 'Goodbye, Geoff. I wish you the best of luck with your new project.'

They shook hands.

Then Geoff and Annabel were driving away from the house. Annabel looked back and saw that Ed was still standing on the gravel: tall, thin and straight-backed. The sky had cleared while the meeting had been going on. The rain had stopped, the clouds had parted and the sunshine was now strong. Dazzling reflections leaped back from the rain-washed roofs and white marble dome of Hartlepool Hall. Each window gleamed as if the panes were not made of glass but silver. The grass in the park shone with that special luminosity good pasture has after rain; the lake was a blaze of colour.

Then the car entered the tunnel of great cedars and limes and wellingtonia that led to the front lodge and Hartlepool Hall disappeared from view.

For a long while after that day Annabel heard nothing from Ed. He no longer answered the phone when she rang. She called at the house once, to see how he was. The gates at the top of the drive were unlocked, but a large wooden sign had been put up beside the lodge:

> GT Hartlepool Developments Ltd
> Luxury Apartments 2,3,4 bedroomed
> Leisure Complex and Golf Course coming soon

Underneath this message were a telephone number and a website address. When Annabel arrived at the front entrance she found that the great door was shut. All the other entrances were locked and bolted. There were no staff about; the gardeners and the groom had vanished, presumably now redundant. She rang the bell at the kitchen door then went back to the front entrance and pulled the bell-pull. She heard a distant clanging but there was no reply. She walked around the house. Shutters blinded the ground-floor windows. Upstairs one or two windows were still without shutters and Annabel gazed up at them in the hope Ed might be there and that he would see her and let her in. But if he saw her she did not see him. There was no movement at any window. And if he saw her, he did not let her in.

She supposed he was off somewhere, looking for the old lady. Annabel got back in the car and drove to the village. There she asked for directions to Springwell Cottage, then drove past it slowly. It was deserted too. Weeds grew in the garden and there was a great crack in the gable end. The windows had no curtains and the place showed signs of neglect. She drove back home.

Annabel learned, when she had dinner with Ed much later, that Ed had, during this period of his life, spent a lot of his time in bed, or else wandering around the darkened corridors and rooms in his dressing gown and slippers. Nobody disturbed him for the first few weeks after the estate was sold. It was as if nothing had happened.

Geoff was busy vetting contractors who would come and remodel the house. The architect was preparing his plans but had not yet visited the building he disliked so much. Geoff's PR agency was preparing glossy brochures describing the haven of executive luxury that would soon be available to prospective owners of the new flats. The auctioneers were drafting catalogues from inventories provided to them by the insurance company. Wheels were turning, but so far their awful creaking was inaudible in the great silences of Hartlepool Hall.

Ed wandered around the house, picked up books and magazines and read a page or two, then put them aside. He prepared meals – when he felt hungry, which was not often – from the supply of frozen food laid in for him by Mrs Donaldson before she left. He sat in his bedroom surrounded by piles of old photograph albums he had found in a cupboard downstairs. These dated back to the last decades of the nineteenth century. He found faded photographs of the Simmonds Iron and Forge Works in Hartlepool, one of the first bricks in the building of the great industrial and mercantile empire his ancestors had created. He found albums of black and grey photographs of his great-grandparents, his grandparents and other relations, attending to the seasonal rhythms of their lives: at Cheltenham, at Ascot, at Lords, at shooting parties, beside salmon rivers in Scotland and Ireland, on the lawns and terraces of their own and other people's houses.

He found one album full of photographs of his own parents. Between two leaves of this volume he discovered an old envelope. Inside was a lock of fair hair and a note scrawled in black ink. It said: *Emily. 1st October 1973.*

Emily was the name of the sister he had never known, the one who had died before Ed was born. There was no trace of himself as a baby. The first photograph he found was a picture of him wearing his prep school uniform, standing beside the car in which the chauffeur was to drive him away to school.

One day, a week after the house had been sold, he entered the library. It was a warm day outside, but the air felt chilly in the darkened room. He switched on some lights and looked about. This was where he and Alice had so often sat and talked. He still missed her. A thought struck him. He went to the glass display cabinet and turned the key in the lock. Then he reached inside and took out the little porcelain figurine of the shepherdess. Her glazed eyes stared innocently up at him. He had no idea whether she was still his property or now belonged to the bank. He wrapped her up carefully in his handkerchief and slipped her into the pocket of his dressing gown.

He would give her back to Alice when he found her again.

Twenty

Annabel's own life during these months was not easy. She had become used to the smell from the dining room or else it had lessened. All the same, after two months, the atmosphere in the house was still not fragrant. Or perhaps the stale, dry odour only remained in Annabel's imagination. The problem was there were few distractions. Geoff was too busy to devote much time to her. As for her entertaining at home, that was now out of the question. How could she possibly use the dining room while her late father still sat there? And if the dining room was out of bounds, the kitchen was far too small to fit in more than two people.

Sometimes Annabel wondered whether it would be more practical to move her father elsewhere: but where? The garage and the garden shed were out of the question, because the gardener visited those once a week. There was a little closet off the kitchen he might fit into, but that was where she kept the vacuum cleaner and the thought of finding him in there every morning when she started the housework was unsettling. She certainly hadn't the strength to move him upstairs.

Anyway, moving him once had been a mistake; moving him twice would only make things worse. She decided against opening the dining room door and resigned herself to a life of continuing loneliness. She couldn't invite anyone over and she couldn't accept invitations from any of the few friends she still kept up with, because then there might be more questions about how her father was. She was beginning to feel that the less said, the better.

She spent a lot of time doing housework. The furniture gleamed; the floors and carpets were spotless. She polished all the glasses and cleaned the silver, even though nothing was ever used. As a matter of fact there was rather less silver to clean these days. She was financing her very modest budget by further small sales to antique shops: a parcel of cutlery in one place; a set of crystal whisky tumblers elsewhere; a pair of silver table ornaments in the form of pheasants that had once been used as a cruet set fetched quite a few pounds; and a picture of the Duke of Wellington paid for two or three weeks' petrol. She took care not to return to the same shop too often. In fact, it was rather interesting exploring all sorts of places, some of which she had not been to for years – Harrogate, Guisborough, Helmsley, Ripon and Richmond; as well as larger cities such as Newcastle, Durham and York.

There were days when Annabel felt that this way of life might continue indefinitely; and other days when she felt she could hardly stand to live like this for another minute. There was too much time to think: that was the trouble. She tried to understand why her life had turned out the way it had. It wasn't just the awkward questions posed by the continued presence of her father; it was more fundamental than that.

All her friends – apart from Geoff and Ed – were now married, and had families. She sat in the cold drawing room, which even the autumn sunshine could not warm, and thought about her age. She was thirty-three, getting on for thirty-four, so even if she was married in the next year, an event that seemed unlikely to say the least, the soonest she might expect to have a child was when she was thirty-six. She worked it out on her fingers. That meant she might be almost sixty before it left home. Time was not on her side.

And anyway, how could she get married in her present predicament? Who would have her? She knew the secret of her father's death would emerge sooner rather than later. Every day, she woke in the morning saying to herself: 'I really must tell someone about Daddy. It's ridiculous. One simply can't go on living like this.'

But then the day would creep by and she would do nothing. The nights were the worst, and there were more of these now Geoff was so busy. She had given up ringing Ed. When evening came she sat in the empty house – but not so empty as she would wish it – and listened to the silences. She did not know how this problem would ever resolve itself.

Geoff called for her one morning. He seemed more cheerful than of late.

'Come and have some lunch at home,' he said. 'It's Marks & Spencer's finest. You don't mind, do you?'

'Not at all,' replied Annabel, who had been living on a very economical diet of tinned soups and chicken drumsticks. 'That sounds nice.'

Geoff's bungalow was very untidy when they arrived. He swept some dirty plates out of sight and closed the bedroom door, behind which Annabel glimpsed an unmade bed.

'I don't have a cleaning lady at the moment,' he said. 'And I've been too busy to pay much attention to housework myself.'

'I'll do some cleaning for you,' offered Annabel. 'Really, I mean it,' she added when Geoff protested. 'I like having something to do.'

'I would have thought your father gives you enough to do,' said Geoff. 'How is the old bugger, anyway? You never talk about him these days. I assume that's a good sign, and he's not giving you quite so much grief?'

'He's not giving me any grief at all,' replied Annabel.

'Good,' said Geoff. 'Now, I wanted to show you something, Annabel. Come and look at the page proofs for the Hartlepool Hall development. I've spread them out on the kitchen table.'

Annabel looked at the coloured sheets. The first page was the front cover of the brochure. On it was an image of Hartlepool Hall. It was not a photograph but a graphic: from the outside the house looked much as it did now but a huge conservatory had been attached to the South Front where the terrace had once been. On the lake were a couple of rowing boats. The gardens had disappeared and been replaced by an immaculate-looking golf course. The legend said:

Hartlepool Hall
A Luxury Community In The Heart Of The Countryside

The next page detailed an interior scene. This had also been generated using computer graphics, but looked quite realistic: a smiling man stood in the centre of a large room with his arm around a pretty woman, both of them holding champagne flutes. In one corner a small girl gazed tranquilly at an enormous television screen and nearby an older boy was playing on a games console. The room contained huge leather sofas and enormous armchairs and was full of light. The caption read:

Modern Living In Classical Surroundings – Twenty-First
Century Technology In One Of Britain's Finest Stately Homes

Underneath the caption there was information about floor area, electric points, broadband and Wi-Fi that Annabel did not bother to read. Another sheet showed a picture of what had once been the stables. These were now transformed into a clubhouse for golfers, and the illustration showed a lot of men standing about, wearing yellow pullovers and tartan trousers.

'What do you think?' asked Geoff.

'Very impressive,' replied Annabel. She was determined to be tactful. It wouldn't help to fall out with Geoff at the moment. What she was thinking was: 'How completely ghastly.'

'Yes, they've done a good job, haven't they?'

'When does work begin?'

Geoff frowned for a moment.

'The development's got off to a slower start than I'd like. I've had difficulties with one or two other projects. Financing troubles. I've had to draw down some funds from this development as a bridging loan to one of my other companies. But we should be under way very soon now. Peregrine is producing detailed plans for the builders as we speak. The auctioneers are going in to remove the contents next week. There will be a huge sale, probably in London. That's not my affair – all the furniture and pictures and stuff went to the bank. But once the house is emptied we can crack on.'

They sat at the other end of the table and had a picnic of mini scotch eggs and prawn cocktail. Geoff opened a bottle of wine and they sat and talked. He was full of plans.

'If this deal works it could form the pattern for many more. It all depends on selling as much as possible off-plan. That's what I need to make the cash flow work. I've got Biggsy lined up – you met him, the little footballer – but

I need to start selling a few more units. You don't think any of your well-heeled friends would take a punt, do you?'

But Annabel declared she had lost touch with her well-heeled friends. After lunch Geoff had to go to a meeting, so Annabel stayed for an hour or two tidying up. It kept her busy, which was the point.

When she got home the voicemail light on the telephone was blinking.

'This is a message for Colonel Gazebee,' it said. 'This is National Savings and Investment speaking. We have you recorded as the holder of Premium Bond number' – here the voice read out an eleven-digit figure – 'and we are calling to inform you that you have won a major cash prize. We will be calling at your address tomorrow morning to present you with details at approximately ten a.m.'

Annabel did not know what on earth to do. There was no number to call back when she tried to return the call. But what would she have said if she had rung them? That she and her father were going to be out? That her father was too busy to receive a cheque for – for what? Ten thousand pounds? Fifty thousand pounds?

A million pounds?

With fifty thousand pounds she could buy herself a decent car and still have change. But what if this prize was the big one? Why would they bother to send people all the way from ... all the way from wherever these people lived, to give her a cheque for ten thousand pounds? They'd just put that in the post, wouldn't they?

There was going to be a prize-giving ceremony. That meant she – that is to say, Daddy – had probably won a lot of money. A single girl with a million pounds in the bank could probably marry whomever she liked. Once she had sold

Lambshiel House and cashed in Daddy's investment portfolio, she might be worth nearer two million pounds than one. She could buy quite a decent little cottage with that, and still have enough left over to live on. She could buy a little cottage somewhere around here, and perhaps a small villa in the south of France. Then she could ask Ed to come and stay with her. They could sit by the pool together, in the sunshine.

Annabel's daydream came to an abrupt end as she remembered the problems. Well, there was nothing she could do about that. She would just have to tell them Daddy wasn't well, and accept the cheque on his behalf. What other choice was there?

The phone rang and Annabel snatched it up, expecting to hear the calm voice of the man from National Savings. But it wasn't him. It was Teddy Shildon.

'Annabel? Teddy here,' he said in his usual brusque manner. 'I'd like a word with Marcus, please.'

'Teddy? Oh, good evening. I'm afraid Daddy can't come to the phone just now.'

'What do you mean, can't come to the phone? He's not dead, is he? He can't still be in bed. It's well over a month since I rang, maybe two. Just go and get him.'

Teddy's voice sounded steely over the phone.

'Oh, I think there's someone at the door,' said Annabel. She was trying not to sound frightened, but she knew her voice was trembling. 'Can I ring you back?'

'No, you *cannot* ring me back. Don't you *dare* hang up on me, Annabel. There's something going on. I've been waiting for two months to speak to Marcus. He never replies to my letters, or signs the papers the lawyer sends him. Don't tell me that for eight weeks he's been unable to read or write. If so, he should be in Intensive Care, not lying in bed at home.'

Annabel hung up. For the next hour the phone rang again at regular intervals, but she did not answer it. When she had recovered a little she dialled voicemail again and this time wrote down the number of the Premium Bond. Then she went to the roll-top desk and found the stack of certificates held together by a rubber band. She went through them in case it was all a mistake. But no, there was a certificate with the right number on it. She took the certificate out and slipped it in an envelope. When she went to bed an hour or two later she put the envelope underneath the pillow so that it would remain close by her. Something told her that tomorrow was going to be a difficult day.

In the morning Annabel rose early. Hazy sunshine filled her bedroom when she drew the curtains. Leaves were just beginning to fall and she saw that there had been a hint of ground frost on the lawn the night before. She dressed carefully in her best country-house clothes, and spent more time than usual doing her face and hair. When she had completed these preparations she went downstairs, clutching the envelope containing the Premium Bond certificate. She made a mug of tea and waited for something to happen.

At nine o'clock sharp the front doorbell rang. Annabel was in the kitchen and hadn't heard a car arrive. It would be the people from National Savings. Her heart hammering, she pulled off her Marigold gloves and apron and walked to the front door. She was thinking: 'I'll say Daddy was taken ill in the night – that the excitement was too much. I'll promise to give him the cheque later.'

But what if they wouldn't give her the cheque? What if they insisted on seeing Daddy? She opened the front door. There stood the Earl of Shildon, and Dr Mitchell. Teddy was wearing a tweed jacket and trousers and looked tidy, for him, and stern-faced. A ball of baler twine had been stuffed into one of his pockets, Annabel noticed, with her peculiar ability to absorb irrelevant details at a time of crisis. The doctor wore a dark suit and carried a black bag. He was not smiling either.

'Good morning, Annabel,' said Teddy Shildon. 'May we come in?'

'It's not convenient at the moment,' said Annabel. 'Daddy isn't well.'

'That's why Dr Mitchell agreed to come with me,' said Teddy. 'Your father hasn't called the doctor for some months and yet he is too unwell to come to the phone or answer letters. We need to see him, Annabel.'

There was a bustle and Annabel found that the two men had pushed past her and were in the hall. 'You can't just march in here without an invitation,' said Annabel, but Teddy gave her an awful look that robbed her of the power of speech.

'I've known you since you were a little girl, Annabel,' said Teddy, 'and Marcus a great deal longer than that. I mean to find out what is wrong with him, and so does Dr Mitchell.'

The two men walked down the hall, and went upstairs. Annabel closed her eyes and just stood there. She pretended she was somewhere else: the south of France, perhaps; or sitting in the heather at Blubberwick with Ed, sharing a picnic. A moment later her visitors came back again.

'His bed hasn't been slept in. Where is he?' demanded Teddy. Annabel didn't open her eyes or speak. They looked in the drawing room. Then Teddy put his hand on the door handle of the dining room.

'*No!*' screamed Annabel, opening her eyes wide. Teddy

opened the door and went in, followed by Dr Mitchell. There was a silence, then both men coughed. Annabel heard Teddy mutter: 'Good God'; and then she heard Dr Mitchell say: 'Neck's broken.' Then there was silence. A few minutes later Dr Mitchell came out, holding a handkerchief to his face. Teddy followed looking pale and grim.

'Do you want to tell us what happened, Annabel?' he asked her.

'I'm afraid that is not our job, Teddy,' said Dr Mitchell. 'We must call the police. It is their job to ask Annabel for a statement. It is an offence to fail to report a death, and poor Colonel Gazebee has quite obviously been dead for many weeks. And he didn't break his neck sitting in a dining room chair.'

'You have a point,' said Teddy. 'I'll go and call the police. Phone's in the drawing room, if I remember rightly?'

He went next door and after a moment Annabel could hear him speaking to someone. When he came back out, Teddy spoke more gently than before.

'We'll wait with you until the police arrive, Annabel,' he said. 'They shouldn't be long.'

Annabel shook her head. Tears streamed down her cheeks.

'It was an accident,' she said.

All this time the front door had remained open. Now a young man with curly blond hair and a red shirt popped his head through the door.

'Morning, all! Ta-raah! I'm Barry, from National Savings and Investments. Am I speaking to Colonel Gazebee?' he asked, addressing Teddy. 'May I come in?'

Without waiting for an answer he entered the house. Behind him were two buxom girls in tight red T-shirts with the word 'Ernie' printed across their chests in yellow lettering. They were clutching a giant cardboard cheque about four feet long. It was written out to Marcus Gazebee, and Annabel saw that it was for five hundred thousand pounds.

'What I thought we might do,' said the young man engagingly, 'is for us all to go out into the garden. It's a nice sunny morning. Then we can take some photographs.'

'I'm not Marcus Gazebee,' said Teddy. Surprise prevented him from explaining any more.

Annabel now lost what remained of her presence of mind.

'Daddy's in there,' she said, pointing at the open door of the dining room.

Without waiting for any further invitation the young man strode confidently into the room, followed by the two girls holding the cheque. There was a scream. The young man and one of the girls rushed out quicker than they had gone in. The second girl had fainted inside the dining room.

'We'd better help her,' said Teddy to Dr Mitchell.

They went in and bent over the prostrate girl, trying to revive her. Annabel went as far as the door and looked across their bent forms at Daddy, who was still sitting where she had left him all those weeks ago, at the head of the table.

With her eyes full of tears and her vision a little blurred, and because she wanted to believe that everything was normal for just a moment, it did look as if Daddy had fallen asleep at dinner the night before. But there was that faint, musty smell. Then there was the way his head had fallen onto his chest. He seemed to have shrunk inside his tweed suit and what she could see of his skin was a sort of dark, parchment colour. His hair looked as if it needed cutting: Annabel had read somewhere that hair doesn't grow after death, it's just that the rest of the body shrinks. It still looked longer than the colonel would have been comfortable with when he was alive. One bony hand lay on the dining room table. Even from the doorway she could see the tendons of the hand, and the marked length of the fingernails, as the moisture in the flesh had disappeared and the hand had dehydrated.

The cheque for half a million pounds was lying on the floor. Annabel picked it up and put it on the dining room table.

'It's all yours, Daddy,' she told him. But her father did not move. She laughed hysterically, and then Teddy put his arm around her shoulders and ushered her out into the hall and then into the drawing room. Dr Mitchell was outside with the visitors from National Savings, returning the girl who had fainted to their care.

'What will they do to me?' asked Annabel. 'Will I have to go to prison? Who will look after Ed?'

Teddy did not reply. Dr Mitchell came into the drawing room and sat down heavily. A few minutes later another car arrived. Teddy went to the front door to let the policemen in. A sergeant and a constable came with him into the drawing room. Suddenly everybody was looking at Annabel, waiting for her to speak.

'Well,' said Annabel. 'Why don't I make us all a nice cup of tea?'

Twenty-One

Ed's reclusive life might have continued indefinitely. He was almost overwhelmed by what had happened. He thought that if he had the courage to visit the Long Gallery, the portraits of all his ancestors would come to life in their frames. They would point their fingers and say: 'We did our duty. We spent the money as it was meant to be spent; we lived our lives as our ancestors expected us to. You have betrayed us.'

This was rather imaginative; still, Ed did not choose to visit the place. He knew that he may not have created the problems that had overwhelmed him, but Hartlepool Hall had gone bankrupt on his watch. He spent the days in sleepy inactivity, and the nights in sleepless restlessness. He began to wonder what was the point of his existence, or why it should continue.

This dreary state of mind was brought to an end by the arrival of the auctioneers.

In honour of their arrival he dressed and shaved for the first time in days, and met them in the hall. There was an elegant figure in a pinstriped suit at the head of a group of porters wearing brown dust coats. The auctioneer, for that was the smart young man, was called William Ellis. He strolled around the house with Ed in tow. The porters followed at a respectful distance, labelling the various objects their master condescended to notice.

First of all they stood in the hall itself, looking at a large canvas that portrayed naked men and women of heroic proportions, several serpents, and a background of burning palaces. Ed had always liked this picture. It had everything you could ask for in a good painting: nudity, mythological animals, pillage. William Ellis studied it, his inventory in his hand.

'Oh dear,' he said after a moment. He scribbled a note then moved on.

This set the tone for the rest of the visit. Either he said nothing at all about the pictures he looked at, or else he simply paused, sighed and looked away.

'Bought on a tour in Italy, I believe?' he asked at one point.

'Some of the pictures were,' said Ed. 'Not the ones upstairs.'

'It is quite shocking how the Italians took advantage of the tourists, even in those days,' remarked William Ellis. He was scarcely more enthusiastic when he came to the Hall of Sculptures.

'Good garden ornaments, I suppose.'

He was impressed by the stuffed white bull, however, which gazed mournfully back at him from its pedestal

'Shot by King Edward VII,' he remarked. 'I wonder what calibre rifle he used. It must have been fun to shoot something as big as that. I dare say this might do well in our New York saleroom.'

He made another note.

Upstairs in the Long Gallery, Ed really thought that William Ellis had been reduced to despair. He visibly drooped; he wiped his hand across his eyes as if he could not quite believe what he was looking at; he made cursory notes.

'I hope you don't mind my saying so,' he remarked to Ed, 'but your ancestors were rather a grim-looking lot, weren't they?'

Ed could not disagree. In front of the picture of Percy Simmonds, however, Mr Ellis paused.

'Ah, this is the John Singer Sargent, isn't it? I'll put that down at ten thousand. Chris Higgins has expressed an interest in this picture himself.'

What good were other people's family portraits? wondered Ed. It was bad enough to have to look at the faces of your own ancestors let alone other people's.

Cataloguing the pictures and furniture took most of the day. After a while Ed couldn't stand any more and left William Ellis to manage on his own. He went upstairs and started to think about packing. He knew that once the auctioneers had labelled and removed what they wanted, the next people to arrive would be the builders and then it would become impossible to live in Hartlepool Hall. It wasn't easy now.

He would need a removal van to carry his few belongings to Springwell Cottage. He decided to book one for the day after tomorrow. There was no point in hanging around any longer.

The next day the house became chaotic. Men in huge vans arrived and took pictures and furniture away. Some of it was going into storage to be returned when the building work was complete; the rest of the items were going to be sold down in London. The architect arrived and spent the day poking about with an assistant, measuring things. He did not bother to speak to Ed, evidently assuming he was a caretaker or servant. Ed did not trouble him.

Pale patches now appeared on the walls and floors where the larger pictures or pieces of furniture had been. Dust rose everywhere in choking clouds as objects were removed and crated and sent away; carpets rolled up and wrapped with twine; oak chests and break-fronted bookcases covered in dust sheets and manoeuvred into the Aladdin's cave interiors of huge pantechnicons. Fragments of bubble wrap lay about the floor where pictures or china had been wrapped. Spiders, deprived of their hiding places, scuttled across the cold marble floors. Stripped of the modifying influence of its furnishings the house became an echoing cavern. Ed could not bear to stay a moment longer. The next morning he enlisted the help of two of the farm men and loaded his bed and a few pieces of furniture into the van he had hired. Then he drove the three miles to Springwell Cottage.

As he left Hartlepool Hall, he tried to pretend to himself that he was just going away for a few days. After all, he was obliged to come back here and live in one of the flats when the house had been converted. This was simply the next stage in a journey, an upheaval in his life that had begun that day, months before, in the south of France, when the letter summoning him home had arrived. He did visit the house once more, but he never again slept in it, or ate in it, or sat on the terrace by the lake smoking and drinking wine.

Springwell Cottage was not as grim inside as might have been expected. Its previous occupant, Billy Thompson, had been a tidy tenant. He had painted most of the walls and woodwork and plugged the gaps in the window frames. The place was draught-free and dry. A back boiler behind the fire, which had to be kept going day and night, heated the hot water and the radiators. A couple of ancient night-storage heaters provided some traces of warmth in the narrow corridor outside the bedroom and bathroom. Ed found an unexpected pleasure in arranging his belongings in the house. They had seemed very few in the surroundings of Hartlepool Hall, but here he was delighted to discover that just the contents of his bedroom nearly filled this little house: bed, sofa, armchair, dressing table, desk, wardrobe, and a small bookcase. He had rescued some scraps of carpet from the Hall, and a kitchen table and chairs. He found there was little else he needed. The cottage already came supplied with kitchen appliances, a few knives and forks and chipped white plates.

For the first couple of days he was too busy settling in to his new home to think about anything else. He lived off scraps of food in the day and went to the Simmonds Arms for supper in the nearby village of Comogan. Nobody troubled him as he sat in the corner of the pub. There were a few curious, not unfriendly, glances. On the third morning he had dressed and was wondering what to do with the rest of the day when he heard a car pull up outside. He went out to see who it was, and met Billy Thompson climbing out of his ancient Land Rover.

'Good morning,' said Ed.

'Morning.'

Billy Thompson was dressed in his usual garb of army surplus clothing and work boots. He looked pale and tired. Ed felt he should say something about ousting him from the house.

'I'm so sorry we had to take the cottage back in hand,' he said. 'You have looked after it very well. Thank you.'

'Aye.'

This was not promising. Ed tried again.

'Have you found somewhere to live?'

'Aye. Out bye.'

'Out bye' was an expression that Ed had often heard used in this part of the world: it conjured up an image of a bleak stone steading on a cold and rushy fell.

'Well, I'm sorry you had to move.'

'These things happen,' said Billy Thompson. He smiled unexpectedly. 'From what I hear you didn't have much choice about it.'

'No,' admitted Ed.

'I've moved house enough times since I lost the farm. I'm well used to it.' There was an awkward silence then Billy added, 'I've come to collect some mole traps I left behind in one of the sheds. Time of year to start catching them, soon.'

That was true. Autumn had begun; the winter months were not far away. On an impulse Ed stepped forward and put out his hand.

'I want to wish you the best of luck, Billy.'

Billy looked a little surprised, but he took Ed's hand in his own, which felt as if it was hewn from rough granite. The two men shook hands solemnly, and then Billy went to find his traps. Afterwards, Ed felt a little less bad about Billy, although, as he admitted to himself, it was not logical to do so: Billy's circumstances since his farm went bankrupt had never been easy, and now it sounded and looked almost as if he were living rough. Catching a few moles wasn't going to pay for a house.

Ed's next visitor came on the same day, in the late afternoon. Teddy Shildon roared up in his old Isuzu, jumping out as soon as Ed opened his front door.

'I've brought you some provisions, Ed,' he shouted. 'Come and give me a hand.'

They removed from the back of the car a ham, a roast

chicken, some cheeses, an enormous meat pie, a roast pheasant and a fruitcake.

'Mrs Beech prepared these for you,' said Teddy. 'We thought it would help to keep the wolf from the door.'

The quantity of food would have fed several wolves for several days. Ed wondered how he would get through it all.

'Teddy, how kind of you.'

'Think nothing of it. Your father was an old friend. He'd give me hell if I didn't keep an eye on you. Now, where did I put that drink?' He leaned into the back of his car and retrieved a couple of bottles of whisky.

'Come on, let's have a dram. I'm the first guest you'll have had here, aren't I?'

'Yes, Teddy.'

'Well then.'

Once they were inside the cottage, the Earl of Shildon poured two enormous glasses of whisky and then added a few drops of water. It was clear that there was more to this visit than simple hospitality. Teddy obviously had some news he was dying to tell Ed. But first he asked what was happening at Hartlepool Hall. He grunted at the answers and Ed thought he was going to offer words of criticism or advice, but in the end all he said was: 'Well, I'm very sad to hear about it all. Very sad.'

They were sitting by the small fire in the sitting room and Ed found the warmth, and the whisky, were making him sleepy.

'I dare say you haven't heard yet about Annabel murdering her father?'

'*What!*' Ed woke up immediately.

'Well, nothing's been proved yet – just found this morning. Of course there has to be an inquest. Marcus Gazebee was

227

never a great friend, but I'd known him for years, almost as long as I knew your father. And of course he was one of your trustees, even if he never bothered to come to meetings.'

'What do you mean, Annabel murdered her father?' asked Ed. He had gone white with shock.

'Perhaps I shouldn't have put it like that. Nothing's proved one way or the other,' said Teddy. 'Still, now you know what I think. Marcus was quite fit, for his age. And what was he doing in a dining room chair with a broken neck?'

Piece by piece Ed managed to extract the story from Teddy, whose anecdotal style was rather terse, making it difficult at first to grasp what might have happened at Lambshiel House.

'I can't believe Annabel would murder anybody,' said Ed. 'She's one of us.'

'I wouldn't expect you to say anything else,' agreed Teddy. 'A lady can do no wrong. But you had to be there – it was something about the way Annabel looked. I've known her since she was four. Always thought she was a bit different, to tell the truth. Maybe that's why she never married. I wondered once if you and she might get together, after poor Catherine died. I'm not surprised you never did.'

'But Annabel?'

'I know,' said Teddy mournfully. 'As you say, she's one of us. But how did Marcus fall backwards down the stairs, and how did he end up in the dining room chair?'

'What does Annabel say?'

'Not a lot. The police came, of course, and she was in quite a state. She said it was an accident, and that she panicked when someone came to the door so she dragged her poor father into the dining room.'

'God,' said Ed. 'I can't bear to think about it.'

'The strangest part is that she then lived in that house with

228

her father's corpse for what – six weeks? More? We don't know and Annabel can't remember. Or so she says.'

It was very odd. They talked about it some more. Before Teddy left he had a quick look around the house.

'You've made it quite snug here.'

'It's not bad, is it?'

'If you hadn't just left somewhere like Hartlepool Hall, you might consider this quite a nice place for a single person to live. Good views, warm little house, plenty of outbuildings if you decide to keep chickens. Let me know if you want any hens, by the way. I've got a surplus of the wretched things.'

When Teddy had gone Ed felt rather unwell and not just from the novel experience of drinking a large whisky at five in the afternoon. He was upset by the news about Annabel. He couldn't imagine what could have happened. Although they were not as close as they had once been, Ed still considered her a friend. Of course he did suspect her of having been in the pay of the enemy when she tried to manoeuvre him into meeting her new man, Geoff Tarset. But what Teddy had accused her of was in a different league. It was almost impossible to believe. At first, he wanted to phone Annabel. But what would he say when she picked up the phone? He decided to leave it until tomorrow or the next day.

The following morning he kept busy installing a television set and buying a new fridge. He went to a supermarket in Darlington and bought a stock of supplies for the house. He was so absorbed in these domestic tasks that it was only when he paused to make himself a cup of tea after lunch, that he became aware of an unfamiliar sensation.

He felt not exactly happy, but content. What had Teddy said yesterday?

'If you hadn't just left somewhere like Hartlepool Hall, you might consider this quite a nice place to live.'

He had enjoyed shopping for his new house. It was something he had never done before he moved to France. He hadn't shopped on a regular basis since running up bills in the tuck shop at school. At home, in the old days, no member of the family had been near a shop, unless it was to visit the tailor or dressmaker. In France he had left the chores to his housekeeper. But now he realised it was quite satisfying to buy things for oneself. Until he went to the local supermarket, he had no idea, for example, of how many different kinds of biscuit there were.

It struck him that there would be more to learn. He could buy a recipe book and teach himself to cook; he couldn't expect Teddy to keep bringing him roast chickens and pheasants. He might teach himself to redecorate the house. He might take down the blanket he had rigged up over his bedroom window and learn to hang proper curtains.

This led to another new idea. If he could do all these new things – and in time he felt he could – mightn't it be possible that one day he could get a job? He hadn't worked out what his needs were yet. He knew he had a rental income from the farmland that had remained in his ownership, probably enough to get by on if he never had any holidays and didn't buy anything expensive. But he knew already that he would need something to fill the time. It is easier to kill time in a large house than in a small one. In Hartlepool Hall he could wander about; pick up a book in one room and put it down in another and then spend another hour trying to remember where he left it. He could go out and inspect the hothouses and see if any of the nectarines were ripe; he could play billiards against himself in the billiard room; if desperate, he could look at the pictures. None of these distractions were available to Ed at Springwell Cottage. Sooner or later he would have to find something to do.

He saw how much of his life until now had been spent in limbo; pleasant enough, but limbo all the same; a state in which no decisions were ever taken, and no conclusions ever reached. Now he was in a different world. He smiled at the thought. Some good might come from all this misfortune after all.

He went outside and surveyed his new domain.

That crack on the gable end of the house needed fixing. He would speak to Malcolm about that. Then Ed remembered that Malcolm no longer worked for him and that he would have to make the arrangements himself. The buildings, stables and kennels were in a shabby state and there were weeds growing everywhere between the cobblestones. The roofs might need a little patching. He decided that he would go and buy some paint and do up the woodwork, then spray off the weeds. He might muck out the sheds and make a space for some hens. Then he could have his own fresh eggs every morning.

He looked about him. Springwell Cottage sat on a hill with a small lane running past it. Below the house were woods of beech and sycamore, the leaves turning yellow and red in the cooler air of autumn. You could not see Hartlepool Hall from here, which was a blessing: it was on the other side of the hill, in the next valley. The valley Ed now looked down into was composed of small compartments of pasture, with sheep or cattle grazing in them. A bright stream sparkled below.

Project after project was occurring to him. The possibilities were endless. In his mind, he was already so busy that he couldn't see how he would ever again have any time to be bored. He was in charge of his own life at last.

Later that morning he decided to drive to a nearby town to buy some paint for the doors and windows of the outhouses. His journey took him along the road that went past the gates of Hartlepool Hall. He hadn't been back there now for nearly a week. He couldn't help himself: he turned down the drive and drove onto the gravel. There, parked in a row, were several vehicles: a builder's lorry; a cherry-picker; and a series of huge yellow skips. These were already filling up with rubble and plaster.

Scaffolding had been run up the front of the house and a platform had been built level with the first floor. From there, buckets of more rubble were being lowered to the ground by one man and conveyed to the skips by another. Ed walked past them into the hall. There were a lot of people about and a tremendous noise of drilling and hammering filled the air.

Inside was a scene of devastation. On one side of the house an internal wall had been taken down, and as Ed looked he could see straight into what had once been the library, where workmen were busy removing the oak panelling below the dado rail.

In the middle of the hall stood the architect, talking to a man who must have been the building supervisor. Both were wearing yellow hard hats. When the architect saw Ed, he called out: 'Can I help you?'

'I used to live here,' said Ed. 'I just wanted to see what's going on. Do you mind?'

'You shouldn't be here,' replied the architect. 'There's a Health and Safety notice at the front door. Didn't you see it? Authorised personnel only.'

The building supervisor had turned away to take a call on

his mobile. Now he handed it to Peregrine Smith, saying, 'It's Geoff for you.' The architect took the call and Ed was forgotten for the moment.

Just then two other visitors arrived in the hall. One was a small dark man. The other was a woman, also dark skinned. Both were muffled up against the cold in fleeces and scarves although it was a mild autumn day.

When the architect saw them he finished his phone call.

'Señor Huayllacahua! So you've come to see your new home!'

So this was Biggsy, the Peruvian footballer, who was now delighting the football fans at St James's Park. The Spanish-looking lady murmured in Biggsy's ear. He nodded, looked around him and exclaimed: '*Qué pena. De hacer esto a un edificio tan bello*!'

The Spanish lady said: 'Señor Huayllacahua says, what a dreadful waste of a wonderful building.'

Peregrine Smith did not take this comment well.

'If Señor' – he struggled with the Quechuan name on his second attempt, and corrected himself – 'if Biggsy doesn't appreciate modern architecture, perhaps this is the wrong investment for him. He was shown all the plans.'

He went on speaking about the architectural significance of the work that was to be done here. While he was speaking, Biggsy's dark eyes were turning this way and that, surveying the devastation. For a moment his eyes met Ed's and Ed felt a spark of understanding pass between them.

Meanwhile the Spanish lady was busy translating Peregrine Smith's remarks concerning his own aspirations for the remodelled house and his views on Biggsy's lack of appreciation of modern architecture. When she had finished Biggsy nodded again, then bowed to the architect and said something in a low voice to his translator.

She turned to Peregrine Smith and said gravely: 'Señor Huayllacahua is no longer interested in this project.'

'Fine! That's just fine with me,' replied Peregrine Smith with a bitter smile. 'Perhaps I can get on with my job now.'

The pair turned away from the architect and left. A moment or two later Ed followed. There was no point in him staying any longer. It was too painful. He wished he had not come.

As he walked back to his car he saw that a chute had been raised to the level of the first floor, replacing the bucket and wheelbarrow. A skip was being manoeuvred to sit underneath its spout. When it was in place, Ed saw, the builders would be able to rip the heart out of his family home even faster.

Twenty-Two

The policemen had been quite unsympathetic at first and some of the questions they had asked Annabel had been very hard. But she found that if she kept her story simple, the questions stopped after a while. It was an accident, she kept repeating. I only moved the body because I was in shock. And then I didn't know what to do.

She had been able to discern little emotion on the faces of the men around her. Teddy Shildon had looked at her with distaste; Dr Mitchell had had an air of scientific enquiry about him; the policemen looked as if they thought that they had better things to attend to. Throughout the interview their radios kept crackling into life, alerting them to other local dramas: a dog had escaped from a farm near Shildon and was worrying sheep; a motorcyclist had run into the back of a milk float. In other circumstances, Annabel would have been irritated by these interruptions, but now she was grateful for them.

After a while the police sergeant had given up and closed his notebook.

'Well, there will be an inquest, of course.'

There were further delays while a police photographer was called in. Teddy had left by then, which was a relief, given how tricky he had been. Dr Mitchell had remained with Annabel until the ambulance arrived to take the body away. When the paramedics came into the house with the stretcher, Annabel went and hid in the kitchen until it was all over and her father's body was gone. Then, at last, she had the house to herself. She was truly alone for the first time in weeks.

It was not surprising that there was a reaction after all that. Annabel's method for dealing with the nervous strain she had undergone was conventional. There was still a nearly full bottle of Gordon's gin in the house, and she spent the rest of that day drinking gin and tonics, until she ran out of tonic. She drank the last few mouthfuls of gin neat, over ice. Then she went to bed.

She woke up the next morning feeling dreadful. It was an hour or two before any form of mental activity was possible. But once she had been sick and felt a little better, Annabel sat down at the kitchen table with a cup of weak tea and tried to decide what to do next. First of all, there was the question of money: her situation was now quite desperate and she was in real danger of starving. She hardly had enough cash to put petrol in the car, let alone buy anything for herself. As far as she could see, she was on the cusp of inheriting hundreds of thousands of pounds and a house, not to mention the half a million pounds prize money from Daddy's Premium Bond. But how could she lay her hands on any of it? This was no longer a question of buying herself a pretty little cottage, or a villa in France: it was about buying a tin of soup before she fainted from hunger.

She rang the bank.

After a lot of time spent listening to polite recorded voices offering her a menu of choices that included buying life insurance, travel insurance and pension plans, she at last managed to speak to a real person. It turned out nobody had the authority to grant her an overdraft.

What about a loan?

Any loan would have to be advanced against some form of security, replied the person she was speaking to. She explained that her father had died and that he had left her the house.

'We would need to have legal proof of ownership,' was the reply.

'Then can I take some money from my father's account?'

'We would need to have written instructions from a solicitor accompanied by a copy of the death certificate.'

No amount of pleading, or requests to speak to someone in authority, had any effect. She needed at the very least legal proof of her father's death.

Annabel rang up Dr Mitchell and asked if he could possibly pop round with a death certificate.

'My dear girl,' said Dr Mitchell, sounding embarrassed.

'I need to get access to Daddy's bank account, to pay the bills,' she explained.

'I'm afraid I can't just write out a death certificate, you know. It's a matter for the coroner to determine the cause of death.'

'But it was an accident,' repeated Annabel for the hundredth time. Why couldn't people grasp such a simple fact?

'We'll just have to wait for the inquest,' replied Dr Mitchell, sounding unhappy.

'But when will that be?'

'Ah, one can't be sure. It depends whether the coroner decides to call witnesses and their availability. I will be called and so will Teddy. But he may want other people to attend.'

'Which other people?'

'I can't say, I'm sure,' said the doctor. 'Will you excuse me now, Annabel? I have a patient waiting.'

He hung up.

Next Annabel rang Ed, not quite sure how he could help, but feeling it was important that he heard her side of the story first. She was becoming conscious that there might be difficulties ahead of her. She had not thought about an inquest before now and she wasn't clear what was involved. She supposed the coroner – she pictured him in her mind's eye as a kindly old man, a bit older and friendlier than Dr Mitchell – would return a verdict of accidental death after listening to her account of what had happened.

There was no reply from Hartlepool Hall. And, if Ed had a mobile these days, she didn't have the number.

What if the coroner *didn't* return a verdict of accidental death? Annabel decided not to pursue this line of thought. There was no point in worrying about something as ridiculous as that. She ought to be more concerned that her friends and acquaintances didn't get the wrong end of the stick. She didn't quite know how she would explain her actions. It might be easiest to suggest she had experienced some form of nervous breakdown brought on by her parent's death. After all, that was more or less what had happened. Something told her it might be a very long time before she entertained her friends in her dining room again.

In the afternoon she rang Geoff on his mobile. She couldn't think what else to do. Besides, Geoff had an uncanny knack of hearing news before most other people. It was important she spoke to him before he too heard some silly story from the rumour mill. He answered the phone promptly, but when he did, he sounded guarded.

'Oh, Annabel. How are you?'

There had been a time not long ago when he answered her calls with the words: 'Hi, babe'.

'Geoff, something's happened.'

'Can it wait? I've got all sorts to deal with this afternoon. Can I call you back?'

Annabel was very firm. No, it couldn't wait.

'Well, go on then. What's the problem?'

Annabel explained as briefly as she could, but it still took some time. At first Geoff kept grunting impatiently, as if to hurry her up. Then he listened in silence.

When she had finished speaking he said: 'You mean all those times I came to the house to collect you, the old man was sitting dead in the dining room?'

'Yes.'

'Jesus Christ.'

'I was in shock, Geoff.'

'Well, you never seemed to be in shock when we went out for drinks together. Or when we went to bed together.'

'Oh, Geoff, don't be so unkind. I was putting on a brave face.'

There was a pause at the other end.

'Annabel, have the police been involved?'

'Only a little.'

'You wait. The first visit from a policeman is never the last.' Geoff sounded as if he had some experience. Then he asked: 'So what can I do for you?'

'I want to see you, of course. This is a bad time for me.'

They agreed Geoff would come to Lambshiel House that evening. There was no mention of drinks, or going out to dinner.

'Could you bring some money?' Annabel added.

'Money?'

'I just want to borrow a hundred pounds or so until Daddy's will has been proved.'

Geoff sounded taken aback, but he agreed to bring what cash he could.

That evening Geoff called at the house about seven. Annabel had made a special effort to look as nice as she could, although she didn't feel very cheerful. When she opened the door she saw that Geoff also seemed to be under some strain.

'You look tired,' she said.

'I'm spitting,' he told her. 'I've just heard that bloody little architect I employ has pissed off Biggsy.'

'Who's Biggsy?'

Geoff reminded her about the little footballer.

'He and a couple of his mates were going to put money down for the first two or three flats we developed. Now Peregrine has made some snotty remark about him not understanding modern architecture. I can't work out what the hell went on, but today Biggsy went to Hartlepool Hall to have a look and Peregrine managed to offend him and now he's pulled out.'

Geoff was so angry he was almost incoherent.

'Who has pulled out? The architect?'

'No, Biggsy, for Christ's sake. Don't you ever listen? Biggsy's pulled out and so has at least one of his mates. We were going to sign them up next week and get their deposits.'

'Oh dear,' said Annabel. She didn't know what else to say. 'Why don't you come into the drawing room and sit down, Geoff?' They were still standing in the hallway.

'I won't come in, if you don't mind,' Geoff said.

Annabel thought he might be feeling a little sensitive about sitting in her father's old armchair.

'Shall we go out for a drink, then?' she suggested. 'There's nothing in the house. I'm afraid I'm completely without a penny until Daddy's will is sorted out.'

Geoff reached into his jacket pocket and pulled out an envelope, which he handed to her.

'There's some cash in there,' he told Annabel. 'A couple of hundred. It was all I could lay my hands on. I haven't got time to go to the bank at the moment.'

'Oh, thank you, thank you,' said Annabel. She leaned forward to kiss Geoff on the cheek but he had backed away from her and she nearly overbalanced.

'Don't worry about paying it back,' he told her. 'The fact is, Annabel, I don't think we should see each other for a while.'

Annabel stiffened.

'What on earth can you mean?'

'I've got troubles with this Hartlepool Hall project. The recession is making things difficult. On top of that I have this problem with Biggsy pulling out. The last thing I can afford at the moment is bad publicity.'

'Bad publicity?' asked Annabel, her tone incredulous.

'Yes. Press stories about me going around with someone whose father died in mysterious circumstances. That's not going to help me sell any flats. Better to wait until we see what happens at the inquest, don't you think?'

'Mysterious circumstances? I've already told you it was an accident.'

Annabel could hear her voice rising. She tried to control her temper.

'Well, they sound pretty mysterious to me, Annabel, and

I'm not betting any money on what the coroner will think.'

Geoff had edged backwards towards the front door. Now he took another step so that he was standing just outside.

'It's for the best, Annabel. It's been fun – but – well, I'm sorry.'

'You contemptible little man!' Annabel screamed. Geoff turned and hurried back to his car, as if fearful she might produce a kitchen knife and pursue him. Annabel did not wait to see him go. She slammed the front door shut, and then burst into tears.

The inquest did not take place for another three weeks. By then Annabel had run out of money again. The bank had frozen her father's accounts and the telephone line was in danger of being cut off, and no more oil could be delivered for the central heating. Annabel could only hope that, when she went to the inquest, someone she knew might buy her lunch afterwards, or even a sandwich.

The inquest itself was mercifully brief. A small, fussy-looking man in a dark suit and spectacles entered the room, and someone called out 'All rise'. When the coroner was seated, proceedings began. When Annabel was called she gave her evidence with economy and clarity.

'So he just fell backwards down the stairs?' asked the coroner.

He was not unkind when he spoke to her.

'Yes, he had been very shaky on his feet. I think he was suffering from the after-effects of a mild stroke. Something happened to him in church a few days earlier.'

The vicar was called and agreed that when he had last seen the deceased, he had not seemed himself. Then the doctor was called and agreed that the injuries he had found on

Colonel Gazebee's body were not inconsistent with what Miss Gazebee had said. Because of the length of time between the event itself and the discovery of the body, there was little else he could add except that the body had been moved from the foot of the stairs to the dining room. Annabel was recalled.

'Can you explain why the body was moved?' asked the coroner.

'Someone came to the door and I didn't want them to see poor Daddy lying dead at the bottom of the stairs.'

'But surely you knew it was not a good idea to move the body?'

'I panicked,' said Annabel simply.

Other witnesses were called. Teddy spoke, very briefly. A police sergeant whom Annabel thought she recognised said that because so much time had passed since the death, the police had no further evidence to present other than the photographs of the body which the coroner had already seen.

While this was going on, Annabel, who was sitting next to Dr Mitchell, whispered to him: 'Who are those men over there?'

There were two youngish-looking men listening to the proceedings. One was wearing a dark suit; the other was more scruffily dressed.

'The one writing notes is a reporter from the local paper. The one in the suit is from the Crown Prosecution Service.'

'What on earth can he want?' asked Annabel.

'He's here to see whether there are grounds for a public prosecution.'

Annabel looked at the man again, this time with a horror she found difficult to conceal. A public prosecution! It had never occurred to her that anyone might take such a strict view of what had happened. She felt hot all over, then cold.

She wondered if she might faint, but then suddenly the proceedings drew to an end. The coroner was remarking in a mild voice: 'To return the verdict of accidental death, I must be satisfied that the death came about as the result of an accident. While the circumstances in this case are somewhat unusual, I have been presented with no evidence that suggests Colonel Gazebee's death was *not* an accident ...' He uttered a few further words of gentle reproof to Annabel for moving the body, and then the proceedings were over.

Annabel left the building still at Dr Mitchell's side. Once they were outside she said: 'I'd be grateful if you could let me have a death certificate as soon as possible. I need to see about Daddy's will.'

'I will deal with it today,' he replied, then walked off without saying goodbye, which Annabel found quite rude.

Teddy Shildon came up to her.

'Well, Annabel,' he said. 'You've got your verdict. You're a lucky girl. Some coroners might have been a lot harder on you.'

'Will you come to the funeral, Teddy?'

'Of course I will. I'll come for your father's sake.'

That was the best Annabel could hope for from Teddy at the moment. In time, she thought, he would come to see how unjust he had been in his opinion of her.

The weather turned cold. Annabel managed to extract enough money from the bank in order to turn the central heating back on and pay a few bills. Lambshiel House was like an icebox. The weather forecasters talked about an early winter. Already frosts had removed the leaf from the trees; only the beech leaves still clung on, brown and twisted, rustling in the cold north-easterly wind. Ice formed in puddles, and on the windshields of cars in the morning. Once or twice there were little flurries of snow, although it never settled for long. The sky was a pale grey, the colour of a pigeon's breast.

Finally Annabel managed to sort out her affairs. Her father's solicitor had offices in Darlington. She went there one morning for the reading of the will. Apart from a small sum of money left to the Army Benevolent Fund, everything else went to Annabel: the investment portfolio and the house.

'What about his Premium Bond?' asked Annabel.

The solicitor, a fat man in a tight-fitting suit, shook with laughter when he heard about the win. Annabel did not relate the full story of how the cheque was presented to her but she still had a letter from National Savings confirming the amount. She showed it to the solicitor.

'My God,' he said. 'That came a bit late for him!'

'It's my money now, isn't it?' asked Annabel.

'We certainly have a claim, and I shall write to them asking them to re-present the cheque in your name. You will be very well off if that comes through. Would you like me to introduce you to a partner who specialises in Wealth Management?'

'Not at the moment,' said Annabel. 'Let me know as soon as you hear anything.'

She left her solicitor's offices feeling triumphant. Once again she had overcome adversity: first the inquest, and now this. Within a few days she would have access to her father's money; the house would be conveyed into her name; and she could do absolutely anything she liked. She wondered whether to ring Geoff. The scent of real money would bring him crawling back to her, she felt certain. Then she could be the one to break up with him.

As she turned the corner, wrapped in her thoughts, she bumped into someone: a large man, with his shirt hanging out. Despite the cold he did not wear a jacket. He stepped aside as if to walk on past but Annabel had recognised him.

'Hello, Eric,' she said.

Eric pretended for a moment not to know who she was, then said: 'Hiya, kiddah!' in a rather sheepish way.

'How are you?'

'How do you think I would be?' said Eric with an angry look on his face.

'I was just asking,' she said, startled.

'The boss has only gone and done a runner, hasn't he? Left me to deal with the creditors, and my own salary not paid for three months.'

'What do you mean, done a runner?'

Eric saw that Annabel had not heard the news.

'I mean that our *pal* Geoff has flit,' he said. 'He's gone off to the Costa Brava and left me to tell the creditors they won't even get a penny in the pound. The receivers say he was trading insolvently. Well, I wouldn't know, I was only his accountant. He was dipping into the loans he took out on the security of Hartlepool Hall to pay off other debts.'

The story emerged, together with a certain amount of bad language. The building contractor had rung up Eric to say that a cheque had bounced. Eric had gone to find Geoff but he wasn't at home. He wasn't at the golf club. He wasn't even at the office. There was a panic. Eric called the bank and the bank panicked too. Everyone was panicking, and the only thing that soon became clear was that there was no money left in any of the accounts to pay anybody anything, including Eric.

'He cleaned out any money that was left and took it with him to Spain.'

'But what will happen to Hartlepool Hall?' asked Annabel.

'The bank's taken it back. All the work has stopped. God knows what they'll do with the place. It's a mess.'

'I'm so sorry,' said Annabel. In a way, she was. Eric was quite as much a dupe as she had been. Geoff had used both of them to help with his schemes; and when his schemes had failed, he'd left them to sink or swim.

'What will you do?'

'I've got a job doing the books at a nightclub in Sunderland,' said Eric. 'But if I ever get my hands on that bastard, they'll have to put me away for murder.'

He expressed no sympathy for Annabel. Either it didn't occur to him that she had been let down as well, or he didn't care. He shambled away and Annabel headed back to her car.

Geoff's departure simplified things for her in a way. She couldn't say she had hated his company. They had had fun together and for a short while he had been a good companion: kind, generous, amusing and sometimes almost loving. But he wasn't suitable for her and that was that.

Her father had been right after all.

Twenty-Three

At last the coroner released Colonel Gazebee's body for burial. Annabel and the vicar decided that a full-dress funeral service was the only adequate send-off for a man whose corpse had spent several months sitting at his dining room table. The Earl of Shildon gave the address.

St Winifred's, the church where Annabel's father had for so many years harangued the congregation with ominous and enigmatic readings from the Old Testament, was scarcely full. Apart from Annabel, decorously dressed in a black coat and a black hat and veil, Ed was the only other person there of her generation. A few of the older members of St Winifred's had turned up: either out of respect for the departed, or in order to make sure he was really dead. Dr Mitchell was there, and a few other faces Annabel recognised from Sunday mornings (how long ago those seemed now); and there were a few strangers sitting at the back that she did not at first recognise. One of these timidly came up to her before the service.

'I'm your father's cousin Matthew from Bournemouth.'

Annabel dimly recalled the name. The thin old man took her hand and held it for a moment.

'I didn't know your father very well. We hadn't met for many years.'

'It was good of you to come,' she replied.

'Oh well, it's the least one can do. I have a senior citizen's railcard and the fare was very reasonable. I'm fond of railway engines. I managed to spot quite a few on the journey.'

When Teddy stood up to give the address, his tall, commanding presence lent the ceremony a solemnity it had not achieved until that point. He wore a white shirt and a black tie knotted somewhere below his left ear. He had not had time to cut his hair since the harvest had finished, so looked more like an Old Testament prophet than a farmer.

Annabel did not listen to the speech. She was trying not to think too hard about the events that had led to this service, in the old stone church that had stood on its hill for more than a thousand years. She wondered whether she ought to cry a little: it might make her feel better. She took a small handkerchief from the pocket of her coat and dabbed discreetly at her face under the veil, but her eyes were dry. Phrases from Teddy's oration reached her:

'A fine officer who served his country gallantly for many years.'

'A well-respected figure in the local community.'

Even Teddy did not dare use the term 'well-liked'. At last he came to the end; in fact he was only in the pulpit for about five minutes, although it seemed longer.

Outside then, for the last exequies: the vicar solemnly speeding his old enemy on his way; the gravediggers shovelling earth onto the coffin as it lay in its pit; the professional pall bearers turning away and lighting up cigarettes as soon as the vicar had set off back towards the church.

Lambshiel House was, for a number of reasons, not considered appropriate for the gathering after the funeral. The wake was held in The Railwayman's Arms, a pub in the village about five hundred yards from the church. Ed trailed in some way behind the others; he had been half-inclined just to get in his car and go. Indeed he had started walking towards it, but then changed his mind. It would be rude to Teddy, and unkind to Annabel, for him not to show his face. As he entered the lounge bar, the first person he met was Teddy, clutching a large tumbler of whisky and a ham sandwich.

'Good speech, Teddy,' he said.

'Hello, Ed. Did you really think so? A frightfully inconvenient time to leave the farm: I was meant to be selling lambs today.' He took a gulp of whisky and added: 'Still, one had to come and see the old boy off.'

Teddy was several years older than Colonel Gazebee had been when he died but he didn't look it. He stood erect and his large frame crackled with energy.

'Was he in the war?' asked Ed. 'You said a lot about his service to his country. I can't remember my father ever telling me where Marcus Gazebee served.'

'He was too young to fight in the Second World War,' replied Teddy, 'if that's what you mean. Plenty of others he could have fought in, but he never saw active service. Spent a lot of time with the army in Germany. But he never fired a gun in anger as far as I know.'

'What did he do?'

'He wasn't in the same regiment as your father and me. I think he had something to do with the men's hygiene. Latrines Officer, we used to call him. He didn't like it much.'

That was Teddy's final word on the subject, and he turned the conversation to the evergreen question of what was to become of Hartlepool Hall. There were rumours going round that work had stopped on the project and that everyone had left the site. Teddy told Ed the latest story: that Geoff Tarset had gone bust.

'Anyway,' he concluded. 'Whatever that man is or is not doing at the Hall, we've still got to shoot the pheasants.'

'It's in a couple of weeks,' replied Ed. 'The keeper knows it is his last season with us. I'm sure he'll give us a good day. We'll meet at the Simmonds Arms in the village, and I've arranged for us to have lunch there.'

'I'm looking forward to it.'

The vicar cornered Annabel. She was longing to talk to Ed, whom she had not seen since the sale of Hartlepool Hall, but she dreaded having to speak to Teddy Shildon, who more than once had fixed her with a penetrating stare. Inquest or no inquest, he had reached his own verdict and seemed unlikely to change his mind. The vicar was reminiscing about the way in which Colonel Gazebee used to read the lessons in church.

'He quite convinced us that fire and brimstone were only just around the corner.' He gave Annabel a conspiratorial look and lowered his voice. 'Of course we are *taught* to believe in the existence of the Abyss, and all the demons that dwell in it, but really, your father managed to bring it all to life with his readings.'

The conversation moved on to the subject of bequests left to the local church by previous members of the congregation. By the time Annabel escaped from the vicar, the Earl of Shildon had left. Ed was leaving too but Annabel caught him at the door.

'Walk me to my car.'

'Of course,' he replied. 'How are you, Annabel?'

'I'm lonely, Ed.'

251

They had not spoken for months. Now Ed stopped and faced her.

'You've been through a difficult time.'

'So have you.'

'It was an odd thing, the way you kept your father's death a secret for so long.'

Annabel lowered her eyes and allowed the veil of her hat to fall over her face.

'I can't explain it just now. But will you come and see me, soon? There are things I want to say to you.'

They set off again. Ed said nothing but as they arrived at the door of her car, he replied at last.

'Yes, OK. I'll call you.'

A few days later Ed remembered his promise to Annabel and visited her at Lambshiel House. It was early evening when he arrived and she welcomed him with a kiss on the cheek. She took him into the drawing room, where a fire was burning merrily. The room looked different to when Ed had last been in it. Some branches of flowering shrubs had been placed in a vase: witch hazel and mahonia. The room seemed more lived in than before, and there were newspapers and magazines scattered about. A few prints of flowers and pretty landscapes had replaced the military pictures that had once adorned the walls before and the place looked almost homely. Ed was sure there had been a clock on the mantelpiece on his last visit, but if there had been, there wasn't one now.

'It's freezing outside,' he said, stamping his feet as he came in. The heating in his father's old Peugeot was not very effective. 'Nice and warm in here, though. You've changed the room around. It looks nice.'

'Daddy didn't like what he called feminine frippery, but

I suppose I can be allowed my own way now,' replied Annabel. Ed smiled and accepted the glass of white wine that she handed to him.

'You'll stay to supper?' she asked. 'It's just salad and cold chicken.'

Ed was going to refuse, but her expression was so vulnerable he changed his mind. There was something different about Annabel, thought Ed, as they chatted together about his new cottage, and other safe subjects. She had been marked by her experiences. Once, a few years ago, she had been quite a striking girl: not exactly pretty, but attractive all the same, with dark hair, thin regular features and large brown eyes. Now there was a hardness in the lines about the mouth, as if she had too often clenched her jaw in defiance or frustration. The lines under her eyes were not yet bags, but the skin had once been smooth there. Her hair was no longer as lustrous as it once was. Of course, Ed told himself, I have aged too. It's more than five years since I saw Annabel regularly.

Annabel noticed him looking at her and asked, 'Do I look awful?'

'Of course you don't,' replied Ed. 'You look very well tonight.'

She had made an effort for him. Annabel had always known how to do a good paint job, and she was dressed in a low cut black dress which wasn't quite a cocktail dress but was really too smart for eating cold supper in the kitchen. There was no question, of course, of using the dining room.

'I know I don't,' said Annabel, 'but it's sweet of you to pretend. The last few months have been awful for both of us, haven't they?'

'Not great,' said Ed. 'But I've decided that unless one looks forward rather than back, one could quite easily go mad.'

253

'Two orphans in a storm,' said Annabel, rising to top up Ed's glass of wine. 'Of course I'm an orphan now as well. You've been one for years.'

'Yes.' Ed did not want to dwell on how Annabel had become an orphan. He still remembered vividly Teddy Shildon's suspicions. He had to admit that Marcus Gazebee might have driven even the sanest person to extreme behaviour. The man had been in a class of his own.

As if reading his thoughts, Annabel said: 'You do know it was an accident, don't you?'

'Whatever the coroner says is good enough for me,' Ed replied. He added quickly: 'And of course I know it could never have been anything else. I think what shook people a little was that you didn't tell anyone what had happened.'

'We all do odd things under stress. Come into the kitchen and we'll have something to eat.'

Over supper Annabel told Ed about her inheritance.

'Dad had squirrelled away quite a sum. I have no idea where it came from. It seems impossible he could have saved it, although God knows we did not live extravagantly. I suppose one of my great-aunts must have left him the shares. There was some money on that side of the family once upon a time.'

'You're very fortunate.'

'And then there's the Premium Bond win.'

Ed hadn't heard about this, so Annabel told him the story, omitting the rather distressing incident in the dining room when the cheque was first presented to the late Colonel Gazebee.

'I've never ever met anyone who won a prize before,' Ed remarked. 'And now it's one of my oldest friends and it's half a million. Congratulations!'

'Well, I haven't got the money yet,' Annabel told him. 'But my solicitor says I'm sure to get it in a week or two.'

She made some coffee and they went back into the drawing room. Ed sat in Colonel Gazebee's old armchair. It seemed in slightly doubtful taste but it was the most comfortable place to sit. Annabel kneeled on the floor in front of the fire, holding her cup of coffee. They were silent for a while, and Ed was wondering whether it was too early to say he should be getting home, when Annabel announced: 'I've finished with Geoff Tarset.'

'Oh. Well, he seems to have let everyone else down. I'm very sorry, anyway.'

'Oh, don't be. I finished with him before I knew he was bankrupt. It was never going anywhere. Just one of those things.'

'He had a certain charm,' suggested Ed.

'The gift of the gab. You must be devastated by what's happened to Hartlepool Hall. Have you been there since the workmen stopped?'

'I couldn't bear to,' said Ed. 'I'm told the place looks like a ruin now. The bank has repossessed it.'

Annabel laughed, but did not say anything.

'What's so funny?' asked Ed, still thinking about Hartlepool Hall.

'Oh, it's just that for years and years, when we were first all running around together, it was always you who looked after us. You were so generous. Mrs Donaldson used to cook the most wonderful dinners . . .'

'. . . and Horace used to mix mind-blowing cocktails,' added Ed. They reminisced for a few moments. Then Annabel leaned forward and spoke in a serious voice. Ed had to lean forward to catch what she was saying and as he did so, he found himself looking straight down the front of her dress. This was unintentional: on his part at least.

'It's my turn to be generous now,' said Annabel.

'How do you mean?' Ed asked nervously.

'Ed, I have money now. I shan't keep this house. It has too many unhappy memories. Once I've sold it, together with everything else, I shall have far more money than I could ever spend on my own.'

There was a pause. Annabel smiled softly at Ed and added: 'I want it to be for us, not just me. For both of us.'

There was no possible doubt about what Annabel was offering. Some of it was there, sitting on the floor in front of Ed, ready for him to take right now. And there was a cash bonus of a million or two. As Ed looked down at her, she began to breathe a little faster. He knew she was waiting for him to lean down and kiss her.

He saw in her a kind of moral blankness or incompleteness that he recognised, because it had once been a part of his own makeup. Annabel had so longed for her inheritance and the liberation she had expected it to bring, that it had consumed her and unbalanced her. Now she had inherited, she did not know what to do about it. There was no sense of purpose in her other than the sense of purpose that a barnacle has when it sees a rock to cling to; nor was there, Ed thought, much more capacity for love than a barnacle might possess.

'I don't see how that could be,' he said.

Annabel reached up and tried to put her arms around him, but he disengaged himself gently. He knew that for him to give in to Annabel would be the most disastrous of all the decisions he could make. He sensed he was on the edge of learning to become a proper human being, and Annabel wanted to drag him back into some kind of half-life. The money would run out soon enough; it always did, no matter how much there was. And with it would go any illusion of love.

In any case he felt nothing for her any more. Once she had been a good friend, but the friendships of one's youth sometimes lapse into indifference, and this was the case with Annabel.

'Annabel, it wouldn't work. You're a friend, a very good friend. But I'd be lying if I told you it could ever be anything more.'

Tears started to stream down Annabel's face: all the tears she could not shed when her own father died; tears of real grief, not the tears of rage that had fallen when her father was still alive.

'Oh, Ed,' she said. 'Please. I do love you, you know. It was only ever you. I never cared for Geoff or any of the others. It was only because I couldn't have you. Please, Ed. Please.'

In her grief she began to unbutton her dress, as if desire might overcome reason, as if there could have been any desire in the first place.

How Ed managed to get out of the house he could never quite remember, but afterwards he drove home feeling hollowed out by sadness: sadness for Annabel, sadness for all the missed opportunities of his own life.

When Ed was safely back home at Springwell Cottage, he sat by the fire, reflecting on what had happened. He realised now that inheritances can destroy people, unless they learn that inheritance has to be earned, and then earned over and over again. He realised that comfortable surroundings, indeed the gilded surroundings of his own life until then, and all the things that went with that, don't tend to produce happiness or fulfilment without some sense of love to go with them.

He thought he had understood these things just in time. He had a purpose now, which was to find Alice. Then he would get a job and look after her as well as he could until she no longer needed him.

Twenty-Four

On the morning of the last big pheasant shoot at Hartlepool Hall, the guns met outside the Simmonds Arms in the village of Comogan.

For most of the previous century, shoot days at Hartlepool Hall had been grand affairs. The Hall would have filled with guests for dinner the night before, then all the guns would have assembled in the stable courtyard where transport was awaiting them. If royalty or foreign guests were staying, the day would start with chilled champagne in silver cups. If it was a day for locals, they would be given a mug of coffee. Then the shooting would begin, with teams of beaters, loaders, pickers-up, and game carts forming a great convoy as they went from covert to covert. Lunch would be in the dining room and would last over an hour, whilst the beaters and keepers sat on straw bales in the stables and sipped their soup, shivering. Then the day would continue until it was nearly dark and the guns would return to the house for tea, more food, and glasses of whisky.

These days, the shoot was conducted with less ceremony and on a more modest scale. But it was still an important occasion that everyone looked forward to, a day on which everyone would do their best to pretend that things were much as they had been, and that Hartlepool Hall itself still survived and had not been pulled down by a bankrupt property developer.

It was a bitter morning. The cold weather of the previous week had intensified, and a frigid landscape greeted the guns as they climbed out of their Land Rovers and Land Cruisers. They were rubbing their hands to keep warm and laughing at the cold. Teddy Shildon was there, and Eck Chetwode-Talbot, and several other of Ed's friends and neighbours, making the party eight in all.

'Good morning for it,' Ed said to Teddy as the latter got out of his car, snorting out clouds of vapour in the cold air like a dragon.

'Not enough wind,' replied Teddy. 'Still, I daresay all the birds will be in the woods on a day like this.'

The keeper arrived and was introduced to those guns he didn't know. A few yards away the beaters were huddled around the horsebox and tractor that were going to carry them from drive to drive. Ed saw one or two of them passing around hip flasks, nipping whatever mixture was inside. Standing apart from them, an elite in their own right, were four pickers-up. The job of these men was to work their dogs to pick up any stray or wounded birds that might fall far back behind the line of guns. One man had five black Labradors that sat up straight in front of him like guardsmen. Another had a couple of flat-coats. Ed recognised Billy Thompson and went over to say hello. He had brought out his two springer spaniels and Millie, his little working cocker. She was a beauty: small, with emerald green eyes and a glossy coat the colour of dark chocolate. Ed could see that Billy adored her.

'She's a pretty animal,' he told Billy, as he petted the dog's silky ears. 'Does she work well?'

'Aye, she'll do the job,' Billy said.

Ed went back to his guests. They drew numbers for the first drive and then set off for the particular wood where the day's sport was to begin. It was a good team of guns: they shot fairly straight, although the bitter cold meant that some of them were a little slow in reloading, dropping cartridges on the ground with numbed fingers and bending down to retrieve them while pheasants soared above the line untouched. But as the day progressed, a respectable bag was accumulated.

At eleven o'clock they stopped for hot soup and sausage rolls and a nip or two of sloe gin. There was a lot of banter about each other's accuracy. Ed was enjoying himself and so were the other guns. They went on to the final drive before lunch at the pub. This was a set-piece: the keeper liked to produce the most difficult birds just before lunchtime, so that everyone would talk about them over the meal, and remember to be generous with their tips at the end of the day.

Ed was a back gun behind the line on this drive, in a place where you could get a good view of the birds coming out of a dark wood at the top of a bank. Behind the guns was a ploughed field and beyond that, the river. He felt almost too cold to shoot: it had been below freezing for days on end, but last night had been the coldest yet. The sky was bright blue, there was hoar frost on the trees and the puddles were solid ice.

The pickers-up arrived and took up their stations. Billy nodded to Ed as he walked past with his two springers and Millie trotting at his heels, heading for his position a field length behind the guns with his back to the river. The drive started.

The pheasants were challenging. They came out of the

wood in twos and threes at a good height, and then they flew higher. As the keeper had hoped and expected, the guns were struggling to bring them down. A lot of cartridges were fired and not much was hit. But Ed saw that Teddy Shildon, in the middle of the line, wasn't missing much. Teddy might have been over eighty, but he hadn't forgotten how to shoot. Every bird he hit was through the beak: it crumpled in mid-air and fell stone dead. It was all done with the minimum of fuss.

Then a hen pheasant came out of the tops of the trees and started gaining height as she saw the guns. She must have been well over forty yards up by the time she crossed the line. You could see the sunlight catching on her wings and breast; she was so high she might have been taken for a golden starling. Ed would have said that she was out of shot, but Teddy shot her. It must have been right at the limit of his range, but she glided down with her wings set towards the riverbank. She hit the ground dead and bounced into the river. Then there was a commotion. Ed turned and saw Billy trotting along the bank, then one or two of the other pickers-up running towards him.

Everyone saw that bird being shot. The beaters, the pickers-up, the guns, all held their breath as she jinked in mid-flight and then began her long descent, like an angel falling out of an Arctic sky. Millie the working cocker was marking her, and perhaps the longing to bring that special bird back to her master was just too much. Perhaps Billy moved, or spoke, or made some unconscious signal that Millie took as permission to go after the pheasant. The next second she was in the river.

But the river was partly frozen after the days and nights of intense cold, and as Millie paddled out into the water and seized the pheasant in her jaws, she did not see the danger ahead. A sheet of ice now covered a section of the river about two hundred yards long. The strong current swept Millie under it before she could turn for the shore. There was nothing anyone could do. They couldn't walk out onto the ice and break a hole; it wasn't thick enough. They recovered Millie's body downstream beyond the ice sheet. She had either drowned or died of cold or both, but the pheasant was still firmly clenched in her jaws.

The rest of the day was overshadowed by that moment. Of course Ed and the other guns went up to Billy to express their sympathy. He nodded but he wasn't really listening. Lunch was a gloomy occasion. The fun had gone out of the day and even Teddy, who loved his shooting, seemed glad when the day's sport was over at half past three. Ed had wanted to find out how Billy was bearing up but he didn't like to bother him just then.

The next day, Ed went into the village to collect some post that had been forwarded from Hartlepool Hall. As he was driving out again, he saw Billy coming in the opposite direction in his Land Rover. Ed stopped his car and wound down the window, so Billy stopped too.

'I was terribly sorry about your dog, Billy,' he said.

'Aye,' Billy replied. 'Bad job that was. Bloody dog ran in, didn't she?'

But there was such pain in his face as he said it. Ed had never heard him swear before.

That was the last time Ed saw Billy, although he heard news of him from time to time in the Simmonds Arms in Comogan. Whatever ties had held Billy to this part of the world, which had called him back from New Zealand, were now severed. The death of his cocker spaniel was the final straw. Ed heard that Billy gave up the tenancy on the little cottage he was in, and sold his other two dogs for whatever he could get.

After that, people said he had found work on a building site in Newcastle; then, later, that he was working as a night-shift security guard in a factory in Manchester. That was the last that was heard of him but no doubt Billy still moves from one place to another, earning whatever he can. There was no longer any reason for him to settle down in any particular place.

Twenty-Five

The bundle of re-directed letters that Ed collected from the post office in Comogan was composed for the most part of junk mail or bills. But there were two items of interest. The first was an envelope, handwritten, with a newspaper cutting in it. He did not recognise the writing and there was no accompanying card or letter. The enclosure was an article from the Fine Arts page of the *Financial Times*. The headline read:

HARTLEPOOL SERGEANT MAKES TWO MILLION

At first Ed thought the story must be about some other lucky person who had won a Premium Bond, or the Lottery. But when he read the article, it turned out to be about the portrait of Percy Simmonds by John Singer Sargent, which had been taken from the Hall. It had been bought by an 'anonymous buyer for ten thousand pounds' – no doubt the auctioneer's private client Chris Higgins – and then sold again at Sotheby's at a much higher price. That was how some men got rich and others stayed poor. For a moment Ed felt seized by a terrible rage. Then he shrugged his shoulders. What was the point of worrying about it? He hadn't been born with the native cunning of his ancestors, and that was that. Ed put the article to one side and looked at the other item of post.

This was a postcard. The picture on the front was of Tynemouth, a coastal holiday resort that, as its name suggests, sits on the north bank of the Tyne estuary. The town curls around from Fish Quay at North Shields, where the trawlers and seine-net boats once used to dock, beyond the old ruined priory on the cliff, to the rows of Edwardian villas that face the beach and the brisk winds that blow off the North Sea. On the back of the postcard a spidery hand had written Ed's former address and the words: '*Missing you . . .*'

When Ed realised what had happened he laughed. He had spent days over the last few weeks trying to find out where Alice had been taken. It had proved an impossible task – there were so many residential care homes, sheltered accommodation centres, hospices and bed and breakfasts scattered across the north of England. She had never given him any hints and the abductors of Humanitas PLC had been about as unhelpful as they could have been.

Now he did have a clue. Alice was in Tynemouth and she had access to postcards and stamps, so she was not being held under too close a restraint. In his worst nightmares Ed had dreamed of Alice lying helpless in some home, subdued by chemical coshes, unable to remember her own name. But on the slender evidence of this card, the situation was not as bad as that.

Ed immediately set aside his other projects: the conversion of the old sheds into accommodation for hens, the further decoration of his new home. All were abandoned while he concentrated on finding Alice. His first thought was to jump into his car and simply go and look; but he had wasted so much time on previous expeditions of this sort that he was wiser now. Instead he began his search on the Internet, went to the library in Darlington and made a list of likely places from telephone directories. Then he spent a few hours on the phone and with surprising ease, he found Alice.

Instead of obstruction, he found nothing but helpfulness. The people who were looking after Alice were delighted to hear she had a prospective visitor. She hadn't been well, they said, but she could be taken out for short walks. Within two days of receiving the postcard Ed had her address and was driving north in the December sunshine to be reunited with Alice.

The home where Alice was staying was not smart, but a converted boarding house a few streets behind the sea front. From here, you could see the seagulls mewing among the chimney pots and hear the dull repetitive thud of the surf; you could smell the salt and see the faint spume that hung in the air on windy days, but you could not glimpse the sea itself.

Inside the house it was warm, and clean, and comfortable. Paper chains had been stuck to the walls with Blu-Tack; sprigs of holly had been hung here and there in a random fashion. In the entrance hall was a small artificial Christmas tree, with gold branches and glass balls. Ed was met by the manageress.

'So you're Alice's friend Ed,' she remarked, when Ed had introduced himself. 'I'm so pleased you've come. Alice has been talking about you, but she didn't want to bother you.'

'How is she?' he asked.

'We were worried about her for a while. Before she ... ran away, I suppose you would call it, although it makes her sound like a naughty schoolgirl, she had become very odd and rather befuddled. She talked such a lot of nonsense about lords and ladies and grouse moors and huge houses. It confused some of the other residents. We wondered if she hadn't – well, frankly, if she wasn't going a little dotty. It happens all the time to our older residents, as I'm sure you can imagine. Not that Alice is that old – she's still quite the baby here. Then she ran away. You could have knocked me over with a feather when I heard about it. I would never have dreamed she had the energy. But off she went, and we had to get Social Services to go and find her.'

'But she's all right now?' persisted Ed.

'Well, she wasn't at first,' replied the manageress. 'She was very weepy and didn't make sense and of course the silly people who collected her had given her far too much sedation. But she's fine now. We gather she had gone to stay with you, but why, or where, we're still not very clear about. Still, all's well that ends well.'

After a few more moments' conversation, Ed was taken through into a sun-room where a number of the residents sat in their chairs reading or talking together or dozing.

'There she is,' said the manageress, needlessly.

Alice saw Ed at the same time as he saw her. She was sitting in a wing-backed armchair, neither reading nor sleeping, but simply waiting. When she realised he was there her eyes widened and before he could say anything she levered herself painfully to her feet. She seemed more arthritic than he remembered. But otherwise she was the same dear Alice: tall, slim – no, painfully thin – with eyes darkened by lack of sleep and with the shadow of her former beauty around her like an aura.

'You've come,' she said.

'Of course I've come,' replied Ed. 'Only you've been difficult to track down, Alice. You didn't leave an address.'

They embraced, and then Ed sat on a chair next to Alice.

'Tell me what's been happening at Hartlepool Hall,' she commanded. Ed gave her an edited version of recent events. He didn't want to distress her, but he knew she would not be put off.

'How horrible the whole business is,' she remarked. 'I want to know more about this, but it's lunchtime soon, and then I usually have a rest. Ed, do you have to rush back or can you stay a little longer?'

Ed promised he would stay as long as she liked.

'Then if they'll let us, will you take me out for a walk? When I say a walk, you will have to push me along in a wheelchair. The cold weather has got into my bones.'

An hour or so later Ed was pushing Alice along the seafront. The wind had dropped and the intense cold of the last few days had relaxed its grip a little. Alice was wrapped up in a coat and rugs and seemed happy to be wheeled along the promenade. They came to a spot where they could sit and watch the sea. A few hardy surfers in wetsuits were riding their boards, waiting for the remaining waves of the swell that had been whipped up by the wind.

When they had watched this scene for a few moments, Ed said: 'I want to ask you a few questions, Alice. You don't mind?'

'I know you do,' she replied. 'And no, I don't mind.'

'Why did you call yourself "Lady" Alice Birtley? I looked you up in all the books and you weren't there. What is your real name?'

'Just plain Alice Birtley. I added the "Lady" because I didn't think I would be able to get past Horace without a title. I didn't dare go there when your father was alive, and it was only by chance that I found out you were expected back home.'

'How? Who told you?'

'Mrs Donaldson. She worked in the care home as a temporary cook when there was nothing for her to do at Hartlepool Hall. I found out about you from her, and she told me you had been away but were expected back home. I had to come and see you. You will forgive me for my deception, Ed, won't you?'

Ed was sitting next to her on a bench, and he patted her hand.

'I forgive you. So you never married?'

'No. Sammy was just a kind man who took me in and made me respectable. In return I looked after him. He was already quite old and ill when we started living together.'

Ed drew a deep breath.

'I think you can tell me the rest of the story now, Alice,' he said. 'I'm ready to hear it.'

'I saw your father two years after he was married, although I hadn't seen him for almost three,' Alice told him. 'He just turned up at Mrs Bright's.'

'Who was Mrs Bright?' asked Ed. Alice stared out to sea, at the waves rolling in and crashing on the golden sand.

'It was a very different world then. On the surface, it was still very correct and formal and what you would think of as old-fashioned, but there was another side to it. I was an adopted child. Joe Birtley was my foster-father. My foster-mother sent me to Mrs Bright when I was only sixteen. She said I would be trained to be of use. "What as?" I asked. "All sorts of things," my foster-mother said. "Mrs Bright will help you get on in life." It took me a while to work out what that meant.'

Ed began to understand.

'Mrs Bright provided the services of young women for the enjoyment of young men such as your father. It wasn't quite a brothel. It was very well-organised. You met Mrs Bright and her girls through a man called Dr Stephenson, who had a clinic in Harley Street. All Simon's friends knew about it. You went there for a consultation first and said you had a problem. Dr Stephenson specialised in advice about sexual health, but he could also arrange for you to be given a letter of introduction to Mrs Bright's house in Bayswater. Of course he wanted a cheque as well, and it wasn't cheap. Only the well-heeled could afford Dr Stephenson and Mrs Bright.'

Ed was less shocked than he might have been. Some consciousness of what had really gone on had filtered into his mind over the last few weeks. So that was the 'room in a house in Bayswater' where Alice had first met his father.

'As I said, it wasn't exactly a brothel,' continued Alice, in an objective tone. 'The clients were screened by Dr Stephenson to make sure they were clean and, above all, wealthy. Only then were they passed on to Mrs Bright's. Many of the girls had their regulars. Sometimes we were just required to go to dances, or nightclubs, with the client. Sometimes the client just wanted company. Mostly whatever happened didn't go on at Mrs Bright's house itself – that was just where you were introduced. The girls would be allocated to their young man, and would be taken to a flat or a hotel. My young man was your father. He tracked me down after we spoke together at Blubberwick.'

Alice stopped talking for a moment. She seemed to be watching two dogs that were chasing a ball on the beach. Ed wondered if she had lost the thread, but she hadn't.

'You were saying you saw my father again after he got married?'

'Yes. He returned to Mrs Bright's and found me. I was still a working girl, but only now and then. I was saving money in order to be free of that world. I knew it wouldn't last once I was in my thirties. Your father came to see me. At first I didn't know whether I was pleased or not that he had walked back into my life as casually as he had walked out of it three years before. He hadn't changed much: he was a little heavier, a little less enthusiastic about things. At first I couldn't understand why he had come, why he would risk his marriage and reputation. But it didn't take him long to get to the point.

'"Maude can't have any more children," he told me. "She's had two miscarriages, and one daughter who died three months ago in her cot."

'"I'm so sorry, Simon," I said. I didn't know why he was telling me this, or what he wanted from me. What a fool I was!'

Ed stared at Alice. He started to speak but she held up her hand.

'Let me finish the story, Ed,' she asked. 'It's quickly told. Your father said – I remember the phrase – "Poor Maude. She's neither use nor ornament if she can't give me a son. It's the one thing I simply have to have, otherwise the whole estate will go to my ghastly cousins." Then he said: "I'll pay you ten thousand pounds if you will bear my son, Alice."

'Well, I was about to tell him what I thought of his offer when he reached over and squeezed my hand. "It will be like the old days," he said. "I've missed you."'

Alice stopped as if she could say no more and turned her face away.

'Please go on,' said Ed. 'What was your answer?'

'You are the answer. You are.'

Simon Hartlepool had been obsessed with producing a son and heir to the Hartlepool Estate. If he had no male heir, the title, the estate – and its debts – might have passed to distant relatives. For old Lord Hartlepool that would have meant failure and disgrace. The one duty he had to discharge was to marry a wife who could give him a son, and in this he had made an unfortunate choice.

'He was starting to run through the Portalbert money as well by then,' said Alice, 'from what I gathered. There was not much money, less love, and a dead child in that marriage. Your father was desperate. The money he offered me meant I could leave the life I had been leading. And I still loved him.'

'Did it take long?' asked Ed.

'I conceived you very quickly,' replied Alice. 'I bore his child in Westminster Hospital. He paid for the best of everything, of course. I had my own room, filled with flowers and fruit. I had the best care you could imagine, and so did you. None of that made any difference when the time came for you to be taken from me.'

'Did he come and take me away?'

'No. It was like the time before – he said goodbye by letter. He sent it by way of the nurse who came to collect you and take you to Hartlepool Hall. She gave me the letter. Your father – I told you I loved him and I still do, in a way – was neither brave nor strong.'

'So some strange woman just came and carried me off and that was the last you ever saw of me?'

'It broke my heart,' said Alice. There was a long pause. She had turned her face away from him, but Ed could see that she was struggling to speak. '... I never saw you again until a few months ago.'

How Ed had been explained away at Hartlepool Hall or what story had been told to the servants or the neighbours, Alice did not know. But what Ed understood at last was something he had always sensed. His father's wife, the woman whom until now he had thought of as his mother, had never forgiven him for his appearance: in her home, in her nursery, at her table, but never in her heart.

There had never been any love in his home. Maude Hartlepool had never forgiven his father for what he had done; Ed had been brought up with no sense of love or belonging; with no sense of purpose; only detachment and a desire to avoid any confrontation with the real world.

He didn't know what to say. He sat silently beside Alice looking out to sea, listening to the rustle and hiss of the waves as they ran up the smooth sand then retreated again.

'Do you hate me now, Ed?' asked Alice.

He turned and put his arms around her. 'I've always known there was something about you. And I wondered why there was such a connection between us. Now I understand.'

'You won't forget me now I've told you?'

'I'm going to be here as often as they will let me come,' said Ed. 'And when my new house is properly comfortable, you can come and stay with me sometimes, if you feel like it.'

'But you've got your own life to live,' protested Alice. She was crying with relief.

'This *is* my own life now,' Ed told her.

Twenty-Six

Horace sat in his flat and waited. His temporary home was the ground floor of a low-rise block on a housing estate near Darlington. It was a run-down, grimy place in a run-down, grimy building. Luckily his flat was on the ground floor, because the lifts didn't work. On the other hand, being on the ground floor had certain disadvantages. Apparently he was on the waiting list for sheltered accommodation, but nothing had happened yet and nobody had been in touch with him about any future move.

So Horace sat on his chair and waited. He was wearing his striped trousers and a white shirt and tie. His old black jacket hung over the back of a chair. Somehow he couldn't get out of the habit of dressing for work – what had once been his work – and in any case, he had very few clothes apart from his butler's uniform.

A bell rang. In his mind's eye Horace pictured the board in the servants' hall, what was now the kitchen, at Hartlepool Hall. Beneath each bell on the board was painted a legend: 'Lord Simon's study'; 'Smoking Room'; 'The Long Gallery'; 'Library'; and so on. So you knew straight away where you were wanted. When this bell rang, Horace stood up, put on his old black jacket and started on his journey to the billiard room. He was certain the bell in the billiard boom had rung.

Halfway out of the door he realised he had become confused again. There was nobody in the billiard room. More to the point, the billiard room at Hartlepool Hall was over thirty miles away. He was here, in a housing estate on the edge of Darlington, in his new flat, starting a new life. The bell that had rung was just the front door. By now he was in the hallway and the half-glass front door was in front of him. He could hear whispering and giggling coming from the other side. Kids! They were always doing things like this. Sometimes they pushed objects through the letter box; this lot just rang the bell. He went to the door, opened it and looked out, but of course there was nobody there.

Annabel did not recover her composure for the best part of a day after Ed left her. At first she was helpless with grief. She could not understand how the relationship between herself and Ed, something which was so evidently meant to be, wasn't going to happen. Who else would look after him, if not her? But all things pass, and this black mood passed too, after a while. The point was, she told herself over a gin and tonic, she had been just a bit hasty in the way she had approached the subject. She had to bear in mind that Ed was quite a shy man, a rather difficult man, and needed to be handled delicately. It was a question of waiting a little and then persuading him to see her again. Perhaps she should offer to help him furnish his new house? Or perhaps she could say she'd been sent two tickets to the theatre and ask him to accompany her. That might be the way. Somewhere safe, somewhere neutral like the theatre. Ed would be too much of a gentleman to refuse.

And then she could begin to reel him in again.

Meanwhile, there was the question of what to do about

Lambshiel House. After another gin and tonic, the question didn't seem that important. Why should she bother to do anything about it just yet? First she needed to work out how to bring Ed back to her. Then she could worry about whether or not to sell the house. It would be much more fun if she and Ed did that together. Then they could go and choose a new home.

Meanwhile, in order to entertain herself, Annabel had been to a bookshop and bought a lot of new books to read. She had all the old Catherine Cookson ones, and some Jilly Coopers upstairs. Now she had come home with an armful of books by a host of other authors. On these short, dark winter days, what could be better than to pour herself a drink, curl up by the fire in the drawing room and read.

In the books Annabel read, charming-and-amusing-but-lonely girls fell for difficult but intriguing men, who often turned out to be surprisingly well off. She sat here by the fire, turning the pages, seeking clues to her own future.

Most days that winter – if it was not too wet or cold – Ed would walk along the seafront at Tynemouth, pushing Alice along in front of him in her wheelchair. They watched the surfers riding on the waves; they heard the seagulls above their heads. They talked of many things, but never about Hartlepool Hall.

The Hall itself stood dreaming in a winter sleep. The gates were padlocked and the front entrance and ground-floor windows had been boarded up. For weeks the bank and the local council, English Heritage, and the Victorian Society, had wrangled about the fate of the Hall and who was to be responsible for it. Meanwhile there had been three reorganisations of the bank, which was going through a difficult time itself, through a combination of the economic downturn and imprudent lending. The person now in charge of stranded assets such as Hartlepool Hall knew nothing of how the house had come to be in the bank's possession, and hadn't time to read the file. He had other, more pressing problems: a bankrupt football club, along with a number of Geoff Tarset's housing developments, all now owned by the bank. Dealing with a semi-derelict stately home was well down his list of priorities.

The house and the estate, apart from one small farm that still belonged to Ed, had been put up for sale, but the condition the house had been left in by Geoff Tarset's wrecking crews put off potential buyers. As the winter progressed, the condition of the house worsened. When the nights were darkest a small team of entrepreneurs from a nearby town had approached along a farm road, cutting the chains on the gates with a bolt cutter. Then they had somehow gained access to the roof and stripped from it quantities of lead flashing.

Now water leaked into the house at several points whenever it rained. Strange flowerings appeared on ceilings and cornices where the damp penetrated; in the roof spaces, leprous growths sprang up. The spores drifted amongst the roof timbers, settling here and there and founding new colonies. Slowly, irreversibly, the house was slipping into decay.

A century and a half ago, things had been very different. Ships built from iron plate manufactured in Simmonds' factories had circled the globe; trains had run on railways built by the Simmonds Railway Company on three continents. Wealth had poured into the coffers of the Simmonds family, wealth on a scale that could hardly be imagined. A great house had been built with a small portion of that fortune: a house that represented everything that was great, that was imperial, that was commercial.

The house had once been surrounded by dependencies: farm steadings with their farmers and labourers; gamekeepers in their cottages; stables with their grooms; gardens and hothouses with their gardeners. Inside the house a way of life went on that, when the house was built, was acknowledged as the proper way to consume that great fortune. But as the twentieth century passed by these dependencies were abandoned one by one. The way of life at Hartlepool Hall became ever more incomprehensible and unimaginable to those who had no direct experience of it. Hartlepool Hall was like a fable, a fairy tale populated by imaginary beings with no connection or relevance to the rest of the world – in the eyes of the rest of the world. And when, at last, the fountain of wealth had ceased, the vigour and effort that had created the original wealth had dissipated and the knowledge of how it was created was forgotten.

The house still stands there by the lake. Its ceilings are coming down; its vast interior spaces are covered in fallen plaster; a Health and Safety notice has been put up forbidding entrance as the structure is unsafe. But who would want to enter it now? Nobody walks any longer in the overgrown gardens, except for a few small boys who come in the autumn to gather conkers fallen from a stand of horse chestnuts. The lake is choked with weed. The woods that once were filled with pheasants are now the haunt of foxes, jays and magpies.

Hartlepool Hall is not needed by the modern world. How could it be? If it had been, someone would have preserved it. Someone would have found a use for that grand building and new life would have been breathed into it. But that is not the fashion, these days. Such houses either become museums, sterile time capsules where tourists gaze at the curator's vision of a bygone age, or they become ruins. There is no salvation for Hartlepool Hall. It does not seem probable that it will ever be rescued.

But if you happened to see it on a morning like this one, early in February, with mist rising from the frozen ground, wreathing the house and the gelid lake in streamers of vapour, Hartlepool Hall still looks unchanged; unchanging. It looks too beautiful to be true, in the early morning light, with the sun just catching the rooftop. You might be forgiven for wondering if it was indeed a dream – this great house with its turrets and dome. You might wonder if it was real, if it actually existed, if it had ever existed.

The
LEGACY of
HARTLEPOOL
Hall

Reading Group Notes

About the Author

Paul Torday was born in 1946 and read English literature at Pembroke College, Oxford. He spent the next thirty years working in engineering and in industry, after which he scaled back his business responsibilities to fulfil a long-harboured ambition – to write. He burst on to the literary scene in 2006 with his first novel, *Salmon Fishing in the Yemen*, an immediate bestseller that has been sold in nineteen countries and is now a major motion picture staring Ewan McGregor. He is married with two sons by a previous marriage and has two stepsons and lives close to the River North Tyne.

The Story behind
The Legacy of Hartlepool Hall

Ed Hartlepool has made brief appearances in two previous novels: *The Irresistible Inheritance of Wilberforce* and *More Than You Can Say*. I wanted to bring him centre stage in this novel. I also wanted to write about a subject that has always fascinated me: how some families can produce enormously entrepreneurial and successful people for a generation or two, and then lose their desire and ability to make money, knowing only how to spend it.

In Conversation with Paul Torday

Q Are you at all like Ed?

A No – most of my life has been spent in working for and sometimes investing in engineering businesses. I don't think Ed would have bothered with any of that.

Q Silence or music while you write? If music – who do you listen to?

A I'm easily distracted, so I write in silence.

Q Do you regret the passing of the world of old Hartlepool Hall?

A The old world of Hartlepool Hall has by no means passed away. I doubt if it ever will, as new money continues to buy up land and large houses, so the process goes on. And there are quite a lot of families who, unlike Ed's, are good at hanging on to their money.

Q *What authors do you admire and why?*

A Anthony Powell, Evelyn Waugh, Kingsley Amis – and many others. These are authors I read in my twenties and thirties, and therefore they have influenced me more than current writers. I admire them for the lucidity of their prose, and their sense of comedy.

Q *Is Hartlepool Hall based on a real building?*

A Yes and no. Elements of Hartlepool Hall exist in various houses I have known, but there is no specific building I can point to and say that was the model.

Q *What comes first for you – plot or character?*

A   Character drives plot, as far as I am concerned.

Q   *How did you physically write* The Legacy of Hartlepool Hall, *and why?*

A   All my novels are written sitting at my desk, on a large iMac, with a view of woods and fields out of the window. I try and keep three or four days a week clear when I'm writing. I write in the mornings and edit in the afternoons. I wrote *Hartlepool Hall* as a way of saying goodbye to the characters and landscapes I have used and returned to in several of my novels. I want to do something different next.

Q   *What's your most treasured possession?*

A   A pair of beautiful 16-bore shotguns, made before the Second World War and as good as new. They are a joy to shoot with. Or perhaps it's my working cocker spaniel, although she thinks I'm her possession rather than the other way around.

Q *How did you set about balancing dark and light in the novel?*

A I'm not that technical. I like to have a redemptive feeling to the end of the book.

Q *What single thing about you would surprise us the most?*

A I still think of myself as someone who has spent his life in business and have difficulty in thinking of myself as a writer.

Q *Would you have sold Hartlepool Hall?*

A No. I'd have struggled on in an un-business-like way and tried to keep it going.

Q *What's your most vivid memory?*

A Sailing through pack-ice around Spitzbergen looking for polar bears.

Q *Any clues about your next book – any snippets for us?*

A A child presents marks or wounds on his body that are consistent with crucifixion. Then the marks vanish – and so does the child.

For Discussion

- What's your first impression of Ed Hartlepool, and how has the author created it?

- What are the 'giant wind turbines' a monument to?

- 'In his world you were what you did; you were defined by your actions, and the consequences of those actions.' How do you think the author feels about Geoff, and people like Geoff?

- Do you like Ed?

- 'You need to love something to be interested in it.' Do you agree?

- To what extent has Ed caused all his own problems?

- Why did Annabel sit her father at the dining table?

- 'But I've decided that unless one looks forward rather than back, one could quite easily go mad.' To what extent is this the theme of *The Legacy of Hartlepool Hall*?

- What does Hartlepool Hall represent?

- 'He saw in her a kind of moral blankness or incompleteness that he recognised, because it had once been a part of his own makeup.' What has allowed Ed to change, while Annabel remains the same? Or has Annabel changed?

- What does the unfolding of Lady Alice's story tell us about the changing world?

- 'He realised now that inheritances can destroy people, unless they learn that inheritance has to be earned, and then earned over and over again.' Has Ed fully grown up, or does he still have a way to go?

Suggested Further Reading

Brideshead Revisited
by Evelyn Waugh

Various Pets Alive and Dead
by Marina Lewycka

The Memorial
by Christopher Isherwood

Something Fresh
by P. G. Wodehouse

The Woman Who Went to Bed For a Year
by Sue Townsend

Wait For Me!
By Deborah Devonshire